Praise for th

MW00989690

A Proper Cuppa

A Proper Cuppa Tea is a smart and sexy romance featuring two professional women. While their relationship first stutters from the distractions of their lives, when they decide to pursue it, the romance develops in a realistic, charming, erotic, and organic manner. These characters are well rounded and fully depicted. They have careers and responsibilities as well as relationships with other people. The blended plotlines and complications are integral to the potential for Lark and Channing's future together. MacGregor's newest romance is a marvelous, entertaining, captivating book as complex and full-bodied as that perfect cup of tea. Put the kettle on to boil, find a cozy chair, and settle in to enjoy *A Proper Cuppa Tea*.

- Lambda Literary Review

The author did a remarkable job of bringing all of the characters to life for me. I was able to form a vivid image of each delightful character in my mind and I felt as though I could hear the witty banter between Channing and Lark. There wasn't a lag in the storyline or any unnecessary drama and I am very pleased to admit that the author made me fall in love with the charming English landscape. This story entertained me from the first word and I can't tell you how many times I had to suppress my laughter while I kept sneaking a read when I was at work. I adore British humor and I tend to fall in love (quite deeply, I must say) with quirky and sarcastic British characters who have a wicked sense of humor. If you love books with picturesque landscapes, feisty women, meddling and well-meaning friends coupled with countless cups of delicious tea, then this story is definitely for you!

- The Lesbian Review

Moment of Weakness

Moment of Weakness... is a romance that doesn't follow the usual track of a les-fic romance. The author's use of time in this story keeps the pages turning as the reader learns bit by bit how Zann and Marleigh met, what happened to Zann in Afghanistan, and who they are. I loved the story and the way I learned about Zann and Marleigh's relationship–not in a straight timeline, but moving backward and forward in time. KG MacGregor's characters are well developed and have flaws. I love that. I loved the romance. I highly recommend this book to KG MacGregor fans.

- The Lesbian Review

MacGregor has written a story that lulls the reader into thinking it will continue along a certain trajectory, then—wham!—we're thrust in another direction with a startling revelation we never saw coming. Every scene skillfully moves this tale along, adding to the tension. From desperation to longing, anger to disappointment, unconditional love to fear, all those moods and emotions and more are well portrayed. The superb writing, characters, and well-timed plot twists are skillfully done to make for an entertaining and revelatory story. *Moment of Weakness* explores the often unexamined tragic aspects of war, the power of true love, and gives the reader a thrill ride that lingers long after the last page has been turned.

- Lambda Literary Review

The Touch of a Woman

What makes this an interesting read beyond the standard plotline are unusual back-histories. The characters are well drawn, complex women, who will resonate with many. And their tender attraction is a reminder that real life isn't always about the grand passion, but a gentle falling.

- *Lesbian Reading Room*

Anyone But You

More than a sizzling romance, a well researched and well-written eco-thriller... I loved the way the story was written: fast-paced, with great punch lines, a tidy, well thought-out and thought-provoking plot, at times witty, at times dramatic. Dating the archenemy added zest to the romance and both heroines were very believable and easy to like.

- *Curve Magazine*

Etched in Shadows

Well written, well edited, thoroughly enjoyable read... The loss of memory and feelings she once had gives Ms. MacGregor the opportunity to show a woman before and after a life changing event, and to explore how starting from scratch as an adult might allow us to make different choices... Johnelle and Alice are strong characters, well drawn and developed.

- *The Lesbian Reading Room*

THE
LUCKY
ONES

Other Bella Books by KG MacGregor

Anyone But You
Etched in Shadows
The House on Sandstone
Just This Once
Life After Love
Malicious Pursuit
Moment of Weakness
Mulligan
Out of Love
Photographs of Claudia
Playing with Fuego
A Proper Cuppa Tea
Rhapsody
Sea Legs
Secrets So Deep
Sumter Point
T-Minus Two
The Touch of a Woman
Trial by Fury
Undercover Tales
West of Nowhere
Worth Every Step

Shaken Series
Without Warning
Aftershock
Small Packages
Mother Load

About the Author

KG MacGregor is the author of twenty-six books, including the romance saga, The Shaken Series. Her works feature strong, career-minded lesbians, and blend romance with intrigue, adventure and dramatic events. She has been honored with nine Golden Crown Awards, a prestigious Lambda Literary Award, and the Alice B. Medal for career achievement. She served as president of the board of trustees for Lambda Literary, the world's premier organization for LGBT literature. A native of the Blue Ridge Mountains, she now makes her home in Nashville, TN. Visit her on the web at www.kgmacgregor.com.

Bella Books, Inc.
P.O. Box 10543
Tallahassee, FL 32302

Printed in the United States of America on acid-free paper.

First Bella Books Edition 2019

Editor: Katherine V. Forrest
Cover Designer: Judith Fellows

ISBN: 978-1-64247-041-3

THE LUCKY ONES

KG MacGregor

BELLA
BOOKS
2019

Acknowledgments

Some books are harder to write than others. Weaving multiple story lines through an ensemble of characters is especially tricky when you're trying not to lose focus on a pair of women destined to fall in love. Fortunately I have my own pair of women to keep me on task.

First there's my partner Jenny, who hears every wayward idea before it hits the page. I can usually tell what she thinks by the tilt of her head. More often than not, I let her reaction be my guide. She also sweeps up at the end, lopping off my extra words and sticking in a few I skipped.

Second is my editor, Katherine V. Forrest. I warned Katherine ahead of time that I'd had some trouble wrangling this one, so she was ready with her pencil. Nice of her not to use a red pen. I especially appreciate her friendship, which shined through in her notes. Sometimes authors need more than pencil marks.

CHAPTER ONE

A voice mail from someone at the hospital had assured Britt Iverson that her father's surgery was successful and there was a good chance for a full recovery. That meant she wouldn't need the black suit after all, nor a dark car for a funeral procession.

From the line of available rentals at Lexington's Blue Grass Airport, she chose a red Toyota Camry and slid her rolling suitcase and carryon bag into the trunk. Her smartphone had mapped the route to Grace Hospital in Leland, twenty-six miles that would take her past one of Kentucky's most beautiful stretches of horse country.

It was hard to feel even a crumb of pleasure from this trip, given the guilt over what it had taken to get her here. Nearly two years had passed since her last visit. Her dad had called only a week ago with a fresh invitation, which she'd answered with her usual promise of "soon."

Exiting the highway onto two-lane Pinckard Road, she allowed gentle traces of nostalgia to calm her anxiousness.

Mile after mile of white rail fences lined rolling pastures, where the occasional cluster of sleek thoroughbreds frolicked in the morning mist. Despite her general aversion to all things Kentucky, she had fond childhood memories of riding along this rural road with her father, the wind blowing through the car's open windows and whipping her hair.

As she neared Leland, the roadside fence ended and a stone chimney rose above the charred remains of the old Iverson homestead, a rickety farmhouse brought down two summers ago by a lightning strike. Four generations of her family had lived there even as it gradually fell to ruin. It was a blessing in disguise, for her at least, since it had forced her dad into a modern home closer to town.

Pinckard Road ended at Main Street, which she found quiet for a Monday morning. Leland was still a small town, but it had grown considerably since she left for college. The downtown area was now several blocks long with shops, offices, the courthouse and the high school. The sidewalk ended at shady City Park, with its picnic pavilions, playgrounds and a municipal pool. Alongside was a modest baseball stadium that was home to the Longdogs, a minor league baseball team that happened to be her father's greatest passion.

Past the high school, a stoplight marked the entrance to the town's medical complex. She parked near the emergency entrance, where a volunteer located her father's room in ICU on the third floor. A quick look in the elevator's mirror reminded her why overnight flights from the West Coast were called the red-eye. The best she could do to freshen up was tighten her ponytail, touch up her lip gloss and straighten her shirt collar. She hardly cared who saw her or what they thought as long as she put on her best smile for her dad.

A nurse looked up from her station and drawled, "May I help you?"

"I'm looking for Vernon Iverson. He's in intensive care. I'm his daughter."

"Oh right, the one from California. He's already had a slew of visitors this morning, 'cept Darlene won't let anybody stay more'n a minute or two. She runs a tight ship in there."

A couple of minutes…plenty of time for him to see that she'd dropped everything to rush to his side.

Her left shoe squeaked obnoxiously as she followed the nurse down the glossy vinyl hall. In the special-care room, her dad was lying connected to drips and monitors, a bandage covering his head. Deep bruises lined his eyes, presumably the trauma of brain surgery.

Fighting back tears, she took his hand. "Dad? Dad, it's me, Britt."

His eyes fluttered briefly, filling her with joy and relief. "My girl."

"That's right, I'm here."

"You should…J…JT."

She recognized the name of his best friend, JT Sharpe, a local attorney he'd known since childhood.

"He's still a little fuzzy but that's normal," the nurse said.

Stroking his hand, Britt added, "Don't worry about a thing, Dad. I'll handle it. All you have to do now is take it easy and get well." To the nurse, she said, "Is there any chance I could talk to his doctor?"

"Dr. Dhawan has finished his rounds for today, but I think he left word. Let me check at the desk."

Alone with her father, she let go of her selfish, impotent tears. She'd never felt so helpless as in the last twelve hours as she frantically made her way across the country. She was all the real family he had. It broke her heart that he'd faced this life-threatening emergency alone.

"Brittany Iverson?"

She turned to face a striking middle-aged woman, tall and trim, with flowing auburn hair women half her age would envy. A lanyard clipped to her dress identified her as part of the hospital's administration.

"I'm Britt Iverson."

"I could see that a mile away. You look so much like your daddy."

Beyond her father's lanky build and fair coloring, she wasn't aware of any other resemblance. That said, she embraced any and all features that distanced her from her mother.

"So pleased to finally meet you, Britt. I've known Vernon for ages, and he's told us all about you. Bragging how he's going out to visit you in sunny California while we're back here shoveling snow. I'm Justine Hall, executive assistant to Dr. Henderson. He's our hospital administrator. I'm the one who left you that voice mail this morning."

"Oh, right." She instantly recognized the soft Southern lilt.

"My goodness, you've flown all night to get here. San Diego, right? How 'bout I buy you some breakfast in the cafeteria?"

She was deeply touched that someone so important would take time to give her such personal attention. "Thanks, but I ate on the plane."

"Coffee then. Let's go to my office and I'll try to fill you in on where things stand."

Britt kissed her father's forehead and whispered that she'd return. Then she fell into step with the long-legged Justine.

"It may not look like it, but your daddy is one lucky fellow. If he'd been by himself...Lordy, let's not even go there. He was at home with a whole houseful of people there to kick off the baseball season. Starts this coming Friday. That bunch does it every year, a big party where they dream how this is gonna be the Year of the Longdogs." She punctuated the last bit with finger quotes and whirled to add, "You know about the Longdogs, right? That's our minor league baseball team. Summertime in Leland, half the town revolves around the Longdogs."

"Right. Dad's always excited about it."

"So's my wife Carly. She and Ninah—that's our friend, Ninah Faust—they went in together on season tickets, and their seats are right next to Vernon's. JT's there too. He's your daddy's best friend, you know…and my ex-husband, the ol' snake. They were all there at the party last night. Carly and I live on Sandstone too, third house on the right, but ours isn't on the lake like Vernon's."

Britt barely processed the string of connections, as she was stuck on the unexpected revelation that Justine Hall had a *wife*. She'd never have guessed it in a million years. That explained her father's insistence that Leland had a visible LGBT community.

Their walk ended in a corner office in the admin wing with an impressive view of the courthouse dome. To one side was a sitting area right out of *Southern Living*.

"Please have a seat." Justine steered her toward the floral sofa and offered a choice of flavored coffee pods. "I don't usually get involved with patient care, seeing as how my job is administrative, but Carly and JT insisted I step in and help bring you up to speed. Just don't take my word on anything when it comes to medical questions. My BA in English lit only gets us so far."

As Justine prepared her coffee, Britt scanned a row of framed photos on the credenza, including a snapshot of Justine and another woman with short graying hair and a smile that warned not to take anything she said too seriously. "Is that your wife?"

"That's her, Carly Griffin. Officially we both try to use Griffin-Hall now that we're married. Now there's a story for you. Some other time though. You wanna hear about your daddy." She collected papers from her desk and perched a pair of designer reading glasses on her slender nose. "I made some notes this morning when Dr. Dhawan was here so I'd remember what all he said. Vernon has what's called a brain aneurysm. They told you that, right?"

"They mentioned it as a possibility. Either that or a stroke." The first call had come shortly after six o'clock last evening, nine p.m. in Kentucky.

"An aneurysm is when a weak spot in the wall of a blood vessel gives way and makes a bubble. They're extremely dangerous if they rupture, but this one didn't, thank the Lord. I'm telling you, he was so blessed to have a houseful of people there with him. And we got that prayer circle going right away."

Britt shrugged off the spiritual platitudes. Her father had been saved by trained medical professionals, not some celestial puppeteer interceding on his behalf. But it was no skin off her back if Justine wanted to believe otherwise. People were entitled to their religious and spiritual beliefs, as long as they didn't push them on her.

"To fix it, they have to open an area of the skull and put a clip in there that basically seals it off. Like a tiny clothespin. It sounds complicated but it's actually pretty routine these days. Dr. Dhawan wants to keep him for a few more days for a full assessment."

"What does that mean, medically speaking?"

"Again, you'll need to speak to the doctor for specifics, but the way he explained it to me was there might be some confusion at first, problems with his speech and motor skills, but that all should come back over time. We've got a residential rehab center too if he needs a little extra help." She joined Britt on the sofa. "I can't really tell you much more than that. I'm already way out of my lane."

"I appreciate it. This is very helpful. Did the doctor happen to say how long a recovery might take?"

"No, but poking around in somebody's brain is major surgery. In my experience it takes most patients at least six to eight weeks to get over that. Best case scenario is he could manage on his own in two to four weeks...as long as he's got somebody on call to drive him to his doctor's appointments and whatnot. Does that help?"

"Yes, thank you."

This couldn't have come at a worse time for Britt. Even two weeks could take her out of the running for a job she wanted very badly and needed very much. She'd aced her second interview and was expecting a callback any day.

"You won't have to handle all this on your own, Britt. Vernon has a million friends who'll be happy to pitch in with whatever he needs."

"Is there anything I can do for him now? Should I be lining up a physical therapist or a home health aide or something?"

"Oh no, the medical team takes care of all that." Justine clasped her hand warmly and smiled. "The rest of us though, we're here to take care of *you*. See, Vernon's been telling Carly and Ninah all about you, said he couldn't wait for you to meet his"—she deepened her voice and smiled—"*lesbian* friends. Since he can't do that, we're gonna have to introduce ourselves."

Britt laughed softly and shook her head. "I take it he told you…"

"That he's extremely proud of his lesbian daughter? He did."

Even at thirty-six years old, she felt like a little girl when she thought of how her father's love and support had saved her at the most critical juncture of her life. "I'm the one who's proud. I've got the greatest dad there is."

"He's a keeper, all right." Justine shook out the contents of a manila envelope, her dad's wallet and a set of keys. "I have it on good authority he's gonna sleep all day, so you might as well go on home and get some rest yourself. We'll look after him, I promise. But then I want you to come on down to our house for supper. Say, six thirty-ish. Nothing fancy, just whatever Carly throws on the grill. Like I said, we're the third house on the right. A big rainbow windsock on the porch. You can't miss it. Oh, and shoes are optional."

"That's so kind of you, but I don't want to—"

"N-n-nnh." She shook her finger. "Not taking no for an answer. Now go look in on your daddy and get on home."

The last thing Britt wanted right now was a social obligation, but she owed it to her father to be nice to his friends.

She returned to ICU just in time to see a young woman exit and hurry to the stairwell at the end of the hall. She was a slight figure with short dark hair, dressed neatly in slacks and a fitted shirt. Probably one of her father's "slew" of friends.

Britt was comforted to know there were so many people who cared about her dad. Not that she was surprised. He was a genuinely nice guy with a fierce loyalty to his hometown.

Finding him asleep, she headed back to her car, encouraged by Justine's optimism but still exhausted and emotionally stressed. Since last fall, she'd lost nearly everything that mattered to her. But at least she hadn't lost her dad.

CHAPTER TWO

Eight teens constituted the entire membership of Leland High School's Gay-Straight Alliance. Three girls, three boys, and two who considered themselves genderqueer.

Ninah Faust had served as faculty sponsor since the club's inception. She knew for a fact she wasn't the only LGBT person on the faculty, just the only one willing to publicly claim it as a central plank of her identity. Moving in with Teri Kaufman the year after she'd gotten tenure had been a defiant statement of pride. Practically everyone in town knew Teri, since her high school glory days had brought Leland a state basketball championship. Teri, now her ex, worked in the radiology department at Grace Hospital.

Today was the GSA's last official meeting of the school year, led by club president Thaddeus Martin, one of Ninah's favorite students. He read from his notes, "It's been suggested we change our name to Gay Alliance since we don't have any straight members."

The idea drew swift opposition from multiple members.

"Only three of us are gay, Thaddeus. If we're going to change our name, I vote we call ourselves the Queer Alliance."

"Not everybody likes being called queer."

"I hate that we have to use labels at all," said Abby McFarland, whose jagged hair was tinted pink to honor her mom's battle with breast cancer. "We should call ourselves the Human Alliance."

Thaddeus continued with his subdued leadership style, allowing the others to conduct the spirited debate. A soft-spoken African-American, he doggedly fought discrimination on multiple fronts, which earned him a mountain of respect from Ninah.

"Miss Faust, what do you think about us changing our name?" Thaddeus asked.

All eyes turned toward her at the back of the classroom, where she sat on a table swinging her feet. "Gay-Straight Alliance has national name recognition, even a court case where the school board tried to stop the club from using the word *gay* in its name."

Leland's club had generated its own controversy when it was founded four years ago. A group of parents, led by a caucus of area ministers, protested against school facilities being used to advance the dreaded *homosexual agenda*. Ninah's friend Carly called them the Local Vocals.

"I prefer queer, but I think we should hold off with a name change for now," said Jordan Smith, whose preferred pronouns were they, them and their. "If queer catches on, the prominent groups will start changing their names. That's when we should do it."

An insightful remark for a sixteen-year-old, Ninah had to admit. Armed with their smartphones and social media accounts, today's kids were much more issue-savvy than she'd been at their age.

"Okay, let's table that one for now," Thaddeus said. "Other new business...Pride Night at Leland Field. It's scheduled for August fourteenth when the Longdogs play the Paducah Dukes. That's the Wednesday before school starts back." He yielded the floor to Trina Jones of the planning committee.

Last year's Pride Night, their first, had been both heartbreaking and exhilarating. With no clue what to expect, the kids had planned a couple of low-key activities to promote visibility—handing out purple PRIDE bracelets as fans entered the stadium, and then sitting together in the bleachers behind a banner with their GSA chapter name.

"Are there more wristbands, Miss Faust?"

"Are you kidding me?" She hoisted herself off the table and opened a storage cabinet to reveal four cardboard boxes. "We ordered in bulk, remember? We still have about four thousand of these babies left."

"We should hand them out again."

Abby grumbled, "Why? Nobody keeps them."

"It doesn't matter," Jordan said. "We need to hand them out anyway. You never know when somebody's going to stick one in their pocket to take home because they're thinking about it, or they just found out their cousin's gay. One little wristband can be a big deal for somebody."

Ninah was impressed by the show of sensitivity. While she took seriously her role as advisor, she usually stopped short of steering them toward specific words or actions so as not to give anyone reason to complain that she was leading them into depravity. It was crucial they learn to navigate their own constituencies—family, friends, church—as individuals.

"Miss Faust, will you get your friends to come again?"

She grinned. "The better question is could I stop them if I tried."

As proud as she'd been of her small group of students last year, there was no mistaking the uneasiness their presence had stirred at the game. They received very little joy from the crowd when they were introduced during warmups as the night's honorees. In fact, random voices shouted the occasional slur or taunt, enough that Ninah began to worry there could even be a physical confrontation before the night was over. Then suddenly a stream of familiar faces arrived and unfurled a rainbow flag—about twenty of her LGBT friends brought together on the spur of the moment by text and social media. What better message for anxious kids than to know they were encircled in a protective cocoon of adults who'd once walked in their shoes?

Trina cleared her throat to bring the club back to their Pride Night agenda. Their March car wash had raised three hundred dollars, which they were donating to the Leland Public Library to help fund the purchase of queer books for children and young adults. They hoped to present a ceremonial check during the game.

Ninah's phone buzzed against the table and she excused herself to the hallway. "Hey, Carly. I was gonna call you. I sneaked off this morning during my planning period and saw Vernon. He was out of it, but the nurse said he was doing great."

"That's what I was calling to tell you. Justine said the surgery went fine, that they'll probably move him out of ICU after supper."

"What a relief." She'd never been so frightened as last night at their kickoff party. Vernon was about to make his toast to the season when suddenly he clutched his head with both hands and crumpled to the floor in agony. She and Carly had soothed him until the ambulance arrived.

"His daughter Britt flew all night from San Diego and got there this morning. She's coming over to our house for supper at six thirty. That's why I'm calling, so you can join us. Justine says she's really nice."

"Sure, sure." She'd been hoping to meet Britt Iverson someday, the elusive lesbian daughter whose brief visits were usually last-minute affairs that precluded Vernon introducing her to his friends. He'd talked about her for years, how she'd made a great life for herself in San Diego with a longtime partner, a successful marketing company and scores of friends. "How long do you think she'll be in town?"

"I guess it all depends on how Vernon progresses. Probably a couple of weeks at least."

"Thanks for thinking of me. I'll be there, six thirty."

Carly and Justine didn't know she had a special reason for wanting to meet Britt. Vernon had confided in her last week that his daughter was going through a difficult time. She and her partner had split up last fall, he said, and he worried she was having some problems with her company as well. He'd invited her for a visit and wanted Ninah to talk up Leland's lively lesbian community in hopes Britt might warm to the idea of returning to Kentucky. He had his eye on a new business venture, and with her company struggling, he hoped she might join him. Whatever he had in the works might be on hold now that he had a health scare to reckon with, but perhaps he could resurrect it once he got it behind him.

She returned to her classroom in time to watch Thaddeus pass the mantle to Abby, who'd been elected to serve as president next school year. As her first order of business, Abby yielded the floor to her.

"I always get emotional this time of year," Ninah said, fluttering her hands around her face as if to dry her tears. "And it seems like every year I say the same thing, that this year's class was my best ever. Honestly, that's how it feels. I'm so proud of every last one of you. You're an inspiration to me."

"Because you're an inspiration to us," Thaddeus said.

To Ninah, that's what teaching was all about. She reminded them to stay in touch through the summer on their Facebook group and to reach out if they needed someone to talk to. "That's the great thing about coming out—you're now part of this giant family we've made for ourselves. Trust me, there are millions of us, and we're always here for each other."

After heartfelt hugs with each of them, she snagged Thaddeus to help carry a few boxes of books and supplies to her car. Summers gave her time to sift through what had worked in her classroom and what hadn't. In eleven short weeks, she'd hit the reset button and start over.

"I hope Abby has as much fun leading the club as I did," Thaddeus said as he hoisted a crate into her Subaru hatchback. "There's a campus LGBT group at Berea, but Ike says I ought to stick to academics my freshman year. I think he's afraid I'll get distracted like he did. What do you think?"

"I think he's looking after his little brother." Ike Martin had lasted only a year at Morehead State before dropping out to focus on songwriting. His day job at The Bean coffee house paid the bills while he toiled in pursuit of his big break. "Everyone's college experience is different. I don't think it's a bad idea to concentrate on your classes when you first get there, but I think you'll eventually find time for both."

As he talked excitedly of his college plans, a dark gray Dodge slowed to a crawl past the high school parking lot, not forty feet from where they stood. Ninah briefly got a look at the two men inside, who were staring them down. Both white, late teens or early twenties. They weren't at all shy about their politics, since the rear bumper was plastered with Trump stickers and Confederate flags. And a paper license plate that implied the vehicle was new, or at least new to Kentucky.

Thaddeus noticed them too and watched through narrowed eyes.

Ninah had little doubt about their intentions, probably triggered by seeing a white woman with a black youth. They meant to intimidate. While she wasn't particularly worried for her own safety, she couldn't afford to take chances where Thaddeus was concerned. "How about riding along to my house and giving me a hand to carry this stuff inside? I can run you home after that."

"Sure, no problem."

If Leland had a white supremacist community, it was operating under the radar. The only sign of the Alt-Right had been a modest rally last fall to protest the town council's decision to remove a Jefferson Davis plaque from the courthouse. According to the *Gazette*, most of the demonstrators were from out of state, recruited over social media. Locals had largely ignored them, thanks to street barriers erected by the Leland Police Department that sent traffic on a two-block detour around downtown.

So who were these guys? It was possible they'd come to Leland for work. The boot factory was taking on dozens of new hires after winning a US Army contract. She'd rather think that than worry they were here to lay the groundwork for another Alt-Right rally, possibly larger and better organized. Leland was divided over lots of political and social issues, but there was broad consensus among locals that they didn't want trouble in town.

CHAPTER THREE

Britt liked many things about her father's contemporary new home, but what she appreciated most was having the whole basement to herself. There was a nice-sized bedroom, an adjoining bath, and a den that opened onto a private patio beneath the main floor deck. If she had to stay a while, it wasn't a bad place to be.

Standing before the bathroom mirror, she piled her long, straight hair into a messy bun in the back and pinned it, taking care to leave a few loose strands for a casual look that was appropriate for a cookout.

She had her father's Nordic features—blond, blue-eyed—and a lean build that had suited the androgynous persona she'd adopted as a rebellious teen. After moving to San Diego for college, she'd fallen under the influence of hip, fashion-conscious friends who modeled a more feminine style that she'd gradually come to appreciate in herself.

Rested from a three-hour nap, she opted to walk the quarter-mile down the street to Justine's house. It was a lovely neighborhood of upscale family homes on wooded lots, with paved driveways that curled toward garden sheds and basketball goals. The early evening air teemed with the scent of a Southern summer—freshly cut grass and barbecue grills.

Her West Coast friends would get a kick out of hearing that her father's social circle included a middle-aged lesbian couple, but anyone who'd grown up in liberal California couldn't possibly appreciate the true significance of that. Britt thought it remarkable that a prominent, professional woman like Justine was living openly in love with another woman in a place so steeped in patriarchy and religious dogma.

Before she could ring the bell, she was met at the door by Carly, the woman from the photo in Justine's office. Barefoot, she wore baggy shorts and a brown polo shirt bearing the logo of a coffee shop called The Bean.

"Britt Iverson, come on in. Justine told me you looked just like your father, minus the five o'clock shadow. She's out on the deck making sure our dinner doesn't turn into a charcoal briquette. You like barbecued chicken, right? I always put a little bourbon in the sauce. Feel free to kick off those shoes if you want." She started through the house before spinning abruptly. "Sorry, I should have introduced myself. I'm Carly, Justine's other half."

"I recognized you from the picture in her office." Same impish grin, and with a buoyant personality to match. "Thanks for having me over."

"Nothing we like better than a houseful of friends."

It was a lovely home, open and inviting. She followed Carly through a great room, where summer ferns spilled from a stone hearth. French doors led to a wide deck overlooking multiple flower beds, all of them bursting with color.

Justine was fussing over a dainty centerpiece of fresh flowers at a round table set for four.

"Look what I found on our front porch, Justine."

"Britt! I'm so glad you came, sweetie. Not that I gave you a choice." Justine immediately pulled her into a hug. "Please tell me you got some rest this afternoon. I checked on your dad before I left work. He ate part of his supper, which gets you a gold star in ICU. They were fixing to move him to a private room."

"I know, I ran back over there about an hour ago. Must have just missed you."

Justine, with her hair pulled back in a ponytail, was dressed in Lycra tights and a shiny green top, apparently fresh from a run. That explained why she looked so *damn* good for a woman in her fifties. She gestured toward a cushioned bench swing. "Have a seat. How about a beer?"

"Sounds great." Britt liked beer as long as it was icy cold. "Anything but coffee. I've had so much coffee in the last twenty-four hours I'm surprised it isn't seeping out of my pores."

"You hear that, Carly? This one's a coffee drinker." She turned back to Britt. "Carly happens to own the best coffee shop you'll find anywhere in Kentucky. It's called The Bean, right across from the law office on Main Street. Which reminds me…" She patted her hips as if searching for a pocket. "What did I do with JT's card?"

Carly produced it from her back pocket, a business card for Jason T. Sharpe, Jr., Esq., Attorney at Law, of the firm Cobb, Finger & Sharpe.

"This is Dad's best friend, right? Dad said he needs to talk with me about something, but I have no idea what."

"Thick as thieves, those two. Did I mention he's also my ex-husband, the father of my children, and an all-round pain in the—"

Carly interrupted, "Pay her no mind, Britt. One look at them and you know they're best friends. And they spoil their grandchildren half to death."

"How can we not? Two girls and a boy. All precious."

"Don't get her started with the pictures," Carly warned. "You'll be here all night."

"JT said for you to come by his office first thing in the morning," Justine said. "Something about papers he needs you to sign on your daddy's behalf, some kind of business contract that has to be done right now. Apparently your power of attorney kicked in on account of Vernon's brain surgery and anesthesia. He just needs to make sure all the papers are legally executed."

It hadn't occurred to her that as her father's next of kin she had authority over his legal affairs and business accounts for as long as he was incapacitated. He'd cobbled together an odd living, first as a maker of a remarkably successful artisanal sausage, which he'd sold to one of the conglomerates so he could settle the divorce from her mother. From there, he'd offered his expertise to other food entrepreneurs who wanted to bring their products to market. His crowning career achievement was a how-to book on the subject, *Bites to Bet On*, which enjoyed a surge in sales after it was promoted on one of the food channels. At sixty-three, he could retire comfortably if he wanted. It wouldn't surprise her if this health scare nudged him in that direction.

Justine delivered her beer in a foam koozie from The Bean and disappeared back into the kitchen, leaving her to exchange small talk with Carly.

Britt said, "I hear you're one of the baseball crazies like Dad."

"I enjoy the Longdogs, but I'm nowhere near the fan Vernon is. Or Ninah Faust." She nodded toward the table. "That's who the other plate's for. She's the one who introduced us to your father, about six years ago. Ninah and her ex, Teri Kaufman"— she lowered her voice and checked the house as if making sure Justine couldn't hear them—"that's a name we don't usually say out loud around here. Anyway, Ninah and Teri had seats next to Vernon for years. When they split up, Ninah bought Teri's half so she wouldn't have to sit beside her every night. Justine doesn't care a thing about baseball, but she indulges me. It's not the game so much as what it stands for. The Longdogs are good for this town, you know? They have a way of pulling us together when it feels like everything else is trying to push us apart."

"That's the great thing about sports, isn't it? Your team hits a home run and you can turn around and hug your worst enemy."

"Exactly. Except now we're all freaking out over what's gonna happen next. The owner got himself in some financial trouble a couple of years ago and had to lay off half the staff. Attendance is way down. There was an article in the paper last month about the Pittsburgh Pirates—the Longdogs are one of their farm teams—saying they might not renew their contract in Leland. There's a rumor some guy from Illinois is working a deal to buy the team and move it to Carbondale."

"Dad's going to be so bummed. Can't they just find a local buyer?"

"Not for two and a half million dollars. The only people around here with that kind of money are into horses, not baseball. And there's a big political fight over whether or not the town ought to buy them, but they'd have to sell bonds to do it."

It occurred to Britt this wouldn't be a bad time to talk with her dad about retiring to San Diego, where they could be close as he grew older and more dependent. He enjoyed his visits, especially the eclectic neighborhoods and beaches. A nice condo in the Gaslamp Quarter would put him on the doorstep of Petco Park, home of the Padres baseball team.

"…think you'd like that?" Carly asked.

"I'm sorry, would I like what?"

"The season opener is this Friday against the Cookeville Moccasins, seven o'clock. I was saying if you wanted to make use of your dad's ticket, you could come along with Ninah and me. JT will be there too. He and his son Trey go to all the games."

"I, uh…" Britt found herself conflicted over whether to be gracious or honest. The only thing she appreciated about baseball was that it gave her dad so much pleasure. "I probably should hold off making plans until I see how Dad's doing."

"D'oh." Carly knocked her forehead with the heel of her hand. "I forget you're not here on vacation. You've got a lot more on your mind than watching a ballgame."

"Anybody home?" It was a woman's voice, surprisingly youthful considering the age of her hosts.

"That's Ninah. Justine will send her out here."

Britt was curious to meet this Ninah, who apparently was closer to her dad than either Carly or Justine. She had her pictured as Lily Tomlin in a baseball cap. "It's so funny to me that my father has all these lesbian friends. I can't wait to tell him he's a lesbro."

"Ha! That's funny. I think it's just us three, but if he wanted to surround himself with lesbians, he could sure do it. Justine keeps an email list of all the locals so we can organize potlucks and picnics and stuff. Everybody knows Justine's List. There must be a hundred names on it by now."

"A hundred lesbians in Leland?"

"If you count the whole county. You should have seen them all turn out when I took on Tiny Watson in the county clerk election." Carly basted her chicken with her bourbon-flavored sauce and fished several foil-wrapped pouches from the coals. "The whole mob of them showed up marching down the street together right before the polls closed. Our very own dyke parade. And we kicked his butt."

"Wait…does that mean you're the county clerk?"

"I am indeed. A living, breathing bureaucrat, if you can believe it. Tiny was one of those homophobic cretins who considered himself the last line of defense against all us gays taking over the world with our *agenda*. A born-again huckster, if you ask me. Calls himself a lay minister."

Her opinion of Carly instantly shot up several notches. She admired anyone brave enough to call out religious hypocrisy in a place where churches dominated government and society.

"Tiny refused to issue Justine and me a marriage license so we got the ACLU to add us to their lawsuit. Which we won, of course. As if that was ever in doubt. The whole thing pissed me off though, so when the next election rolled around I ran against him on a promise that I'd do my job instead of grandstanding and wasting a bunch of taxpayer money on lawsuits just to be mean to people I didn't like."

"Good for you." Britt never would have guessed an out lesbian could win an election in rural Kentucky. Perhaps Leland wasn't the same place she remembered. Today's Leland had cafés, boutiques, even a brand-new Whole Foods, probably due to the influx of Lexington's young, well-educated families in search of bigger homes for less money. Now if they could just close down all the churches.

"Hi, guys. Sorry I'm late. I managed to lock myself out of the house with my car keys inside." The new arrival smiled and extended her hand. "I'm Ninah Faust. And you must be Britt."

This was no Lily Tomlin. In fact, she was Britt's age, with bright hazel eyes and *very* short dark hair that accentuated her delicate facial features. In thigh-hugging shorts and a sleeveless, pale yellow shirt opened to the hollow of her breasts, she presented a girl-next-door look that was undeniably appealing.

"Did I see you this morning at the hospital? About a quarter after ten."

"Guilty as charged," Ninah said. "I sneaked in to see Vernon but he was out of it. I'm gonna try to go back sometime tomorrow."

Britt couldn't help but notice that all three women spoke in a distinctly Southern cadence and dialect, just like her dad. *Gonna, wanna, fixing to.* While she didn't mind it in others, she'd worked hard to erase her own Southern accent after being mocked years ago by her college classmates.

She said to Ninah, "I hear you helped save the day when Dad went down. I'm grateful, more than I can say."

"He scared the living daylights out of all of us. I hope you gave him what for." She had a roguish smile like Carly's.

"Trust me, no one was more scared than I was. And being two thousand miles away didn't help. I felt a lot better after Justine told me he was surrounded by a bunch of people who cared about him."

"That's one of the great things about Leland, right Carly? Neighbors look out for each other. Stick around awhile and you'll see that for yourself."

Britt had gotten her fill of Leland as a teenager, but this was admittedly a new perspective. This warm welcome unexpectedly eased her anxiety about having to be there. In fact, it was probably the most comfortable she'd ever felt in Kentucky since coming out in high school. These three women might even make her visit bearable.

CHAPTER FOUR

Ninah watched Britt from the deck as Justine toured her through the flower beds. The woman was captivating. She was also vulnerable right now, so much that a soft-sell of Leland's friendliness felt underhanded. Vernon might not want her plowing ahead with his scheme under these circumstances.

"You're looking especially lovely tonight, Nines," Carly said teasingly.

"I should have known better than to think I'd make it through the night without you being a smart-aleck."

"Some people just don't know how to take a compliment."

So what if she'd fussed a little over lip gloss and worn something that showed off her fit physique? "I wanted to make a good impression."

"I'm sure you have. Seriously, you look great. For that matter, so does she. Just don't go falling in love with her and running off to California."

"Ha! If I was ever gonna leave Leland, it would have been to get away from Teri."

"You've got me there." Carly cupped her hands and shouted, "Dinner's ready."

Returning to the deck, Britt said, "This is so beautiful. If there's one thing I miss about Kentucky, it's the green. Most of San Diego is xeriscaped on account of the drought."

"There's an idea, Justine," Carly said. "Plant things you don't have to water, weed, or mow."

"Not in my yard, you don't. I love my flowers." Justine pointed to assigned seats that had Britt and Ninah sitting beside each other. "Correct me if I'm wrong, Britt. You didn't grow up here in Leland. I seem to remember that Vernon moved here from Louisville."

"He was from here originally, but yeah, we lived in Louisville before he and my mom got divorced. I actually graduated from Leland High School, but I did my first three years at duPont Manual."

"Impressive," Ninah said. For Carly and Justine's benefit, she added, "Manual's been the top high school in Kentucky for about thirty years running."

Throughout dinner, she found herself staring at Britt. The resemblance to her father was uncanny. Same deep-set blue eyes and long lashes, rounded lips that were quick to smile. She'd often thought Vernon would have been an attractive woman. Britt was living proof.

"Was everything all right at the house when you got there?" Carly asked. "Ninah and I stayed after the party last night to clean up. Gosh, was that just last night? Anyway, blame us if your dad gets home and all his stuff's in the wrong cabinet."

"It was fine as far as I could tell. I couldn't believe all that food in the refrigerator. I should have had you over for dinner instead of coming here. It must have been quite a party."

"We always have a big blowout at the start of baseball season," Ninah explained. "Last year it was at JT's, the year before at City Park. It's just a bunch of friends, about ten of us. We've all had season tickets for years and our seats are close together. This party gets everybody amped up for the opener. Except this year we're all bummed out because the Pirates are making noise about pulling out. I've got a bad feeling this might be their last year in Leland."

"Yeah, Carly was saying some guy wants to move them to Illinois."

It felt petty to be talking about baseball when Britt was probably fretting about her father. On the other hand, she might appreciate the diversion.

Coincidentally, Justine had reached her limit on baseball talk. "What sort of work do you do, Britt?"

Ninah knew the answer already, having reviewed Britt's LinkedIn profile. Had she used a personal photo instead of her company logo, her phone would be ringing off the hook.

Britt described her work as a freelancer doing promotions for product launches and corporate events. "My girlfriend Candice and I had our own consulting company, just the two of us. Former girlfriend, I should say. She took an in-house job with our main client, which basically gutted our business and left me holding the bag."

Gutting their relationship too, according to Vernon. Apparently Candice had moved to Reno to work at that company's headquarters.

"I'm hoping to hear back from the Regent Hotel in downtown San Diego. They had me in for a second interview last week for an opening as their convention planner." She knocked twice on the deck rail for luck. "Or I could probably go to work tomorrow for one of the biotech firms. I like being my own boss, but I'm ready to transition into working for someone else. There's a lot of stress in a job where you're constantly having to sell yourself."

How could Vernon ever hope to lure Britt back to Leland when she had exciting prospects in such a vibrant place? Leland's lesbian community could never compete with a place like San Diego. Only a handful of the women in their social circle were single, and most were Carly and Justine's age or older.

"What about you, Ninah? Justine said you were a teacher."

"That's right, social studies at Leland High School. In fact, that scream you hear Wednesday around three o'clock will be me celebrating the fact that school's out."

"A tough year, huh?"

"No more than usual, but it gets really crazy during the last couple of weeks. All any of us can do at this stage of the game is hold on till the ride stops."

"I'd kill for summers off. Anything special planned? Besides watching baseball, I mean."

Justine answered for her. "Ninah doesn't just watch baseball. She gets *paid* for it. Can you imagine? That would be like paying me to plant flowers."

"That's right, my dream job. Professional baseball watcher. I've always liked to score the games, just as a hobby. But then Archie Davenport—he's the GM of the Longdogs—he asked me a couple of years ago to be the official scorekeeper at home games. I was doing it anyway, so now I get paid. Twenty-five bucks a game."

"I had no idea that was an actual job. I thought the scorekeeper just flicked a little button every time somebody scored." Britt chuckled and shook her head. "Okay, I'm being facetious...kind of."

"The official scorekeeper records every single play. That's how they keep up with player stats. I used to do it old school on a scorekeeper pad with a pencil, but the Valley League uses software so the scouts can calculate everything and analyze it to death. Like who's the best hitter with runners in scoring position, stuff like that."

Carly started clearing the dishes, refusing Britt's offer to help. "Justine and I will handle this. You guys just relax and keep each other company."

Alone together for the first time, Ninah sensed that Britt was winding down. "You must be exhausted. You've had a wild twenty-four hours. I bet your dad was glad to see you this morning."

"Not as glad as I was to see him. You try not to think about these things, but our parents get older. I figure this is our cue to start talking about what we want the next ten years to look like, and the ten after that, and so on. It's just him and me, so we need to look out for each other. I'd love it if he'd move out west so we can be closer. He won't, not yet anyway. But the conversation has to start somewhere. Maybe he'll be ready in a couple of years."

"Have you given any thought to coming back this way?"

"Me back in Kentucky?" she scoffed. "Sorry, this place isn't for me."

"It's definitely not California."

"I can't deal with the church culture. Mostly because of my mom, but it's ingrained in everything. They've taken over government, schools, doctors' offices, bedrooms. And why are they so obsessed with other people's sex lives?"

From the sound of it, Britt and her mother were estranged.

"We've definitely got our share of Bible thumpers, but most of the churches around here are Mainline Protestant, middle of the road. Conservative, sure. And that's a challenge when you wanna start a Gay-Straight Alliance at the high school, which I did. But then Carly being elected shows we're getting to be more open-minded. You'll probably see that once you meet some of your dad's friends."

"Dad's always been my rock." Her voice cracked with sudden emotion. "Sorry, it hits me every now and then what a close call this was. I don't know what I'd do without him."

"He's gonna be okay." Ninah covered Britt's hand with hers. "That's what Justine said. She wouldn't lie to you, not about that. Trust her."

"I do." Clearly embarrassed by her tearful display, she brushed her cheeks and stood. "I guess I should be getting home. This jet lag's going to do me in. Thanks for everything you guys did last night at the house. It means a lot to know that Dad has so many good friends looking out for him."

"We're looking out for you too. Want me to run you home? I don't mind."

"Thanks, but the walk will probably do me good."

"Okay, sure. But let's get together again while you're here. We could go for a walk, grab a bite to eat. Maybe even take in a ballgame. I bet your dad would get a kick out of hearing you put his tickets to good use."

They took out their phones and traded texts to capture numbers.

"Here, I'm sending my address too in case you ever wanna stop by. I'm just a couple of blocks off Main Street. We could walk over to The Bean and grab a latte or something."

Britt nodded, but it was distinctly noncommittal. "I'll shoot you a text once I get the lay of the land."

Ninah blamed herself for the gloomy turn in Britt's mood, having dredged up ill feelings about churches and her mother. Added to the worry over her father, it took an obvious emotional toll that spilled over into her goodbye.

Justine sensed it and responded in her usual nurturing way—with a motherly embrace. "I know you're worried, sweetie, but it's all gonna be okay. I promise. Anything you need—I don't care if it's a hug, a bedtime story, or a piece of chocolate pie—you're gonna hurt my feelings if you don't ask. Do you hear what I'm saying?"

They stood motionless in the foyer for over a minute, the only sound an occasional sniffle. When they parted, Justine took Britt's face in her hands and kissed her forehead, a tender gesture that sent Britt back into her arms with a sob.

Ninah and Carly recognized the depth of their connection and stepped away to give them privacy.

"Do you think she's okay?" Carly whispered.

"She is now. I have a feeling what she needed was mothering, and Justine was there to give it to her. Like she does for everybody."

CHAPTER FIVE

Britt perused a shelf of mugs and T-shirts as she waited for JT Sharpe to collect her soy latte. The Bean was a popular spot, with every table occupied by coffee sippers chatting with friends or working on laptops. It had the genuine warmth of an indie shop, but with the tried and tested vibe of the iconic chains.

This JT was a likable fellow, she had to admit. Smiling and folksy, he too had a silver Southern tongue that probably played well with juries. While she could easily see him as her father's best friend, it was harder to wrap her head around the idea that he'd once been Justine's husband. That they remained good friends was a testament to his decency.

"Here ya go, one soy latte," JT said as he handed her a cup. "Too bad we missed Carly. I've got some papers for you to sign back at my office, but what say we take a little walk through town first?"

It was a gorgeous day, sunny and warm but without the sticky humidity that would overtake Kentucky by midsummer.

"A walk would be nice, I think." Following him outside, Britt excused herself to hand a couple of bucks to an apparently homeless man who greeted passersby with random flattery. Earlier he'd complimented her shoes, which were ordinary canvas flats. He was partial to red, or so he said.

"That was nice of ya," JT said. "Ol' Judd's an institution around Leland. And he doesn't miss a thing, so watch yourself."

"Good to know."

"Saw your daddy last night. He's sure glad to have you home."

Britt cringed at the word. Leland wasn't her home. "I saw him early this morning. He's definitely on the mend—got real food for breakfast. Except he called it break-*food*. They said his aneurysm was in an area near a language center, so they expect him to have those little flubs for a while. He'll come out of it over time. They want to keep him another few days at least and then slot him into the rehab center."

JT lowered his sunglasses from his forehead and loosened his tie. "However hard it is, I know Vernon. He'll deal with it."

Their walk took them past a handful of shops that lined the town square, its centerpiece the antebellum courthouse where Carly worked. At City Park, JT guided her to a shaded bench across from the baseball stadium. Behind them was a historical marker that honored town founder Benjamin Leland, a Revolutionary War hero.

"Here we are, home of the Longdogs," she said. "Carly and Ninah said you guys are all bracing for bad news. Dad's going to be devastated if this team gets sold and moves away."

"Nobody wants to see the Longdogs go. They're woven into the fabric of this town." He stretched his arms along the back of the bench and crossed his ankle over his knee. "The casual fan might not realize it, but just about everybody who's made it to the Baseball Hall of Fame got their start in a little town like Leland." He sat up and scrolled through his phone to show her a ticketing app. "Season opens Friday night against the Cookeville Moccasins. Got my tickets already."

"Dad has his printed out and stacked on his desk. He hates that he'll miss the opener, but I promised him I'd go in his place."

"Bet that made his day." He raised his sunglasses and squinted in the sun. "Vernon said you never really took to Leland."

"I don't have anything against it." Other than its role in the most miserable time of her life. "I just prefer the anonymity of a big city. Plus there's something about California that speaks to my soul. I feel at home there, like I belong."

"I get that. I feel the same way about Leland. I'd say your daddy does too."

It was beginning to sound as if her father had sent JT on a mission to head off her attempts to persuade him to move to the West Coast. Or worse, that he was planting a bug designed to make her feel guilty for not coming back.

"My wife and I have a daughter, Alex…she's special needs. When she was little, we had help from Trey and his sister Emmy, the kids I had with Justine. And from my mother-in-law, God rest her harpy soul. But when Alex got bigger, we had to start looking at the big picture. She wasn't thriving, not like she could've. What she needed was to be in a group home with people who knew how to bring out the best in her. It was gut-wrenching, all that guilt about sending her away. But it came down to doing what was best for her. That's how parents roll, you know?"

She acknowledged a grudging respect for the challenges he and his wife had faced, while tamping down her irritation that he probably was setting her up for a guilt trip.

"Your daddy and me, we're the same age. Played high school ball together. Now you wouldn't know this to look at me"—he sucked in his gut and slapped his stomach—"I was a real porker back then. Coach always sent me down the field to block so Vernon could run it in for a touchdown. All the girls,

'Oh Vernon, you're such a hero.' And there I'd be lying flat on my back with somebody's footprint on my face."

"Took one for the team."

"Took a *bunch* for the team. See, I'd do anything in the world for Vernon. Back when he divorced your mama, I tried to get him a better split, but he said, 'No, give her whatever she wants. As long as I've got enough left for Britt.' That's why he came home to the old farmhouse here in Leland, so he'd have what he needed to send you to college in California."

Playing on her father's sacrifices was way below the belt. "Dad's always been very good to me. He was there for me no matter what I needed. And I'll be there for him too."

"I know you will. My point is this: Parents—*good* parents, that is—they don't ever stop wanting to help their kids. We're all gonna get decrepit one of these days and that shoe'll wind up on the other foot, but Vernon's not there yet. He still thinks it's his job to look after you, and he's been worried lately that things aren't going so well out there in San Diego. Is he wrong?"

The truth was irrefutable, if temporary. "My business went off track last fall, but I've got feelers out. I'm very good at what I do—product launches, rebranding, setting up conferences. My skill set is always in demand."

"Oh, I have no doubt. In fact, it's in demand right here in Leland."

She cast him an indulgent look.

"Suppose somebody came along and offered you the opportunity to get in on the ground floor of something that was flat-out *guaranteed* to make you a multimillionaire in five years or less?"

"No business comes with a guarantee like that."

"Don't be so sure. Sometimes Lady Luck sits herself right in your lap."

"Go ahead, I'm listening." She willed her crossed leg to stop swinging with impatience.

"Good, 'cause I've got a helluva story for ya. It all started a couple of years ago with that fire out at the Iverson homestead. Vernon thought about rebuilding something new out there but then Carly pointed him to that house on the lake and he couldn't imagine anything he'd like better. He held onto the land though...sentimental reasons, I guess. But then about three months ago he decided he ought to just clear up the mess and sell it. Problem was his papers all got burned up, so he went down to the courthouse to get a copy of the deed. You'd never guess what he found."

Probably not.

"You know all that fenced-in land along Pinckard Road? Folks around here always figured that was Clyde Hickson's 'cause he runs his horses on it. Turns out it was part of the old Iverson farm. We're talking over three hundred acres of prime Kentucky bluegrass."

He definitely had her attention now. "Are you saying that gorgeous horse farm I've been driving by my entire life actually belongs to my family?"

"*Belonged*. See, Clyde's daddy took out a fifty-year lease on it way back in the day, but it was expired. So I set up a meeting between your daddy and Clyde to smooth it all out. Any given day Clyde's got a dozen or more thoroughbreds out there grazing, so he *had* to have that land. And he's rich as Croesus so he didn't care what it cost."

Grinning at her father's luck, she said, "And now Dad's rich too, it sounds like. Good for him. He's set for life."

"Sure, but my story's not finished. Not by a long shot," JT said coyly, nodding toward the stadium. "Your daddy ever mention Duffy Barnett? A right good fella, played ball with us in high school. Started these here Longdogs back in 1985 when the league was expanding. It was all humming along till a couple of years ago when he went in with some investors on a riverfront development up near Prospect. Looked good on paper I guess, till the guy putting the deal together turned out to be a scam artist. Took everybody's money and ran off. Next thing you know Duffy's having trouble meeting payroll here at the ballpark. He tried doing things on the cheap, but the fans noticed and started complaining. Attendance fell, sponsors pulled out. Next thing you know the Pirates serve notice that the Dogs might be in breach of contract, and they start threatening to go looking for a new prom date."

Suddenly she didn't like where this was going. It would be just like her dad to lend his new fortune to an old friend, especially if it meant saving the team he loved.

"So in came this guy, Raymond Gard, owns Gard Trucking. You've probably seen his trucks out on the highway. Big red letters on the side, 'Let us *Gard* your shipment.' Guess he reckons that's clever. He made Duffy a fair offer considering the Dogs were losing money and couldn't draw more than six hundred head a game. Two-point-one million. But he wanted to move the team to Carbondale and change their name to the Big Rigs."

He teased her with a long silence, forcing her to say, "I get the feeling Dad had something to say about that."

"You're doggone right he did. He had a check from Clyde for a million-three burning a hole in his pocket, and two hundred grand from me, 'cause I wanted a little piece of the action too. He borrowed the rest against his 401K."

Her next breath caught in her throat.

"That's right. The league papers went through this morning. They're Vernon's team now. And mine too, a little bit." He spread his arms on the back of the bench and crossed his legs.

"That doesn't…" She shook her head. "Dad made his living in the food business. What does he know about running a baseball team?"

"He knows he needs smart people on board. In particular, he needs someone who knows how to turn out a crowd and show them all a good time. Seems that particular skill set is always in demand."

"Whoa! You're not serious."

"I am, and so's your daddy. We're sitting on a golden opportunity here, and all we need is a marketing whiz like you to make it blossom. Picture this, Britt. You've got two thousand seats in there. Those are fans who think they've come to watch a baseball game. Sure, but they've also come to eat your hot dogs, drink your beer, and buy your T-shirts. That's the baseball experience. And since this is the minor leagues we're talking about, it's all that plus raffle tickets and ugly dog contests and Cowboy Night and grown men racing tricycles around the base paths. Your job is to come up with all those silly ideas so you can show fans a rip-roaring good time whether the Dogs win or not. Tell me that's not right up your alley."

It was. *Exactly*.

Except annoyingly, this had all the fingerprints of her father trying to bail her out of her own business failure. Surely he could find someone better suited to the job. "Look, the idea of me having anything to do with a baseball team is frankly ludicrous. And in case you missed it, I live in California. I have a business out there that needs all my attention right now."

JT chuckled as he wagged a finger in the direction of the stadium. "You gotta admit, it's a heckuva coincidence, you being an expert on promotions, and that being exactly what the Longdogs need help with. Come on, walk with me."

It was no use arguing about her professional capabilities when the real issue was Leland itself. She didn't want to get into that with JT, but her dad would surely understand.

They passed through an open iron gate and trudged up a winding ramp to a concourse lined with vacant concessions stalls, kiosks, and public restrooms. A short tunnel took them into the stadium, where about three dozen uniformed players were taking batting practice, fielding practice, and conditioning drills. It was a decent-sized park inside, with bleachers on both ends and a section of premium club seats that spanned from one dugout to the other. Above those seats was an awning, painted black and red in the Longdogs motif. At the very top were a pair of box suites she assumed were for VIPs.

"Now some people might look at this and see an ordinary sports field. Those of us who love the Longdogs, we see a community institution, something we can rally 'round and be proud of."

Words that sounded too familiar to be a coincidence. Carly also had spoken about the importance of the Longdogs to the community, which left Britt to wonder if she was part of this conspiracy to lure her to Leland. "Am I the last person to hear about this?"

"Why no, you're the first. After me, that is. And I know Duffy hasn't told anybody 'cause he called me just this morning scared to death the deal was gonna blow up along with your daddy's brain bubble. I said no, that you were here to sign off."

That made her feel better. Carly and Ninah were going to love this news, even if she didn't.

"Now Vernon, he looked around and saw all the places where Duffy could have been making money but wasn't. And he's got a plan to fix it—a plan that involves you."

As he pleaded his case, she noticed a guy on a small tractor mowing the outfield with such precision that it yielded a giant green checkerboard. The aroma of fresh-cut grass was intoxicating, but hardly enough to lull her into saying yes when every cell in her body was screaming *No!*

"I know nothing about baseball. As in zilch, nada, diddly squat."

"You don't need to. The Longdogs are what's called a farm team for the Pirates. All the baseball decisions get made in Pittsburgh. Your job is to bring folks out to the ballpark, show 'em a good time, and send 'em home feeling like they got their money's worth. Heck, the Dogs don't even have to win for that. Lord knows we've sat through our share of duds and had fun just the same."

Fine, so the job was right up her alley. She'd sold everything from toys to medical devices to investment services, all by designing special events that created curiosity and passion for new ideas. That didn't mean she wanted to move back to Kentucky to sell a night at the ballpark.

"Don't underestimate your daddy's business acumen. He's one shrewd son of a gun. Before he shook on this deal with Duffy, he worked up a new lease with the town council that gives him *all* park-related revenue for a rock-bottom rent. That's because the council wanted to keep this team in Leland. We're talking advertising, concessions, merchandising. And tickets for everything under the sun. You can stage concerts, motivational speakers, whatever your pretty little head dreams up."

She admittedly was impressed by her father's inspiration. Still, it was a mammoth undertaking for a man nearing retirement age, especially one who now had cause to be concerned for his health. "But I'm worried about Dad. What if he's not the same guy he was two days ago?"

"That makes you being here all the more important, Britt... especially since we already signed the loan papers." Red and sweating from the midday sun, he led her along the aisle to a shaded section directly behind home plate. "Last year, the Bloomington Bicycles sold for twelve million dollars, and they've only got fifteen hundred seats. You know why? Because they sell out. They've got a waitlist for season tickets. That's what somebody like you can do for the Longdogs."

Twelve million dollars?

"We practically stole this team off Duffy for a paltry two-point-two. You give it one good summer, maybe two. It'll be worth twice that, easy. All it takes is steady work and smarts." He tapped his finger to his temple. "You get this place humming and next thing you know some dot-com billionaire's gonna waltz in here and wave ten or fifteen million dollars under our noses."

There wasn't a whole lot she wouldn't do for ten or fifteen million dollars, but she was enough of a realist to know that most get-rich-quick schemes were too good to be true. For JT's plan to work, every single piece would have to fall into place. "What happens if the Pirates pull the plug before we get things turned around?"

He blanched. With his hands in his pockets, he began to rock. "Obviously, that'd be the worst-case scenario. We'd have to convince another team to move operations to Leland. That'll be hard to do if we've still got a thousand empty seats."

"And Dad's investment?"

"Gone."

As far as she was concerned, that changed all the calculus. Her dad didn't just want her back in Leland. He *needed* her to help make a go of it. If she turned her back on him, he could lose everything.

One summer, maybe two.

"All right, so assuming I say yes…what happens next?"

He broke into a broad grin. "We hit the ground running… right this minute."

CHAPTER SIX

After a workout at Grace Hospital's wellness center, Ninah dreamed of melting into her sofa with a crisp salad and a broiled filet of salmon. She wrinkled her nose and perished the thought. Surely an hour of cardio and weightlifting deserved a guilt-free plate of chicken fettuccine.

Her apartment was on the lower level of an eighty-year-old white frame house. She arrived home after sunset but before dark, what her mother called "the lightning bug hour." Upstairs neighbor Emmy Sharpe was milling about on the wide covered porch they shared.

"I thought you'd be in bed by now," Ninah said as she climbed the gray plank stairs. "Seeing as how you had such a late houseguest last night."

A pharmacist at Grace Hospital, Emmy also happened to be Justine and JT's daughter. "Is there no such thing as privacy?"

Ninah snorted. "Not when your stairs are next to my headboard. Why the secrecy? You afraid I'll tell your mom about your sleepovers?"

"Technically, they aren't sleepovers if nobody sleeps."

"TMI, girl. TMI."

At twenty-nine years old, Emmy was almost a contemporary but for the fact that she'd been a junior in high school the year Ninah began her teaching career at Leland High. Over the years, Emmy's occasional presence at parties hosted by her mom and Carly helped dispel their teacher-student dynamic, but it was only when they became duplex-mates that they established themselves as adult friends and confidantes.

Dressed in cartoon pajama bottoms and a tank top, Emmy was pinching dead leaves off her potted begonias and geraniums. Tall and fit like Justine, and with the same auburn hair, she also shared her mother's interest in plants. "Not to belabor the obvious, Ninah...we've been neighbors for three years now. When are *you* going to have a sleepover?"

"I'll have you know I'm taking a break."

"For three years? That's not a break, it's a coma. You need to get laid, woman."

It so happened the thought of dating someone had unexpectedly crossed her mind last night as she'd gazed across the table at Britt Iverson. Leland needed more women like Britt. Even one would be a vast improvement.

She collapsed on the porch swing and kicked the floor to set it in motion. "As luck would have it—bad luck, that is—I ran into Teri Kaufman at Whole Foods yesterday. That usually puts me off thoughts of sex for a month or so."

"You give that girl too much power. Cut the cord already."

"Don't worry, it's cut. I think she's down to two friends, Robbi and Liv. I'm afraid to ask what they see in her. Some things you're better off not knowing."

Emmy pitched the clippings over the rail and signaled with her shaking hips that she wanted Ninah to scoot over on the swing. "So get your butt back out there and find somebody better."

"Right, I'll just pick one from the multitudes throwing themselves at my feet," she replied sarcastically, snapping her fingers. "What's really pathetic is—thanks to that list your mom keeps—I know practically all the lesbians in town, and there's not a single one I wanna date."

"I kind of felt that way too…about the guys, not the lesbians. But then all of a sudden there he was."

"Lucky you. So how come you're sneaking him in and out of your place at all hours of the night. Oh wait, he's not—"

"He's *not* married. It's just that we'd like to have a little more time with each other before we announce it to the world. You know how Mom will be if she finds out I'm seeing somebody. She'll have a million questions, the first being whether or not he's ever voted for a Republican." After a couple of seconds, she pointedly added, "I'm almost positive he hasn't."

"And your dad will wanna see his bank statements."

"Exactly. Let's hope I'm better at keeping a secret than Mom. I'll never forget when she fell for Carly. She thought nobody knew but it was all over her face."

Ninah chuckled. "It still is. I've never seen two people more perfect for each other."

"You had that with Teri once, right? Obviously not at the end, but you must have loved each other at some point."

Surely they had…though it was hard to remember any loving feelings given the acrimony surrounding their demise. "We had our moments, I guess, especially the first couple of years. All those endorphins have a way of making you oblivious to somebody's flaws. Considering what I know now, I can't believe we lasted six years. I must have been sleepwalking."

"Six years. It scares the shit out of me to think I could spend that long with somebody and not have anything to show for it." She hissed and sheepishly added, "Sorry, didn't mean for that to come out so brutal."

"No point in sugarcoating it. Our relationship ended in a raging dumpster fire. At least when your mom and dad split up, they stayed friends."

"You weren't there for the fireworks. But yeah, they eventually worked through it. Maybe one of these days you and Teri..."

"I don't want Teri for a friend. In fact, I'd prefer never to see her again, but Leland's too small for that. Let's just hope I don't ever need an x-ray or CAT scan. She'd probably kill me with radiation."

"She's not the only imaging tech at Grace Hospital, you know. They've got two or three others on staff who could kill you too." Emmy bumped her shoulder playfully.

"I thought about moving when we split up so I wouldn't have to run into her anymore. There was an opening at Dunbar High in Lexington but by the time I finally made up my mind to go for it, they'd hired somebody else."

"I can't believe you'd let her run you out of town. This is your home. You've been here what, fifteen years?"

She'd chosen Leland High School from the list of job openings posted in the placement office at Western Kentucky University. "Thirteen, but Teri's lived here all her life."

"You at least have squatter's rights, especially since you teach at the high school. You know practically every family in town."

It was true she felt at home in Leland, especially with her rich network of friends. But friends weren't enough to fill the hole since her breakup.

"I love this place, Emmy. I know it's just a wide spot in the road to some people, but it's like New York City compared to where I came from. It's friendly, it's quiet. And we've got our own baseball team. All we need now is a busload of single lesbians under forty and we're talking nirvana."

"Look around, Ninah. People find each other. Could be the right person is somebody you've known for years, and one of these days it's going to click. That's what happened to me. Or maybe she's with somebody else right now, but for whatever reason it doesn't last."

There was yet another possibility...but she couldn't wait to get back to San Diego.

CHAPTER SEVEN

Britt tightened her grip on her father's elbow as she noticed his hesitation. They were in the hospital's stairwell, where he was practicing alternating feet as he went up and down. Stair climbing was one of the skills he'd have to master before his doctor would consider releasing him home, since his bedroom was on the second floor.

"You got it, Dad?"

"It's harder than it feels."

Harder than it looks? Despite his occasional odd word choices, most of what he said made sense if she took it in context. Moreover, his doctor was generally pleased with his mental assessment, though he was recommending at least two weeks at the rehab center to help recover his speech and motor skills.

"Once you get these stairs mastered, we're going to strap a box on your shoulders. You can go up and down the bleachers hawking beer and peanuts."

"Wish you could break me out of here for the game."

"Dr. Dhawan thinks it's too soon and I agree. We can't risk you falling and landing on your head. Besides, you can't stay awake long enough to watch a baseball game. They take forever."

Fans who'd followed the Longdogs' recent misfortunes would be thrilled to hear the team was back on solid financial footing and staying put in Leland. With JT looking over her shoulder, she'd dutifully signed the closing documents yesterday. All they were waiting for was formal recognition by the league office, expected by end of business today. Then she'd send out a press release announcing the change in ownership.

"So Dad, when were you going to tell me about the Longdogs? Or was this little brain stunt of yours all part of your master plan to get me back here?"

"I was gonna send you a first-pass ticket." First *class*. "And take you with me to the ballpark. I wanted you to see for yourself what a good..."

A good opportunity? A good fit with her skills? As he seemed to search for the appropriate word, Britt contemplated whether to make suggestions or let his brain do the work.

"I planned on talking you into being my business partner. I can put you on the...so you can be a co-owner." Clearly exhausted from the physical and mental effort, he shuffled to the door that would lead them from the stairwell. "But only if it's what you want. I didn't mean to dump it on you like this."

"It's okay, Dad. I'm not promising to stay forever, but I told JT I'd stick around till we got it off the ground, the first season for sure. That means you'll have me under your feet for the whole summer."

If she'd had any second thoughts about staying in San Diego, they were crushed last night by an email from the Regent Hotel, a form letter addressed to "Dear Applicant." They'd chosen someone from their many excellent candidates. Thanked her for her interest. Wished her well in her career endeavors. Yada-yada.

So it was the Longdogs or bust.

Lucky for her, JT was right that minor league baseball actually had very little to do with baseball. She'd spent much of the last twenty-four hours in a deep dive on the Internet exploring what her new job would entail. Initial hopes that she could shuttle back to California when the season ended were dashed once she realized just how much there was to do in the off-season. Lining up vendors and sponsors, hustling for group ticket sales. Cultivating community relationships.

Then there was the event calendar, in which every single home game needed to have at least one hook. A theme night, a sponsor promotion, a contest, a special guest. Plus she needed to come up with an endless stream of audience participation activities to keep fans engaged between innings. Prizes, contests, giveaways. The challenge was figuring out what would resonate with Longdogs fans. To do that, she'd have to find a way to connect with Leland itself.

"JT should be calling any minute with the news," she said as she helped her father back into bed. "And it better be good news, because I've already written the press release for tomorrow's *Gazette*. JT confirmed that I'm your sole heir, by the way, so watch your back. I might decide to cash out."

He barely managed a smile as sleep threatened to overtake him any second.

She tucked the sheet to his chin and kissed his forehead. "I'll be back to see you in the morning. Love you."

The decision to stay in Leland for a year or two triggered a cascade of steps needed to unwind her life in San Diego. First would be a call to her accountant to dissolve her LLC. There was no point in continuing to pay corporate license fees for a business she couldn't sustain. Next she'd need to move her belongings into storage and convince her landlord to let her break the lease. And figure out how to get her car to Kentucky.

On the drive home, she placed a call to longtime friend Holly Burchard. She'd always felt a special connection with

Holly, a Dayton native who'd headed west after college for a job with a biotech magazine. Like Britt, she worked at home with no boss to scold her for taking personal calls on the clock.

"Hey, how's your dad?"

"A lot better. Thanks for asking. It's possible he'll get moved to a rehab center tomorrow. A couple of weeks there and he should be able to come home."

"Fucking-A. Did you find out if he got the Phynox? Those are all the rage right now." Leave it to Holly to be as interested in the manufacturer of the aneurysm clip as she was in the patient.

"All I know is it won't set off the metal detector at the airport. Look, the reason I'm calling...this is really nuts." No way was she telling her friends that her father had just sunk his retirement savings into a sports team and expected a klutz like her to help run it. The jokes would never stop. "I won't go into the gory details, but it turns out Dad signed on to a major business deal right before this brain thing hit. He can't manage it right now, so I need to stick around and see it through so he won't lose his investment. Not forever, but it could take a while to get the right people in place to run it. It's a great opportunity, a lot of money up for grabs if we play our cards right. We're talking millions."

"Wow, what kind of business? Something to do with that book he wrote?"

"No, this is..." *Oh, screw it*, she thought. If she couldn't talk to her best pal, who else was there? "Please don't tell everybody this. They'll laugh their asses off. He bought the minor league baseball team that plays here in Leland. Their mascot is a dachshund, but do they call themselves the Dachshunds? No, because the minor leagues are wacky. They're called the Longdogs."

"Oh. My. God. That's fucking hysterical. Britt Iverson, the second coming of Marge Schott."

Britt recalled the name. Schott was a former owner of the Cincinnati Reds, notorious for her bigoted remarks about minority players. After repeated offenses, the league finally forced her to sell the team.

"Don't worry, Marge's legacy is safe. I'll be working mostly behind the scenes doing the stuff I'm actually good at. Once Dad gets back on his feet, he'll be the public face of the team."

"I read something on Bloomberg not long ago about minor league sports teams being the new collectible for billionaires. You could be sitting on a fucking gold mine, Britt."

Three. Whenever they talked on the phone, Britt was in the habit of counting the number of times Holly used the word "fuck."

"That's what the lawyer says. This one needs a lot of work to build up the fan base, but once we get there…"

"How long are you talking about?"

"I don't know, could be a year or two. Obviously I'm not thrilled about having to move back here, but I'll be so busy I won't even have time to think about it." No, because she'd be thinking about San Diego, with its beaches, gardens, and canyons. "Who am I kidding? I can't believe I'm doing this. I'd sooner take a running jump off the cliffs at La Jolla."

"Aww, it can't be that bad."

"Prodigal daughter returns home alone and penniless."

"So fucking what, Britt? You're looking at this all wrong. Face it, Candice fucked you over. Break up with somebody, fine. That bitch took your livelihood too—"

Five. "And my house. Don't forget my house."

"And she left you with jack shit. Now you get to rub her fucking nose in it. Candice did you a big-ass favor, girlfriend. You know why? Because you're about to get very fucking rich. She shit all over you for a job in Reno—fucking Reno—making what, eighty thousand a year? You would never have done that to her. And now you're going to make millions and you don't have to give a single fucking fuck about her."

"Right, all I have to do is go back to Kentucky with my tail between my legs."

"Are you listening? Because fuck that right now, Britt." Reading the moment, the tenor of Holly's voice had gone from teasing to compassionate to fiery, which was why she was Britt's favorite friend. "Flip the script. You're not going back home. You're *relocating* for a better job. That's how successful people advance their careers. So go for it. What's a little change of scenery? Work your magic and get filthy, stinking rich. Then you can live wherever the fuck you want."

Twelve.

Britt could get on board with that. Rather than feeling humiliated that her father was trying to help rescue her career, she could celebrate the fact that he was giving her this tremendous opportunity because of what she brought to the table. There needn't be a stigma attached, no tacit admission of failure. Just the opposite, in fact.

"Thanks, Holly. You're good to have around whenever I need a kick in the ass."

"Fucking-A. What are friends for?"

As she pulled into the driveway at her father's house, another call beeped in, JT Sharpe. She quickly made loose plans with Holly to hook up when she returned to San Diego to pack up her apartment.

"JT?"

"Hey, I just got the certification letter hand-delivered from the league. We're good to go. And I sent the press release over to the *Gazette*, so all of Leland is gonna chase you down tomorrow and hug your neck."

"If they really want to show their thanks, they can come to the ballpark."

That made it official. First thing tomorrow, she'd walk into the offices at Leland Field and introduce herself to the folks Duffy Barnett had hired to run his failing team. With luck, she'd find them competent and hard working, missing only the leadership she and her dad would provide.

Still sitting in her car, she scrolled through her recent calls for the number she'd added two nights ago. Ninah would be thrilled with her news, Carly too. Of the two of them, Ninah was more devoted to the team. Though tempted to show up at her door to deliver the news in person, she found herself too excited to wait.

Ninah answered on the second ring, her voice holding a trace of panic. "Hey, is everything all right with your dad?"

"Yes…yes, he's doing great. Sorry, didn't mean to scare you. You got a minute?"

"Sure, I just walked in the door right this second. Only one more day of school and I'm done for the summer. It's totally insane. Wish me luck."

"You got it. Now let me know when you're sitting down."

"Uh-oh. Is this gonna be good news or bad news?"

"I think you're going to like it." She tried to picture Ninah's face. "You remember Justine saying JT wanted to meet with me? You're not going to believe this." She paused for dramatic effect. "Dad bought the Longdogs."

"He *what*? Are you serious?"

"That's what the meeting was about. He called two minutes ago to say the league signed off on it. It's a done deal. We just sent out a press release so it'll be in the paper tomorrow, but I wanted you to hear it from me first."

"Oh my God, this is so cool!" She was almost shrieking. "We've been worried about an out-of-town buyer and it was your dad all along. You had no idea?"

"Not even a hint." She briefly explained about the land on Pinckard Road, and how JT and her dad had thwarted the sale to Gard. "They were going to make the announcement that night at the party, but then Dad's aneurysm hit. And get this. He needs me to stay and run all the events at the ballpark. Contests, games, theme nights. I had no idea how big a deal that was at—"

"Wait a minute. Back it up, Lucille."

Britt chuckled at the expression. She'd give anything to see Ninah's face right now.

"Does this mean you're moving to Leland? Because that would be freaking awesome. The Longdogs are gonna be so much fun now. I can't wait to see what—*holy crap!* This means you're my boss."

"Oh, right. You're the official scorekeeper. Assuming you survive the first round of personnel cuts. You know how these takeovers go."

"Britt Iverson, corporate raider." Ninah laughed. "I can't believe Vernon pulled this off, that old sneak."

"Tell me about it. He didn't even think to tell his own daughter. And he won't be showing up for work for who knows how long. I have to walk in there tomorrow and act like I know what I'm doing."

"If there's anything I can do to help, ask away. I mean that. You need a crash course in the Longdogs? I'm your tutor."

It was an intriguing offer, especially since JT said Ninah knew as much about the team as anyone. "I might just take you up on that. Let me go in tomorrow and get the lay of the land. Just don't be surprised if you find me waiting on the schoolhouse steps when you come out."

"This is fantastic news, Britt. Not just the team, all of it. This is gonna sound totally selfish, but I'm really glad you're staying."

Only for a while, she almost said. Her eagerness to make it clear that she wasn't attaching herself to Leland was quieted by a sudden intrigue over the fact that Ninah was glad she was staying. Not exactly what she'd call a silver lining, but definitely an attractive consolation prize.

CHAPTER EIGHT

Iverson, a Leland native and longtime season ticket holder, secured the team's commitment to the town with an extended lease on Leland Field to the year 2042. Councilman Aaron Cobb proclaimed the deal "a home run for generations of Leland baseball fans."

Ninah read the story again as she waited for her coffee order. She couldn't have been happier if the Longdogs had won the World Series. Especially given that two days ago she and Carly were practically mourning the team's inevitable exit. This was Christmas in June.

Brittany Iverson, a promotions planner from San Diego, joins the Longdogs office as vice president. "Our goal is to make Leland Field the place to be on game night. Come for the baseball, stay for the family fun. We promise something for everyone." The Longdogs open their 32nd season on Friday night against the Cookeville Moccasins. Game time is 7 p.m.

"You sly dog," she said under her breath. Vernon had this up his sleeve all along. That's why he'd sought her help to convince Britt that Leland was a great place to live.

The barista called out, "I've got one *hot* mocha latte for Ninah."

She snaked through a group of people waiting at the counter to claim her drink.

"Someone's in the kitchen with Ninah," he sang, a convincing impression of his music idol, Nat King Cole. "Strumming on the old banjo. Fee-fi-fiddly—"

"Nice try, Ike," she said sharply, cutting him off. Waving the newspaper in his face, she added, "The Longdogs are staying in Leland and it's the last day of school. You can't possibly spoil this day, not even by sticking that stupid song in my head for the next six hours."

A former student of hers now in his mid-twenties, Ike Martin styled himself the World's Greatest Barista. Jokes, impressions, and irrepressible earworms were a hallmark of the service he delivered to his regular customers. He'd also sold a few tunes of his own and hoped one day to write the mega-hit that would launch his songwriting career.

Folding a dollar into his burgeoning tip jar, she added, "By the way, your brother did a bang-up job this year as president of the GSA. You can tell him I said that."

"But then I'll have to listen to an hour of Thaddeus moaning, 'Oh, Miss Faust. She's my favorite teacher ever.'" He batted his eyes to mock her.

"And that's a problem because?" She craned her neck toward the back room of the shop in search of Carly. High fives were in order after the news about the Longdogs. "Is Carly back here?"

"You missed her by a couple minutes. Maybe she saw you coming."

"Or maybe she heard you singing."

As they shared a laugh, an unfamiliar young man abruptly approached the counter and sniped at Ike, "How about you fix our coffee instead of monkeying around for tips?"

The language was jarring, a white man telling a black man not to monkey around. Judging from the hush that fell over their side of the shop, Ninah wasn't the only one taken aback. The Bean was known for its neighborly vibe. Painted placards all around the shop promoted kindness to others.

She immediately connected this man, with his high-and-tight haircut and white polo shirt, to the muscle car that had stalked her and Thaddeus two days earlier. Clearly he had a problem with African-Americans. Not so long ago, her impulse would have been to step back and leave Ike and this stranger to hash it out, but she was woke, as her kids would say, to the new reality that silence in the face of racism was tacit consent. Addressing the man, she said coolly, "Ike's job is customer service. Judging from all that cash in his tip jar, I'd say he's pretty good at it."

"He won't be getting any tip from me."

Al Pennington, a loan officer at Bank of Leland, looked up from his phone and said calmly, "Take your time, Ike. Extra buck from me."

"Me too, bro." That from Tim C, whose business cards identified him as the guy to call to fix your computer.

Before the young man could escalate the confrontation further, Ike nonchalantly slid a covered cup toward him. Under his breath, but loud enough that those nearby could hear, he said, "One delicious *vanilla* latte for…Seth Seth bo-beth, banana-fana-fo-feth."

Seth's jaw twitched with anger and humiliation as he stormed out, leaving Ninah and the others to trade looks of indignation and relief. Ike appeared unfazed, at least on the outside. It was remarkable how he'd met the insult with humor.

The last three years had seen a rise all over the country in people like Seth, men and women captured in viral videos setting upon people they felt were beneath them, either because of their race, ethnicity, religion, or sexual orientation. Hillary Clinton had famously called them "deplorables," a word Ninah found perfectly descriptive. With Leland slowly becoming more diverse and inclusive, she hoped Seth and his ilk would soon discover their views were no longer welcome.

As she turned for the door, a pair of teenage girls shuffled in, each glued to her cell phone. Ninah recognized them as Sabrina and Kylee, rising seniors from her civics class. In the fashion of the day, their long T-shirts obscured their very short shorts, making it appear as if they were wearing nothing underneath.

"I can't believe they let him stand there on the sidewalk. He smells like a garbage can," Sabrina groused. "And why's he wearing that nasty coat when it's, like June already?"

Clearly she was talking about Judd Stover, a homeless Vietnam veteran who lived on the streets of Leland. Judd sometimes hung out near The Bean in the morning, panhandling customers as they came and went.

Kylee sarcastically replied, "Could it be—I don't know—because he doesn't have a closet to hang it in? He can't just leave it lying around, Sabrina. Somebody will steal it, and then he won't have one when it gets cold."

"Then he should get a job so he can buy a new one."

One girl callous, the other compassionate. For the life of her, Ninah couldn't understand how two people so fundamentally different remained such close friends.

"'Morning, girls."

"Miss Faust. Got your caffeine fix?"

"You bet. I need all the help I can get on a day like this."

"Us too," Sabrina said. "I couldn't function without my frappé."

"Better get a move on. Rumor has it they add an extra hour of detention on the last day of school."

Still stewing over Seth's treatment of Ike, Ninah stepped out onto the sidewalk and scanned the street for the gray Dodge.

She hated to think its owners were staying somewhere nearby. That would put them within walking distance of The Bean, the high school, and more importantly, her house.

Handing a folded dollar to Judd, she described Seth and asked if he'd noticed which way he'd gone.

"Got in a 2014 Dodge Challenger, granite crystal. I seen one like it at B&T Motors. Might be the same one." He stroked his grizzled chin. "It sat right there in the handicapped spot with the motor running."

"Figures." The Alt-Right movement was bigger than white supremacy. It disrespected virtually all marginalized communities. "What's this world coming to, Judd?"

"I try to focus on the nice people." He smiled and tipped his worn cap. "People like you."

It was a good philosophy in theory, but Ninah knew from thirteen years in the classroom that ignoring the troublemakers only went so far. She suspected Seth and his friend were intent on causing havoc.

"Oh, and it had a boot sticker in the back window."

"A boot sticker…" That was a parking permit for the boot factory, which confirmed they'd come to Leland for work.

As she started up the sidewalk toward Leland High, she recognized a familiar face closing in from the next block. "Well, well. If it isn't the new owner of the Longdogs." She greeted Britt with an exuberant hug, which Britt returned. "I'm a hugger. Hope that's okay."

"I'm not complaining," Britt said. "It's funny that I've only been in town for three days and already I'm running into people I know."

"That's a small town for you. It's why we're all so nice to each other, because if you make enemies, there's no way to avoid them. Makes us try harder to get along."

Britt was stunning in a smart black pantsuit and crisp white shirt that exuded authority and seriousness. She shuddered to realize it was also the sort of thing she might have packed for a funeral.

"I take it you're on your way to work?"

"Assuming they don't laugh me out of there."

"That would be unwise, considering you're the boss now. And something tells me that in a matter of days you'll know more about their jobs than they do."

"I wouldn't go that far, but I need to learn as much as I can if I'm going to make this work. I just wish Dad were walking in with me. Or JT, for that matter, but he had to go to court in Frankfort."

Ninah didn't know what to make of that. Britt didn't strike her as a shrinking violet who depended on men for support. "JT and your dad obviously think you can handle it. So do I, since I can't imagine they'd drop this in your lap otherwise."

"Let's hope you're right. It's hard to overcome first impressions."

Sabrina and Kylee emerged with their frappés, bouncing in the direction of the school. "Don't be late, Miss Faust. Last day of school, you'll get detention for the whole summer."

"I'm right behind you," she called, trying to stretch the moment with Britt. "If I weren't running late, I'd buy you a coffee."

"Your last day, my first. And later this afternoon, I'm supposed to meet the guy from the *Gazette* who wrote up our press release. Wesley Hodges. Do you know him?"

"Yes…yes, I do." She didn't want to say something that might bias Britt and get her off on the wrong foot with the paper's primary sports reporter. Wesley took seriously his belief that the press should be adversarial to those in power and hold them accountable for mistakes. And he never pulled his punches. While it made for interesting reading, his blunt criticism of high school coaches and athletes didn't always go over well in the community. "Wesley has a tendency to focus on the negative. You'd do well not to give him too much ammunition."

"Thanks for the heads-up." Britt shook her head and sighed. "You wouldn't believe how much web-surfing I've done on minor league baseball in the last forty-eight hours. Thousands of articles and videos, and I swear I've seen them all. I can't believe how much I don't know about baseball. As soon as I open my mouth, everyone's going to realize I'm an idiot."

"Only an idiot would take you for an idiot." Ninah gave her shoulder a reassuring squeeze. "You're the owner now. That automatically makes you the authority on everything."

"Yeah, except baseball."

"I've got that covered. All you have to do is ask." She took a reluctant step toward the school, briefly toying with the possibility of calling in sick. *Nope.* Sabrina and Kylee would hang her out to dry. "After three thirty today, I'm all yours if you want it."

"Be careful what you ask for."

The bell sounded as Ninah reached the schoolhouse steps. She'd replayed Britt's last line a dozen times in her head, giddy to think it might have been flirtatious. Alone in the stairwell, she laughed to herself. "Careful what *you* ask for, Britt Iverson."

CHAPTER NINE

The operations center of the Longdogs was on the top floor of the stadium, one level above the concessions concourse. Accessible by private elevator and a stairwell tucked behind the ticket window, it housed a conference room and several offices, and provided entry to the press box and owner's VIP suite.

Five of the offices were presently unoccupied, with the administrative staff down to only two—general manager Archie Davenport and his daughter-in-law Misty, an administrative clerk. Right away, Britt staked out the office farthest from Misty's jazzy ringtone. While the room itself was small, a wide window yielded a grand view of the baseball diamond below.

Now seated at her desk across from Archie, she began to massage her temples. "How long has it been like this?"

"A little over two years," he replied grimly. "Started right after Junie died. Ovarian cancer. She was kind of a den mother to all the players. Junie loved the Longdogs like they were her own boys. Once she passed, Duffy kind of lost interest. I could see it in his face when he came to the park. He was gutted."

It made sad, convoluted sense from an emotional standpoint. Duffy should have divested sooner…but then he probably would have squandered even more in the development deal. At least this way, he now had a couple million dollars of her father's to see him through retirement.

"What kind of marketing did you do last year?"

"Misty helped me dredge up some of the old promotions, plus we had a bunch of stuff saved back for giveaways. T-shirts and caps and the like."

"I don't suppose there's anything we can hand out for the opener tomorrow night?"

"As a matter of fact, we rustled up a bunch of foam rubber balls to throw out. About a hundred or so. Got the Longdogs logo on one side and Simmons Funeral Home on the other."

That was too much irony to unpack, she thought.

According to his personnel file, Archie had just turned sixty-eight and had held the general manager position for six years. Short and paunchy, with a flattop haircut that squared his face, he bore no traces of ever having been an athlete. Apparently he wasn't much of a general manager either, but that probably wasn't his fault. He'd only taken the job as a favor to Duffy, accepting a salary that was half the league average, with no revenue responsibilities. His career goal at this point was to retire, but he hated to see the Longdogs go out on his watch.

"Let's talk about some of these others. What all does Misty's job entail?"

"She handles the phone, the mail, payroll…basically all the paperwork. Ask her for whatever you need. She'll get it done."

From her quick review of personnel files, Misty was a solid hire. She had an associate degree in business from the community college, and her pay was reasonable. But that ringtone had to go.

"And Coy Guthrie?"

"Coy's our clubby. That's what we call the clubhouse manager. Every team has one. He puts out the spread, does the laundry, keeps all the equipment in order. Takes care of whatever the guys need."

"He does all that for only four hundred a month?"

Archie went on to explain the clubhouse dues structure, whereby the players paid for their upkeep out of their meager salaries and signing bonuses. On game days, Coy laid out a light afternoon meal following batting practice and a full meal postgame. "Plus they give him tips. But just between you and me, he likes his job so much he'd probably do it whether they tipped him or not."

Britt scribbled a note on her pad to remind her to seek Coy out so she could get a clearer picture of how the money flowed in the clubhouse. Yet another item on the long list of things she didn't totally understand.

"And Pervis Yates. Who is that?"

"Pervis is…Pervis. He does a little bit of everything. Cuts the grass, chalks the lines. Fixes things that get broke. Oh, and he's Banger."

"Excuse me?"

"Banger's our mascot. That's Pervis all dressed up in a dachshund costume. Dances and does handsprings across the infield. Kids love him."

"I see." A mascot could figure prominently in promotions, appearing at birthday parties and shopping centers. "All right, then…who have we got selling advertising?"

After an awkward silence, Archie shook his head. "I asked Duffy about maybe hiring a couple of interns from the business school at UK, but that kind of fell through the cracks."

And by now the best prospects would be locked up in other internships. "What about you, Archie? Ever done any advertising sales?"

"No, I'm the baseball guy."

"The baseball guy...okay, now I'm confused. It's my understanding the Pittsburgh Pirates make all the baseball-related decisions. How does that mesh with your duties?" She honestly didn't want to come off as confrontational, but she needed to know just exactly what the GM of a business did if he wasn't concerned with revenue.

In a tone that bordered on defensive, he started his list. "Well, for one thing, I'm responsible for the condition of the field. It has to meet Minor League Baseball standards—the height of the mound, the clip of the grass, the width of the chalk. Everything's got to be perfect."

"You do that?"

"Not me personally...but I supervise Pervis and make sure he does it right. I do the hiring and firing, make all the travel arrangements, hand out the per diems, pay the vendors. That is, I give all the invoices to Misty and tell her who to pay and how much. And I'm here most days to accept deliveries. You'd be surprised how often they have to order food and beer. You can't just let the driver drop off a keg at the door if nobody's here. It has to go in a locked cooler right away, or somebody'll sneak by in a pickup truck and tote it off."

"Heavens, yes." An important job, for sure. "And in the off-season?"

After a noticeable squirm, he turned his eyes to the floor as he spoke. "That's when I line up the vendors, and order supplies and stuff. Naturally, the workload's a little lighter...but it balances out on account of all I have to do in the summer. By the time the guys shower and eat, it can be twelve thirty, one o'clock in the morning. I'm always the last man out so I can lock up and turn the lights out."

It occurred to her that she had two choices with regard to Archie. She could let him retire and absorb his supervisory duties herself while distributing the rest of his responsibilities across the remaining staff. Or she could double both his salary and his workload and lure him into staying at least two more years so she wouldn't have to take on a new GM. The latter wasn't feasible unless he possessed an aptitude for sales.

"I appreciate what you're saying, Archie. It's just that…" She spread out a set of printouts with expenses and revenues. "The baseball end of this business gets handled in Pittsburgh. Sure, we provide them a little support for that, but basically we're here to sell stuff—tickets, concessions, advertising, and merchandise. If no one's doing that, we can't keep paying people like Pervis, like Coy…like you. Are you following what I'm saying?"

He nodded, but that was about the extent of his concern, which she found worrying. Still, he was indispensable. For now, anyway. He'd forged relationships with the staff and vendors, and he seemed to know all the day-to-day minutiae of operations. She'd hate to find herself mowing the field and chalking the lines.

"Look, Dad and I plan on turning this franchise around. We'll be putting a great deal of effort into making Leland Field the place to be on game nights. Before this season's over, we're going to fill every seat and sell them all the hot dogs and popcorn they can eat. I assume you want that too, right?"

"Yes, ma'am."

"Can we count on you to help us get there?"

He nodded eagerly. "There's nothing I'd like better than to see this stadium rocking again."

"Okay, then. Friday, opening night. What are we doing to get fans pumped up for the season?"

"Well, there's the rubber balls…and we usually do a drawing from the ticket stubs to bring some lucky family from out in the bleachers over to the club seats behind home plate. And we've got Mayor Wilson throwing out the first pitch. He does that every year. And Deke Sullivan, that's Misty's uncle. He's the choir director at First Baptist. He'll lead the singing of the national anthem."

Thrilling. How would she ever contain the crowd with that kind of mayhem?

"The big news this year is Cory Hanover. He's that kid from Vandy that threw a no-no in the College World Series."

"A no-no? Is that like a spitball or something?"

Archie had the good sense not to laugh at her expense, but she could tell he wanted to. "A no-no is short for no runs, no hits. It means he shut down every batter who came to the plate. It's a good thing."

"Right, got it. So is he pitching for us or the other team?"

"Oh, he's a Longdog. I reckon that'll get fans excited. It's been a while since we had an ace. Except he's probably *too* good for Leland, which means by August they'll probably call him up to Bradenton or Altoona." He became more animated as he talked about the team. "And there's this kid from Panama, Oscar Lopez. Eighteen years old but he's a real bruiser, plays third base. Scouting report says he can hit the ball a country mile. And Scotty McCall out of UNC, all six-foot-eight of him. That's who you want on first, somebody who can stretch like Gumby and pull in a throw. We might win a game or two with those guys before somebody calls them up."

The more he talked, the more she realized how little she knew about the most basic aspect of her business—the game itself. JT had assured her it didn't matter, and she'd convinced herself that her dad knew enough for both of them. But it could be weeks before her dad was around to take charge. In the meantime, every stupid question she raised would cost her credibility, which would lead to whispers of incompetence and erosion of support for her leadership. She was caught in that old maxim, whether to remain silent and be thought a fool or speak up and remove all doubt.

Setting her papers aside, she conceded that for now she was at the mercy of this skeleton staff and whatever meager plans they'd made thus far. Until her father came back to point them all in the right direction, her best hope was not to tank his investment in her very first week on the job.

"Thanks, Archie. I know you've got a lot on your plate for the opener. Why don't we pick this up next week when we have a better idea of where things stand."

Alone in her office, she methodically ripped her list of questions into strips too small to read, dropped them in the trash, and poured the dregs of her coffee on top. Then she buzzed Misty to have her call the *Gazette* and cancel the interview with Wesley Hodges, who would have had a field day with her ignorance.

Fortunately, she knew someone who could help.

"R u busy 2nite? I need a crash course in baseball."

CHAPTER TEN

Ninah had no doubt Britt was a smart cookie. Anything she absolutely needed to know about baseball was at her fingertips on the web, so it was possible her urgent request for a "crash course" was a pretext for something else. A reason to call, an excuse to see each other. That's what she wanted to think, and she was happy to oblige.

After a hurried farewell to her students and colleagues, she'd raced home to change into shorts and a shirt she could unbutton an extra inch or two. It was all she could do not to call Emmy with the news that Leland was getting a new lesbian and she'd appointed herself the welcoming committee.

It was odd to drive by Carly and Justine's house without stopping. These posh houses in the Sandstone development were out of reach on a teacher's salary, with each lot carefully carved among ancient oaks to preserve a woodsy character. All the homes were two stories high and shared certain architectural features—multi-level rooflines, arched windows, and exteriors faced with natural fieldstone from the Elkhorn Quarry. A girl could dream.

Vernon's house, the last one on the street, fronted Lake Leland. Last year he'd added a gazebo to the dock, and that's where Britt had suggested they share some beers and talk baseball.

Britt met her almost as soon as she pulled into the drive, dressed in denim shorts and an oversized purple V-neck tee. Her hair was twisted in a knot on top and held in place by a large clip. Hands on hips, she declared, "I hope you're as fed up with adulting as I am."

"All that and then some." Ninah presented a dripping six-pack of Blue Moon ale. "I officially survived year thirteen without getting shot, assaulted, arrested, fired, or sued. For a public school teacher, that's a banner year."

"Welcome to freedom."

"What's up with your dad today?"

"His doctor says he's at ninety-six percent. So precise. I feel a lot better now that he's starting to act like his old self. He can't wait to be discharged, and he's obsessive about his therapy. But then I say something about the Longdogs and he forgets everything else exists. He's so excited about this."

"No wonder. He's got his two favorite things—baseball and you." Ninah was happy to see the emotional turnaround in Britt, especially after her breakdown in Justine's arms. Fear and exhaustion never played well together.

Britt handed her a couple of beers. "Let me put the rest of these in a cooler and we'll take it with us down to the dock."

Ninah took a moment to appreciate Vernon's house in the afternoon sun. The living room was sparsely furnished and decidedly masculine. On one side, a towering stone fireplace dominated the room, softened by plush leather seating and colorful accent rugs across the knotty pine floors. Floor-to-ceiling glass lined the back wall, granting a spectacular view of the lake.

"I love your dad's house. It's like Carly and Justine's, grand without being ostentatious."

"Anything beats that old farmhouse on Pinckard Road where he used to live." She returned with a large bag of lime-flavored tortilla chips, as well as the cooler. "Grab that door, will you?"

When they stepped outside, Ninah took the cooler from her hand. "But what a shame about the fire. Your dad must have lost a lot of precious memories."

"He'd already given a lot of stuff to the historical society, so it wasn't as bad as it could have been. In fact, it probably turned out to be the luckiest day of his life. That's how he found out his family owned nearly half of the Hickson pasture. He sold it for a bundle just in time for a baseball team to fall in his lap."

"I can't believe he kept it secret so long. Especially with JT as a partner. Justine says he blabs about everything."

"They kept it quiet so that guy from Carbondale wouldn't up his offer. Dad didn't want to get into a bidding war. But you'd have thought he'd tell his own daughter. I think he was worried I'd try to talk him out of it."

Ninah kicked off her flip-flops to enjoy the feel of grass between her toes as they traipsed across the lawn toward the dock. "Would you have tried?"

"Probably not. He's crazy about baseball and it's *his* money. But if I'd known his plan was for me to help, I'd have told him I didn't want to be involved if it meant moving back here. Which—"

"Do you really dislike Kentucky that much?"

Britt ignored the question and pointedly continued, "Which clearly would have been a huge mistake on my part. Because now that I've had a chance to study the business aspect, I see what an extraordinary opportunity it is, both financially and career-wise. It'll be fun to work with Dad on something where we can see tangible results. Right now the promotions calendar looks like a clothesline at a nudist colony."

Ninah had to think for a second. "Nothing on it?"

"Just a couple of lame ideas they recycled from thirty years ago. It's no wonder the Longdogs have been circling the drain. But there's nowhere to go but up. All they really need is a fresh approach to ballpark entertainment—which is exactly the sort of work I've been doing for the last fifteen years."

"I can't wait to get this party started. With the two of you calling the shots, the Longdogs are gonna be fun again."

The wooden dock ran forty feet out over the water to the gazebo, which sheltered some Adirondack chairs and a picnic table. On it, weighted down by a cell phone, was a small stack of papers and files.

"Nice office you've got here. Adulting isn't all bad."

"It doesn't totally suck with a view like this." Britt twisted off their bottle tops and raised a toast. "To summer."

"To summer." She sat at the table opposite Britt with the bag of chips between them. "How did it go with Wesley Hodges?"

"It didn't. That's what set me off today." She tasted a chip and made a face. "These are stale. You want me to go back in and find something else?"

"I'm fine."

"Anyway, I got to thinking about what you said about him, how he honed in on the negatives. It occurred to me that I didn't know enough about baseball to wing it all the way through an interview, so I had Misty call him and cancel. He wanted to reschedule for tomorrow, but I said we were too busy right now with the changeover. I'm going to try to hold him off till Dad gets back."

"That's probably smart. If he gets an inkling you aren't into baseball, it'll be like blood in the water. Once the season starts, he'll probably lose interest in a profile. He'll have game stories every night, plus all the player news."

"It's not just him I have to worry about. It's all the vendors, the potential advertisers, even the fans who might stop me to talk. As soon as I open my mouth to someone who knows anything about baseball, they're going to find out I'm basically clueless."

"Play it like a politician. Come up with your own talking points and stick to them, no matter what the questions are. We practice this in my civics class. It's a debate technique. Here, write these down." She nudged a pen and pad toward Britt and counted on her fingers. "Good clean fun for the whole family. The best value in town for your entertainment dollar. Top quality concessions to round out your ballpark experience."

"Damn, you're good at this."

"I'm making stuff up but you get the idea. Figure out what messages you wanna push and practice saying them ten different ways. And don't let anyone knock you off script."

"This is great. Why don't I just hire you as our spokesperson till Dad gets back? Then you could answer all the baseball questions too."

"You don't want me for a spokesperson. I'm way too opinionated when it comes to baseball. Besides, you're totally gonna rock this. Promise me you'll do an Elvis contest. Oh, and Johnny Cash Night, where everybody has to wear black. They're gonna love it, Britt. Mark my word, three years from now we'll be jotting down your talking points for when you run for mayor."

Britt laughed. "Thanks, but no thanks. Three years from now, I hope to be filthy rich and sitting on a dock in San Diego looking out over the Pacific. Trust me, I am *not* cut out for small town life in the Bible Belt."

With the smallest hint of teasing, Ninah reminded her, "Don't look now, but three days ago you couldn't imagine being here at all. Maybe you'll have another epiphany."

"It would take a lobotomy."

"Come on, let's make another list." She commandeered Britt's tablet and pen. "What's great about living in Leland? I'll start. The people are friendly."

"When they aren't being homophobic, misogynistic Bible-thumpers."

Clearly religion was a hot-button issue. "I'll concede that we probably have more than our share of holy rollers, but we also have plenty of church people like Justine Hall. She goes every Sunday and she's about as liberal as they come."

"Point taken."

"Okay, number two: People in Leland care about each other."

"Which also means there's no privacy. Everybody's all up in your business."

"You'd be surprised how many secrets there are in this town," Ninah said, remembering Emmy's mysterious boyfriend. "How about this? We never have traffic jams."

"Because half the cars are sitting on blocks in somebody's front yard."

"Now you're being mean." Ninah swung her foot beneath the picnic table, missing Britt's leg but kicking her bench. "We're laid-back."

"Because there's nothing to do." The sudden sharpness in Britt's voice signaled a serious turn in what had been a playful exercise.

"There's plenty to do." Ninah gestured toward the lake. "We go canoeing, hiking, biking. Or if you're Justine, you go out running every day in the fresh air. We have sports leagues at the rec, the wellness center, Rotary."

"Sounds thrilling."

Ninah bristled at the sarcasm. "It is for us…but I guess that's because we're such *simple* folk. You may not be able to get avocado toast on every corner, but I guarantee you we were local-sourcing and sustainable-farming our tables long before hipsters in California decided it was trendy." Regrettably, her voice also had taken on an edge that turned their companionable conversation combative. "Sorry, now I'm the one sounding mean."

Britt tortured her with an excruciating silence before stating calmly, "I was rude and I apologize. If you like living at a slower pace, more power to you. All I meant was that it's not for me. I've been coming here to visit all my life, and to me this place feels... Never mind, I should shut up now so I don't say something else to insult you."

Ninah bit her lip to keep from apologizing again.

"Look, I've had these conversations with Dad a hundred times. He loves this place, obviously. And I'm happy for him. He deserves it after living with my mom for twenty years. But it grates on me how he always tries to get me to say I love it too. 'Isn't this a great view, Britt? Don't you like how peaceful it is here?' And if I say yes, he adds, 'You could always stay and enjoy it.' I should get a little string here in my side, something he can pull and make me say whatever it is he wants to hear."

"And I just did the same thing to you."

"It's not your fault I'm still hauling baggage from this place. I'm here willingly. I promised to help Dad get the Longdogs up and running. It's a good career move, so I need to quit bitching about it and own it instead of acting like I've been forced into indentured servitude." She blew a breath upward that lifted the hair on her forehead. "So much for talking baseball. Maybe we should take a raincheck, try this again when I'm not in such a shitty mood."

What Ninah had noticed about the shitty mood was that she'd triggered it with her sales pitch on Leland. That was probably something Vernon did too, and clearly Britt resented it. Next time they sat down together, she'd pay more attention to what Britt wanted. "I'll take a raincheck under one condition—you have to guarantee it. Call me when you're ready and we'll do this again. I swear I'll listen better. But just promise you'll call me."

CHAPTER ELEVEN

It had taken Britt hours to get clear on what she needed to do. She was relieved to see the lights still on at Ninah's house.

What was going through Ninah's head right now? Another list, probably: All the things she'd rather do than listen to a faux snob whine about how bored she was living among the hicks in Leland.

She tentatively climbed the steps of the old frame house, angry at herself that she might have ruined her chance for friendship with someone she actually liked quite a lot. The front door stood open behind an old-fashioned wooden screen that allowed her to see all the way through the living room to the kitchen. "Knock knock."

Ninah emerged from what Britt assumed was the bedroom. She'd changed into blue boxer shorts with white piping, and a gray T-shirt touting the Leland Wildcats. "Britt, is that you?"

"Hey…sorry it's so late. I came to apologize. I don't know what came over me, but none of it's your fault." She stepped inside the opened screen and followed Ninah's gesture to take a seat on the couch. "I'd like it a lot if you'd forget what an asshole I was and give me another shot."

"If anyone was an asshole, it was me. I knew you weren't all that happy about being here. I shouldn't have pushed you. You're entitled to feel however you want...and I'm sorry for being so flippant about it. I should have been more sensitive to your feelings, especially with all you've got going on."

"It's just a bunch of old baggage. Most people would have outgrown it by now." Every telling of the story, which Britt had shared with only a handful of close friends, always triggered visceral feelings of humiliation and rage. Trusting Ninah with it was a leap of faith. With a deep sigh, she relaxed against the pillows behind her. "It goes all the way back to my senior year in high school."

Ninah snorted. "If it makes you feel any better, high school's pretty complicated for everybody. At least that's what my students tell me."

"Especially the gay ones, I bet."

"Oh, yeah. There's so much pressure on kids to be like everyone else. Bullying's a huge problem."

"I could handle the bullying. I just flipped them off, you know?" Britt shook her middle finger. "What got to me most was how some of my friends—I'm talking people I'd known since first grade—decided they couldn't be friends with me anymore because I was going against the Bible."

Ninah's face fell. "Aw, that's such crap. I'm so sorry that happened."

"It hurt, I'll admit it. And the really sick part of it...I'd gone to the Presbyterian Church my whole life, so I knew why they were saying it. I worried about it all the time, that God was mad at me for not trying harder. I even prayed about what to do, but all that did was make me feel guilty."

"That's just not right." Ninah scooted close enough to rest a hand on Britt's knee. "I'm not all that religious, but I firmly

The Lucky Ones 77

believe *if* there's a God, he made us this way. If that turns out to be wrong and it keeps me out of heaven, then so be it. I am who I am."

"Exactly. Except I don't wonder about God anymore. I've decided he doesn't exist." She'd tried for years to understand why God would allow so much suffering and injustice. If he was all-powerful like everyone said, the least he could do was step in and stop his followers from spreading hate in his name. "Whenever I'm in Leland—or for that matter anywhere in Kentucky—I feel like there's this pervasive cloud of judgment hanging over me everywhere I go."

Ninah sighed. "Unfortunately, there's still plenty of that to go around. But it's not as bad as it used to be. Look at Carly. She ran for county clerk against a blatant homophobe and beat him. Not by much, but I like to think it means we're turning a corner." Whether she realized it or not, she was stroking Britt's thigh. "From what you were saying the other night, I got the impression your feelings about Kentucky had more to do with your mother."

"Oh, it does. But that's the church too." She shuddered, recalling her experience with irrepressible rage. "My mom's one of those deluded wrath-of-God types who gets off on telling everyone else they're going to hell. But she wasn't always like that. Like I said, we were normal, run-of-the-mill Presbyterians. When I was about fifteen, she went with a friend of hers to one of those Pentecostal revivals, then came home all flustered and breathless saying she got *saved*. She wanted Dad and me to get baptized in this new church of hers, the Assembly of Whatever. We both said no. Or in my case, *hell* no. She turned into a different person overnight. Off to Bible study all the time, praising Jesus fifty times a day."

"Must have been weird."

"More like bizarre. I think she was infatuated with the minister, Brother James. She aligned all her beliefs and values with his, parroted everything he said, including the absolute certainty that gay people were going to hell."

"Were you out?"

"Not to my parents. I came out to them the summer before my senior year. I figured they already knew, but me not saying anything let them live in denial. Dad was a little shook up at first—I could tell—but he kept his cool. Whereas Mom went completely ape-shit. Off she goes moaning to Brother James, then she comes back crying about how I'm breaking Jesus's heart. Poor Jesus."

"That's right, lay on the guilt." With a small laugh, Ninah added, "Something tells me that wasn't working on you anymore."

"Just the opposite. I started flaunting it. Talked about it all the time, kissed my girlfriend in front of her, stuff like that. I said if I had to go to hell, at least I'd get to ride the party bus with the cool kids. Your basic rebellious teenager stuff. You know what I mean?"

"Uh, I've taught high school for thirteen years, sistah. I've seen a few obnoxious little shits in my time." Ninah snickered again and shook her head. "Where was your dad in all this? Didn't he take up for you?"

"He tried to reason with her and get her off my back. But then he'd get on my case for baiting her, said it only made her worse. Which it did, but that was kind of the point. Then right before Christmas she came to me and said there was only one present she wanted that year. That was for me to come talk with Brother James, like he was going to sprinkle some magic fairy dust over me and make me straight. I should have refused, but I was feeling full of myself. I thought it would be fun to yank his chain too."

"You didn't."

"I would have if I'd gotten the chance. I thought he'd be some old guy, all hellfire and brimstone. Instead, he was about Mom's age, mid-forties, kind of soft-spoken." She drew a deep

The Lucky Ones   79

breath through clenched teeth as the memory enveloped her. This part sometimes gave her a sensation of bugs crawling up her legs.

Ninah sat up straight and twisted to face her. "Hey, you okay? You don't have to talk about this for my sake, Britt."

It was too late to avoid the emotions. "I remember it was cold that day. Brother James had one of those electric kettles in his office and he offered me a cup of spice tea." Feeling a familiar knot in her chest, she tried to relax. "We chatted for a few minutes and he was actually nice. I started thinking it wouldn't kill me to be polite. I knew he wasn't going to change me, no matter how many supposed treasures were waiting for me in heaven. But then I noticed I was feeling sluggish, that my eyes wouldn't focus. He kept asking me questions and I couldn't form the words to answer."

"Oh my God, he drugged you."

She nodded, a rocking motion that helped soothe her fury. "Probably ketamine. Not enough to knock me out but it kept me from running out of the room. Then he opened the door and Mom came in carrying a pillow. They put me down on the floor. I remember feeling like I was standing off to the side watching them. Brother James got down and put his hand on my forehead and started speaking in tongues and commanding all the demons to get out in the name of Jesus. Mom was just chanting hallelujahs and stuff."

"Britt, that's just evil."

"I haven't even gotten to the evil part. Keep in mind I'm only seventeen years old. Still a child in the eyes of the law. So after all their wailing, this other guy comes in. Early thirties maybe. What I remember most—it's burned into my brain like a cattle brand—is all the hair on his hands. Like he was Bigfoot or something." She tugged at her collar and swept her fingers across her chest. "It curled out from under his T-shirt halfway up his neck. I'm a dyke, right? So all I can think is how physically repulsive he is. He kneels down beside me, holds my hand and starts brushing his hairy fingers on my face. Like he's my boyfriend or something. It was gross. He keeps saying how beautiful I am, how God's going to send me a handsome husband and our family will serve the Lord."

Ninah rose and started to pace, her face a mask of horror. "Please tell me you reported all of them to the police. That's kidnapping...and they gave you drugs!"

Britt reminded herself that Ninah was only trying to be supportive. She couldn't know that such a remark was effectively a judgment of how she'd handled the situation. "Everyone imagines they'll be brave and stand up for themselves, but it's not so cut and dried when it's your own mother. I didn't want her arrested and thrown in jail...though it would have served her right."

"Of course not. I didn't mean...God, you poor thing."

"After a while, whatever they gave me started wearing off. Brother James stopped his gibberish and they sat there and watched me, like they were waiting to see if their little miracle had worked. I was so freaked out, I could hardly talk. Plus my legs were so wobbly that my werewolf boyfriend had to help me out to the car. When we got home, Mom sent me upstairs to lie down. I locked the door and stayed in my room for two straight days except to go to the bathroom." She hugged herself and shuddered. "I kept thinking about his hairy knuckles on my face."

"I'm so sorry." Ninah returned to her seat and clutched Britt's hand with both of hers. "I can't imagine a mother doing that to her own child."

"The next night I heard her arguing with Dad. He came up to my room and made me tell him every detail I could remember. He was furious. Told me to pack a suitcase, that we were going to spend Christmas here in Leland with my granddad."

What began as a respite soon became a symbol of ruin. Every visit since had triggered a visceral sense of angst tied to that awful memory.

"I figured we'd only be here till New Year's, but Dad went to JT and filed for divorce. Her lawyer froze their assets so we couldn't rent anything in Louisville until they had a settlement, and she kept rejecting everything. So I had to finish my senior year here at Leland High School."

"What an awful thing to do to a kid. You probably felt like you were the one being punished."

"And to make matters worse, Dad asked me not to tell anyone I was gay. It wasn't that he was ashamed—at least that's what I choose to believe—he was worried they wouldn't accept me, that I might get hurt. He promised if I made it through graduation, he'd send me to college wherever I wanted to go."

"So you chose California because it was as far away as you could get." Ninah flopped back against the pillows and drew Britt's hand into her lap. "No wonder you feel the way you do. How could you like a town when your memory of it is so oppressive?"

"I haven't told that story to many people, but it's why I don't see myself staying here very long. It's a good career move for the time being. If I can turn this team around, it ought to put me in a position to get the job I want. A nice little bullet point on my résumé." With a frustrated sigh, she added, "But I doubt I'll ever overcome this vibe."

"It breaks my heart that you go through that every time you come back. Maybe this time we can help you write over the wretched parts, leave you with some happier memories."

Britt turned to find smiling eyes as a wave of emotion seemed to fill them both. Then to her surprise, Ninah slowly closed the distance between them until her mouth hovered only a breath away, asking permission.

She eased into the kiss, her mind a jumble of sensations. What was Ninah thinking?

I like you. Let me comfort you. You excite me.

Any of those was perfect.

CHAPTER TWELVE

As their kiss deepened, Ninah found herself falling backward onto the couch, with Britt looming above her. She was acutely aware of her scant clothing, shorts and a T-shirt with nothing underneath. If Britt dared to reach inside, they'd quickly be past the point of no return.

Feeling an urge to even the odds, she slid her hands under Britt's shirt until she located the clasp of her bra. She released it with a simple twist, and getting no resistance, gently caressed her back as their breaths turned to gasps.

Of all the ways she'd imagined her evening with Britt, having sex hadn't been anywhere on her list.

A warm hand stroked the back of her thigh, all the way to the top, where fingertips brushed her bottom. "Is this okay?"

Showing more confidence than she felt, Ninah answered by wriggling free and tugging her T-shirt over her head. Then she lay back to admire Britt's lustful gaze.

"You're gorgeous," Britt hissed, pulling off her own shirt and bra together.

Tingling with arousal, Ninah drank in the sight of full breasts with pale pink aureoles and rose-colored nipples already stiffened with excitement. They fell together again in a succession of kisses that seemed fueled by a shared hunger for passion itself. Her three lonely years melted away. Tonight would be her new touchstone.

Voices outside reminded her that her front door was standing open. If Emmy came home right now, she'd get an eyeful. "Bedroom," she said.

While Britt scooped up their shirts, Ninah hurried across the room and kicked the front door closed. Then she led Britt to the bedroom, where a ceiling fan lowered the temperature a good ten degrees. With a swift yank, she flung the bedcovers to the bottom.

"This is nice," Britt said. "It's very…you."

It was, as long as "you" meant neat and subdued, her soft floral sheets the only real splash of color.

Britt quickly dropped her shorts, but kept her panties on as she crawled beneath the sheet.

By the light of the bedside lamp, Ninah stepped out of her shorts and briefly stood for a silent appraisal. Then she stretched out alongside Britt and cupped her cheek. "I'm so glad you're here."

"I don't usually… What am I saying? I don't usually anything. I haven't been with anyone but Candice since my junior year in college."

Ninah laughed softly and tickled the hair on Britt's forearm. "We've already exceeded my expectations by several light years. If you wanna lie here and talk, that's fine."

"That's not quite what I had in mind when we got naked. The moment I kiss you—which I'm about to do—I'm going to want all of you."

Ninah trembled with anticipation as their lips met again, this time languid and inquisitive, as if kissing were all there was. With a gentle nudge, she pushed the panties down until Britt peeled them off and tossed them aside.

For the next several minutes, Britt lay perfectly still with her eyes closed while Ninah traced every curve of her body within arm's reach. From her thigh to her round bottom, to the womanly curve of her hip. To her heavy breast, which Ninah covered with her mouth as Britt softly moaned. Then to the hollow of her neck and collarbone. Exquisite, all of it.

When she tried to follow the path with her lips, Britt stopped her with a hand to the chin, lifting her face for another soulful kiss. Without realizing it, she'd begun a wavelike roll against Britt's leg, which alternately hardened and relaxed in a matching rhythm. The heat of their bodies grew until finally Ninah curled a hand into the soft, delicately shaped patch of hair between Britt's legs. A gentle teasing induced a quiet hitch in her breath and a steady writhing as her excitement built.

"Go inside me."

Ninah slithered into the velvety crevice. One finger, then two, while her thumb tugged at the outer edges of her sensitive center. She studied Britt's furrowed expression as she became more focused, more controlled. The muscles in her hips and thighs tightened as if to summon all her energy for the crescendo.

"Ohhhh!" Her body jerked as her climax struck, and she arched into the touch as long as she could, holding her breath until the throbbing subsided. Then she gasped and wilted all at once.

Ever so gently, Ninah withdrew from inside her. Robbed of the chance to taste her directly, she brought her fingers to her mouth to savor the essence. She'd never felt more powerful.

As she basked in her prowess, Britt began her own discovery, a fingertip journey under the cover of another kiss. Ninah's senses were already inflamed. She threw off the sheet and surrendered her whole self.

Britt answered with a spirited growl. Licking, nipping, she brought Ninah's nipples to a torturous, tender peak before embarking on a more disciplined crawl. Caressing, inhaling.

Weaving her hands through Britt's silky hair, Ninah encouraged her mouth's odyssey. The anticipation alone nearly undid her, as warm, wet breaths opened her thighs. When Britt's tongue finally parted her, she fought the first tingles of release. *Too soon.* But when fingers slid inside, she gave it up.

Her climax still pulsing, she reached again for Britt, who countered with a captive hug. "I still need a minute. You destroyed me."

"I know the feeling. That was amazing."

Britt nuzzled her ear. "I had no idea how much I needed that."

They lay still and silent as Ninah tried to make sense of what it meant. One thing was plainly obvious—tonight, they'd needed each other.

CHAPTER THIRTEEN

Outside the press box, Ninah stood solemnly in the aisle with her hand over her heart as Deke Sullivan warbled the last lines of "The Star-Spangled Banner." Deke was an institution in Leland, having led the Baptist choir for more than forty years. He also was perfectly emblematic of all the ways the Longdogs were stuck in a rut. The Iversons would be a breath of fresh air.

"Thank you, ladies and gentlemen. And welcome to another great season of Longdogs baseball!"

Cloudless and with only the barest hint of a warm breeze, it was a perfect night for baseball. The stadium was more than two-thirds full, a decent crowd considering the stunning drop in attendance last year after Duffy's neglect. Ninah had hoped for a full house, this being opening night under new ownership.

There was no sign of Britt. In fact, she'd been off the grid since disappearing the night before last from Ninah's bed. No note, no text. Nothing. It was hard not to take that personally.

Ninah trudged up the stadium stairs to the press box with the starting lineup in hand.

"Ninah Faust! Aren't you a sight for sore eyes. I was beginning to think you weren't even gonna come up and say hello." Stu Tomberlin, set to turn seventy-five on the Fourth of July, rose from his chair to greet her with a hug. Three decades in the booth as public address announcer had earned him the moniker Voice of the Longdogs.

"I wanted to make sure you guys saw this," she said, acknowledging reporter Wesley Hodges, who wore noise-canceling headphones to cover Cookeville's radio announcers sitting two seats away. "Hank made a last-minute change to the lineup. He's using Austin Farmer as DH."

"Thanks for the heads-up." Stu penciled in the change of designated hitter in his notebook. "What did you think of Vernon Iverson buying the team? That's what them corporate raiders call a white knight. I tell you, I sure hoisted a cold one."

"Yeah, me too," she said. "I went by the hospital to see him this afternoon. He's doing pretty good, said to tell everybody hi."

"Too bad he had to miss his very first game. That's some bad luck."

"I showed him how to tune in to the Cookeville radio station on his phone. Maybe you'll get that guy to give him a shout-out. That would be cool."

What would be even cooler was for the Longdogs to sign a radio contract of their own. Maybe the Iversons would see the wisdom in making folks wish they were at the ballpark.

The VIP box next door was empty and dark, which made her wonder if Britt was even watching the game. Perhaps she was too nervous. It was better to think that than to worry she was avoiding the place because of Ninah. If she regretted having sex, they could set it aside and focus on being friends. To do that, they'd have to talk eventually.

She waved a hand in front of Wesley to get his attention. "That was a great piece this morning on Cory Hanover. I hope you'll write up some of the other guys like that. It's good to see the personal side." It was a gratuitous compliment, designed more to flatter than engage. Her willingness to play to his vanity might prove useful should he go after Britt or Vernon for their management of operations.

"Thanks," he grunted. "If the other guys do something to earn it, I'll write 'em up."

"Throwing out the ceremonial first pitch of the Longdogs season, five years and counting, Mayor Paul Wilson."

At the pitcher's mound, general manager Archie Davenport conducted the ritual, presenting a new baseball to the mayor as they smiled for the *Gazette's* photographer. Hamming it up as usual, Wilson loosened his arm and pretended to shake off a sign from Longdogs catcher Angel Alvarado. Then he went through an elaborate windup before hurling a pitch that fell to the dirt a good three feet in front of home plate.

Predictably, the home crowd booed.

"Yep, five years to practice and he still can't get it there," Ninah muttered.

Stu nudged her. "Better go grab your seat. The Dogs are about to take the field." He pressed a button on his sound system that played a chorus of—*what else?*—"Who Let the Dogs Out?"

"See you guys later."

She scampered down the concrete steps to the fifth row, second seat. The empty aisle seat beside her was Vernon's, and the one on the other side belonged to Carly. They'd chosen these seats specifically for the view over the shoulder of the umpire as he called balls and strikes.

After logging in to the Longdogs' secure network with her iPad, she opened the scorekeeping app and entered the lineup change. A part of her missed the old days when she tracked the games on a tearaway pad of scoresheets, but it was fun to imagine fans and talent scouts following her every click in real time from as far away as Japan, home to Longdogs prospect Yuki Yakamoto.

"Hey, kiddo." Carly arrived carrying a giant bucket of popcorn and a red souvenir cup of Sun-Drop. "You tired of summer vacation yet?"

"God, no. But I woke up at five o'clock this morning, right on schedule. By the time I train myself to sleep till seven, it'll be August and I'll have to drag myself out of bed at five again."

"A little bird told me you are seriously crushing on the new girl. What's up with that?"

Had they seen Britt's car in her driveway? "How could you possibly know that already?"

Through a mouthful of popcorn, Carly garbled, "You just told me. All I knew for sure is you drove past our house the other day, didn't even stop to say hi. Now we need you to settle our bet. Justine said you wouldn't have gone over there unless you were invited, but I said you were probably just stalking her."

"Exactly what I don't need, you two starting rumors. But you can let Justine know she wins the bet. Britt needed some advice on how to deal with Wesley Hodges from the *Gazette*. He can be sneaky sometimes, so I gave her some tips for not falling into his trap." She pretended to shift her attention to the field, all the while knowing Carly was waiting for more. No way would she confess to more than that, since Britt had backed off already. "So we sat out on the dock and talked, had a couple of beers. No big deal."

"Sounds nice. But then Emmy said you had company later that night, somebody in a red rental car."

Ninah stiffened. "Britt's right about one thing. Living in a small town means everyone knows what you're up to."

"So...how was it?"

Her face warmed with what had to be a crimson blush, but she kept her eyes straight ahead. "Carly, remember that time you accidentally weed-whacked Justine's impatiens, and you got me to say I did it because you were already in the doghouse about something?"

Carly twisted her lips as she bit back a response to Ninah's playful threat. "Hey, how about this Hanover kid? He's the real deal, huh?"

Ninah sighed with relief as Cory Hanover threw the first of his warm-up pitches, a curve that dropped like a rock over the outside corner of the plate. The crowd responded with an appreciative hum.

"Holy wow," Carly said. "Something tells me we're in for a treat tonight."

"Wouldn't it be something if this really turned out to be the Longdogs' year? That would be so cool for Vernon. And for Britt...and for all of us."

Hanover's next pitch was a fastball that thumped loudly in Alvarado's mitt.

"Back to Britt," Carly said. "The Pride picnic's coming up soon, which means she's about to meet all the single ladies." She interrupted herself to do a dreadful Beyoncé impression. "And mark my word, it's gonna look like Guido's when they bring out a fresh hot pizza for the buffet, everybody rushing up there with their tongues hanging out. And that includes Teri."

Another breaking ball, this one on the inside corner.

Ninah shuddered with disgust. "I could have gone all night without hearing that name."

"She's here with Robbi and Liv, by the way." Carly twisted in her seat, spilling part of her popcorn in Ninah's lap. "They're sitting one section over at our eight o'clock, all three of them. Mark my word, Teri's gonna make a move on her."

"If Britt gives Teri Kaufman the time of day, I'll eat my own mouth. That woman is toxic."

"Of course she is, but the point remains that Britt's gonna turn a bunch of heads when she shows up...especially if she shows up by herself." She stuffed another handful of popcorn into her face. "Which is why you walking in *with* her sends a useful message."

Even as Ninah hated the idea of behind-the-scenes shenanigans, the wisdom of Carly's words weren't lost on her. "What are you suggesting?"

"You need to close this deal, Ninah. Justine wants to have a small welcome party next week…just for couples. And you."

"That's not very subtle." Plus it would be humiliating if Britt turned her down.

"Leading off for the Cookeville Moccasins, second baseman Jorge Sanchez."

They rose with the crowd in anticipation of the first pitch as the batter took his stance at the plate.

Carly tossed herself a puffed kernel and caught it in her mouth like a trained seal. "The subtle part's up to you, Nines. You don't have to keep throwing yourself at her. Seems like she already likes you. This is an opportunity for you guys to be a couple. But only if you wanna come."

"You're so full of shit, Carly. Of course I'll be there. But don't get your hopes up about me and Britt. I've got a feeling she's not all that interested in being somebody's girlfriend."

Or maybe it was only Ninah she didn't want.

"Look at this kid," Carly said, pulling out her phone to snap a pic of the new Dogs pitcher. "Twenty years from now when Cory Hanover goes into the Hall of Fame, we're gonna be able to say we were there when it all began."

The first pitch of the game—of the season, of this future star's professional career—was a slider, obvious from the clockwise rotation that produced the illusion of a red dot as the ball's seams spun. As it tailed toward the plate, the ball hung ever-so-slightly over the outside corner of the strike zone. The home plate umpire had already started his dramatic gyration for a called strike when Cookeville's Jorge Sanchez connected with a thunderous *crack!* that sent the ball over the right field fence.

CHAPTER FOURTEEN

Britt massaged the small of her back and shifted her aching butt on the aluminum bench. Three hours was a long time to sit on bleachers without back support. No wonder some of the fans nearby had already packed it in. But at least out here in right field, wearing sunglasses and a panama hat until the sun went down, she didn't have to worry about being ambushed by Wesley Hodges or the *Gazette*'s photographer.

After giving up a home run on his first pitch, the young pitcher everyone had been raving about settled down, recording nine strikeouts as he retired the next fifteen batters. Meanwhile, the Longdogs got back in it with a two-run homer by third baseman Oscar Lopez. By the seventh inning, it was looking like a Longdogs win when back-to-back errors by the same Lopez allowed two runs to score. Now down to their last three outs, Leland trailed by one.

On the bright side, Britt's hurriedly arranged wagon race had been a hit with the crowd. At a break between innings two couples, the Greenes and the Bartons, had set off in opposite directions from home plate, the men pulling their wives in a red wagon. When they reached second base they had to switch so that the women pulled their husbands the rest of the way. The particulars needed tweaking if they were to try this game again, she noted. If not for the spill Jake Greene had taken rounding third, there might have been a calamitous collision at home plate.

"Leading off the bottom of the ninth for the Longdogs, right fielder Troy Cline."

Her foray into the cheap seats had given her insight into the experience of budget-minded fans. A family of four could catch a game from these bleachers for a mere twelve bucks, though they'd still get hosed on concessions. Using the note function on her phone, she reminded herself to come up with a basic food package—hot dog, chips and a soda—she could sell in the outfield concessions at a bargain price. She'd also look into what it would cost to add seat backs to these bleachers.

A deep male voice behind her said, "Too bad about that Hanover kid. One unlucky pitch and a couple of bad hops, and he gives up a beauty of a game. At least we've got the top of the order coming to the plate."

She cast a tentative glance over her shoulder, unsure if the speaker was addressing her or a companion. A forty-ish man in dress slacks and loosened tie, he apparently had come to the ballpark from an office job. His most distinctive feature was the cleft in his chin, which straight women probably found boyishly handsome.

"He's got a heckuva slider though," he went on. "Best I've seen on a rookie, and I've been watching this game a long time."

Since there was no one else within reasonable earshot, she glumly concluded he was talking to her. Less certain was if he was actually talking baseball or laying the groundwork for hitting on her. Accustomed to being approached by men, she contemplated how best to shut him down. She could try a few words of Spanish, like *Please don't spray fragrance in my car.*

The crowd let out a collective gasp as the first pitch careened off Cline's batting helmet with a loud *pop!* Visibly shaken, he trotted slowly to first base, where he represented the potential tying run.

"We'll take a base runner any way we can get it," the man said, clapping his approval. Apparently deciding he'd done enough to engage her, he scooted like a giant crab down two rows to sit beside her. "Kip Barlow, hopeless fan of these hapless Longdogs."

Barlow…she'd come across that name earlier today but couldn't recall where. After only a cursory nod, she turned her attention back to the field.

"At the plate, second baseman Rolando Castillo."

"It'd be nice if Castillo knocked one out of here, but I don't think he's much of a slugger. He's fast though."

After a couple of bluffs, Castillo laid down a perfect bunt that advanced Cline to second, and he almost beat the throw to first. One down.

"Not fast enough," she said dryly.

"Unfortunately, those of us who've followed this team for years are kind of used to losing. You know what they say—can't beat the Longdogs for a night out. Unless you're the other team."

"Now batting, shortstop Malik Terry."

It occurred to her that if Kip was the ardent fan he claimed to be, she might learn a thing or two from him that would help with marketing to others like him. "How come a diehard fan like you is sitting all the way out here? You should be in one of the club seats closer to the action."

"Right you are. It so happens I've got a couple of season tickets in the fourth row right behind home plate. Most nights I come with my daughter—she's nine—but my in-laws are visiting this week from Cleveland, so I let her sit over there with her grandpa. Talk about a hardcore fan, that girl's absolutely crazy about this team."

So Kip Barlow was a family man. She hoped that meant he wasn't hitting on her after all. "A longtime fan, huh?"

"As long as I can remember. I'm friends with the new owner, Vernon Iverson. Now there's a real fan for you. The last guy, Duffy Barnett…boy, he let things fall all to heck. If you ask me, he took advantage of fans' loyalty, raising prices, cutting back on the extras. Didn't even keep the bathrooms clean. For a while there it looked like some rich guy was gonna buy the team and move it to Carbondale. But then out of nowhere, Vernon swoops in and saves the day for all of us. Shame he's not here to celebrate tonight. Had a brain aneurysm last week and had to have surgery." He pointed to a wide sign near the 385-feet marker on the center field wall. "That's me, by the way. Better Smiles by Barlow."

"You're an orthodontist." That's why his name sounded familiar. His was the only billboard ad in the entire park that was prepaid through the end of the season.

"All righty, here we go," he said, rubbing his hands together as he turned his attention back to the action on the field. His folksy Southern cadence reminded her of JT. "Base hit ties the game."

Tension rippled through the park as fans came to their feet. Even Britt found herself tingling with anticipation, though it dissipated instantly when the Moccasins manager ambled from the dugout and signaled to his bullpen for a left-hander. The last pitching change had caused a delay of about five minutes. The crowd grumbled in unison and returned to their seats.

"Let the players play!" Kip yelled. Then to Britt, he said, "I don't think I've seen you out here before. Have you been a Dogs fan long?"

She was torn over whether to come clean or remain incognito. Since he was a friend of her father's, he was sure to find her out eventually. She extended her hand and smiled. "I'm Britt Iverson. Vernon's my dad."

He lit up with recognition, then wide-eyed delight. "Well, of course. I should have known. You look just like him. Same smile, same gum symmetry. I bet you don't hear that every day."

"I don't, but I'll take it as a compliment. I've always thought my dad was handsome."

"And he's one of the nicest guys in Leland." He blew out a breath and visibly shuddered. "Boy, I sure am glad your father's Vernon and not Duffy Barnett. I shouldn't have said all those things about Duffy."

She laughed. "No worries. I've already heard some of it, and I imagine I'll hear more as the season wears on."

He asked how her father was doing, and that she convey his well-wishes. Amazingly, he too had been at the house party the night of the health scare.

"I take it you know Ninah Faust then, and Carly Griffin."

"Oh yeah, we all sit together over there. That Ninah, she's an encyclopedia about baseball. I don't mean like she knows facts. I mean she understands the game better than anybody. Her dad played in the majors for a season. I think he passed a couple of years ago."

Funny that Ninah hadn't mentioned that...but then Britt conceded she'd rudely made every single moment about herself. "I didn't know that about her father. No wonder she's an expert."

In case she needed another reminder, Kip was further proof that in Leland everyone knew everyone else. With her luck, the whole town already knew she'd left Ninah's house in the middle of the night.

"On the mound for the Moccasins, Randy Jacoby."

"If you don't mind me asking, Britt, what are *you* doing out here in the rabble? You ought to be sitting up there in that air-conditioned suite eating shrimp cocktail and drinking champagne."

"Can you keep a secret?" When he nodded, she told him about canceling the interview with Wesley after being warned about his critical approach. "Dad should be back in two or three weeks. It's better if he handles the baseball end. I'm here to focus on the fun stuff, like that silly wagon race. I paid my secretary's son ten bucks to assemble those wagons in time for the game. All the entertainment you see over these next few games will be some idea we cobbled together at the last minute, so be sure to cut us some slack. I hope we'll be a little more organized by the time the team gets back from its first road trip."

"My daughter loves all the games and contests. If you ever need a volunteer for anything, she's your girl."

They turned their attention back to the field, where the relief pitcher was finishing his warm-up. That brought Malik Terry back to the plate and the crowd to its feet.

Britt was glad she'd engaged with Kip instead of brushing him off. He could be an important ally in building more advertising support. She scribbled her name and email on the back of a generic Longdogs business card. "Let's have a beer sometime and talk some more about the ballpark experience. Or whatever else you drink. I'd like to know if that billboard of yours is doing what you want it to."

"Sure thing."

"In fact, shoot me an email in the morning and I'll leave some tickets at will call. No point in that suite sitting empty. Bring the whole family out tomorrow night."

"Oh wow, Tanya's gonna like that. That's my wife. She'd be here every night but the mosquitoes eat her up. I reckon that's because she's so much sweeter than the rest of us."

A crack of the bat sent a fly ball their way, but the right fielder made a running catch for the second out. Cline tagged up and advanced to third, just ninety feet from home plate. Two outs.

A base hit would tie the game, possibly sending it into extra innings. Win or lose, the concessions stands would take in a few more bucks. Even an idiot had to appreciate that.

"*Now at the plate—Osssscar Lopez!*"

"Let's see if Oscar can redeem himself for those errors in the eighth," Kip said as the third baseman took his place in the batter's box. "He's got some power, this guy. A walk-off home run would be just the ticket."

Lopez connected sharply on the first pitch to send it soaring into left field, so high it nearly disappeared against the dark sky. Fans drew a collective breath and held it. Going…going…

"*Foul ball!*"

"Damn!" She smacked her hat against her thigh. That was precisely why people sat three hours on a hard bench, because there was always a chance it would pay off with a dramatic, come-from-behind home run that would send everyone home jubilant.

"Boy, he sure tagged that one. You don't see much power like that in A-ball. Something tells me this guy's gonna be fun to watch." He cupped his hands and yelled, "Straighten it out, Oscar."

The next pitch was wild, sailing over Lopez's head all the way to the backstop. Troy Cline stumbled in the dirt as he broke for home. It was only a small slip but it gave the catcher an extra half-second to corral the carom and flip it to the pitcher, who'd scampered in to cover the plate. As Cline slid, the glove came down on his calf and the crowd went deathly silent waiting for the call.

"*Out of there!*" the umpire finally roared, setting off a chorus of boos—and a cascade of sponge balls, courtesy of Simmons Funeral Home.

CHAPTER FIFTEEN

As the game crowd thinned, Ninah looked about in hopes of catching a glimpse of Britt. But for a controversial call, they could have celebrated kicking off the "Iverson Era" with a win. The least she could do was offer consolation for the loss, or kudos for the hilarious wagon race. Or just an upbeat message of support for how well Vernon had looked this afternoon. Frankly, any excuse would do.

She hadn't expected to feel so anxious. Why was Britt avoiding her? Maybe it dawned on her that Ninah had taken advantage of her vulnerability.

"You need a ride home?" Carly asked as she scooped up the trash pile she'd created around her seat.

"I feel like a walk tonight, but thanks." She patted her pockets. "I think I left my new pen in the press box. My GSA kids just gave it to me two days ago and I lost it already. I better go grab it before they lock up."

At the press box, Stu answered her knock and presented her pen. "Bet you're looking for this. I thought about stealing it, but seeing as how it's got your name engraved on it…"

"You don't have it in you to be a thief, Stu."

Wesley and the Cookeville radio announcer had packed up but were standing around chatting about Oscar Lopez's impressive debut.

"Too bad about that call," she said to Stu. "We were sitting right on top of it. Carly and I both thought he got in under the tag."

"That's the way we saw it from up here." Stu leaned in and whispered, "Me and the radio guy, that is. You-know-who was of another opinion."

"Of course he was."

Ninah smiled politely at Wesley and noticed a flash of light behind him in the owner's suite, which had been dark all evening. Someone had briefly opened the door from the offices and shut it again. It couldn't have been Archie Davenport. She'd seen him only moments ago going into the visitors' dugout. Nor the janitorial staff, who were at work already sweeping popcorn and peanut shells from the stands.

"Excuse me," she said, stepping around Wesley to the door that led to the administrative offices. Archie always left it unlocked so members of the press could access the executive restrooms, which were off-limits to the public. From the hallway, she observed a light coming from an office at the far end. "Hello?"

Britt's face peeked from the doorway. "Ninah?"

Her pulse quickened as Britt started toward her. Aiming for nonchalance, she folded her arms and leaned against the wall, pasting on her warmest smile. "Was it something I said?"

"I was going to call…sometime over the weekend when it wasn't so crazy."

"It's not that big a deal. I just want to make sure everything's okay."

"Of course, I just…" Britt scuffed her sneaker-clad foot like a child caught with her hand in the cookie jar. "Like I said the other night, that's not something I usually do. I don't want to…"

"Seriously, Britt. Whatever you say is fine. We got ahead of ourselves…our emotions got the best of us." She hated that her voice was shaking while she was trying to sound casual. "If you don't want to go in that direction, all you have to do is say so. Then we're back to being friends."

Britt mirrored Ninah's stoic pose and pinched her lips. "I hate to sound like such a cliché, but it's me, not you."

"Of course it's you. I was freakin' amazing." Ninah laughed awkwardly in an effort to dispel the tension. "In fact, it wouldn't surprise me at all if I was too much to handle. I get that a lot."

"You *were* freaking amazing, for the record. The thing is, I don't plan to be here very long, and you're way too nice to be just a…"

"Fuck buddy?"

"That." Britt managed an embarrassed grin. "A freaking amazing fuck buddy. But this isn't a good time for me to start a relationship."

"Or a good place, I suppose. I understand how you feel about Leland." Summoning the maturity of her thirty-five years, Ninah willed herself to smile. She'd known all along it was too good to be true. Women like Britt never gave her a second look. But then Leland didn't have any women like Britt. "So on that note, I have a favor to ask. A baseball favor."

"Whatever it is, I'll do it."

Ninah took out her phone and scrolled to a series of photos taken last year at the ballpark, a small crowd waving signs and rainbow flags from the bleachers behind first base. "Remember me saying I'm the faculty sponsor of the Gay-Straight Alliance at Leland High? This was last summer, Pride Night with the Longdogs. Duffy agreed to let us do it as long as it didn't cost him anything. We did all the organizing. The kids handed out purple wristbands and sat together behind the Longdogs' dugout. And there was a moment of silence for victims of the Pulse massacre."

"How did that go over?"

"Not as well as we'd hoped, but it comes with the territory, you know? We publicized it ahead of time with flyers and social media, so one of the churches showed up for a mini-protest in the parking lot. Like you said, the Assembly of Whatever. You can probably imagine what they looked like, with their little signs about loving the sinner, hating the sin."

Britt rolled her eyes and made a gagging gesture.

"My sentiments exactly. We also got a few random boos when Stu announced that it was Pride Night, but we got some applause too. The hardest part for me personally was after the game, watching the kids pick up all those wristbands people threw on the ground. Talk about an apt metaphor. No matter how much progress we make, too many queer kids are still being thrown away."

Britt shook her head with disgust. "One thing I like about California is Pride supporters outnumber protesters ten to one."

"Right, which is why events like these matter so much. With most of the churches against us, we need to get the business community on our side."

"So you want to do another Pride Night?"

"Duffy already gave us the go-ahead, but that was ages ago. We had it down for August fourteenth when the Paducah Dukes come to town, if that still works. This year we have a check to present to the library so they can buy some queer books. It would be really cool if we could do that in a ceremony at home plate before the game. Oh, and hand out more wristbands at the gate. Please tell me we're still good to go."

"I'd be lying if I said I wasn't a little worried about the protests. People don't hold back like they used to. I'll probably need to hire some extra security."

Ninah thought of the men who'd stalked her and Thaddeus at the school, one of whom had also confronted Ike. Britt didn't need to hear more negatives about Leland.

"Believe me, we went over the potential risks, how important it is for everyone to stay cool. These kids need something to feel proud about. You know what that's like. We won't get respect unless we demand it."

After a studied silence, Britt nodded. "All right then, Pride Night it is. August fourteenth. And we'll promote the hell out of it."

Ninah might have kissed her cheek had Wesley not suddenly emerged from the press box.

"Brittany Iverson, right? I'm Wesley Hodges, sports editor for the *Gazette*."

Because sports editor sounded loftier than beat reporter, she thought cynically. In addition to being prickly, Wesley sometimes tried too hard. Too bad he hadn't tried harder to iron his shirt.

He looked past her to Britt, as if she weren't even standing there. "I tried to get back in touch with you but we kept missing each other. We need to reschedule that interview. My readers are interested in your thoughts on the direction of the team. Like, what's your strategy for winning back those fans who feel priced out of a night at the ballpark after last year's increase in ticket prices?" He made a point of holding out his phone so Britt would know he was recording her response.

"That's a question I expect to study very carefully. But I've only been here a few days, so I've not yet familiarized myself with the team's financial records."

"Understood. About that wagon race and the sponge ball toss...can we expect to see more diversionary entertainment designed to increase the fun quotient?"

"That's a great way to describe what we're aiming for, the fun quotient. And yes, absolutely. We'll be putting a lot of energy into making a night with the Longdogs a fun-filled experience for the whole family."

He put his phone away but showed no inclination to return to the press box. "I don't suppose you have a window, say forty minutes, sometime tomorrow when we could sit down and talk in more detail about your vision for the team? More of a friendly chat, really. We could even do it on background over lunch if you want. You decide what's on the record and what's not."

Ninah found his cajoling smile borderline creepy. In the years she'd known Wesley, she'd never seen him attempt to charm his sources into comments. But none of those sources were as attractive as Britt. Given that he'd probably talked to several of Vernon's friends and associates already, it was odd that he didn't seem to know Britt batted for the other team.

"I don't think tomorrow is…" Britt's forehead creased with a hint of panic, and she glanced at Ninah for help.

"You're too late, Wesley. I just this minute put the squeeze on her so we could go over plans for Pride Night. I'd offer to reschedule, but my students have a lot to do to get ready. It's harder to get everyone organized now that school's out."

"Some other time then." A feigned smile did nothing to cover his annoyance that Ninah had beaten him to the punch. Or for that matter that she hadn't yielded to him as soon as he butted into their conversation. He grumbled a cursory goodbye and returned to the press box.

"Thanks for that," Britt said when he was gone.

"No problem. Oh, and my offer's still good for a baseball chat anytime you want. Now that school's out, I can even come to your office." That was her way of letting Britt know she could pull back and stoke their friendship without the suggestion of more.

"I might take you up on that as soon as I come up for air. You wouldn't believe how much there is to do. With Dad still in the hospital, I'm having to go solo."

"I understand." Ninah decided to accept that at face value since the alternative was Britt giving her a brush-off. "You've got my number."

Britt caught her arm as she turned away. "Ninah, I really wish…if the circumstances had been different…"

"I know. Me too."

CHAPTER SIXTEEN

In a rocking chair on her front porch, Ninah adjusted her Bluetooth earpiece so she could continue her conversation while applying a fresh coat of pink polish to her toenails. "I warned you Wesley Hodges was a downer. But this was really a low blow."

She'd called to give Britt a heads-up about Wesley's blog, which appeared in the *Gazette*'s digital edition but not in the actual paper. In today's post, he'd blamed Britt for the team's loss.

"Okay, I found it," Britt said. *"Thrown out at home: New Longdogs owner costs team opening night win."*

"He's pissed because you blew him off, so now he blames you for the Longdogs losing last night. *You!*"

"What the actual fuck?"

"He claims the wagon race left ruts in the field, and that's what caused the bad hop on Oscar Lopez in the eighth inning." The error had allowed the runner to reach first, and he eventually scored what ended up being the winning run. "He also says it's your fault Troy Cline lost his footing when he broke for home, that if the field hadn't been torn up by the wagon wheels, he would have been safe by a mile."

Britt read aloud, "...*defaced the infield to the detriment of play, almost certainly in violation of MiLB standards. While these players give it their all, their dreams are undone by the spectacle of a third-rate reality show.*"

"He's being a real douche about it, Britt. Read on, it gets worse."

"...*you'll want to double-check your ticket just to be sure you haven't wandered into a carnival by mistake. While previous owner Duffy Barnett tested fan loyalty with higher ticket prices, he at least maintained respect for the game the way it was meant to be played. Not only has Miss Iverson retained the exorbitant ticket prices, she's abandoned baseball altogether to focus on diversionary entertainment. She calls it the 'fun quotient.' I call it a shameful bait and switch.*"

Britt viciously ground out the last words. "That bastard. He's the one who called it the fun quotient. For a guy who's supposed to be a sports reporter, he doesn't know shit about the business end of minor league baseball. I ought to yank his press credentials."

"It would serve him right," Ninah said evenly, trying to sound supportive. "But that won't stop him from buying a ticket and covering the game from the bleachers. Plus then he'd call you out for being thin-skinned."

Voices filtered down the stairs from Emmy's apartment, one of them male...and familiar, but Ninah couldn't place it. She wondered if she finally was going to meet the mysterious boyfriend.

"I have to respond to him or it's going to snowball. The last thing I need right now is a war between the baseball purists and the new customers I'm trying to reach. I'm going to have to crawl back to him and beg for an interview whether I want one or not."

"You can't reward him for being an asshole. We'll find another way."

"We?"

"Okay, you. But I have a vested interest in the outcome. Not only are the Longdogs gainful summer employment, they also happen to be one of my favorite things about living in Leland. I don't like seeing them trashed. And I especially don't like seeing *you* trashed."

She hadn't meant for that to come out quite so emphatically. Britt could take care of herself.

"Maybe I should just ignore it. You say it's not in the paper?"

"Digital only. He's got a decent-sized following though, which you can tell from the comment section. They're mostly hardcore sports fans, but they don't all hang on his every word. The more provocative he is, the more discussion it generates. And that gets him clicks, which gets the paper more advertising dollars." A long silence followed, during which Ninah finished painting her toes and scrolled through her phone to the comments. "You still there?"

"This guy calls himself Longdong. That might be all I need to know about who follows this blog. He says, '*It was worth losing to see Jake Greene bust his ass falling out of that wagon. LMAO.*'"

"Longdong wisecracks about everything."

"So you read this crap?"

"I'm a sports fan. I don't comment though. Public school teacher is public enough for me, thank you."

"What if Hodges is right? It never even dawned on me the wagons would tear up the ground. Maybe my best PR move is to put out a mea culpa and promise to take better care of the field in the future."

The voices inside escalated to laughter, followed by the sound of running, then all quiet. Tease, chase, kiss. Deciding she didn't want to hear what followed, Ninah dragged her chair to the far end of the porch.

"You could've rolled the infield with a Zamboni and the Longdogs still would've found a way to lose. Give it up already."

"Right there, that's a perfect example of what I was talking about," Ninah said. "That's the attitude Wesley fosters with his negative approach."

"Here's another one from Three…he uses threes instead of e's. How cute."

Ninah laughed. "That's Trey Sharpe, Justine and JT's son. He's a sports fanatic, especially UK basketball. I think he and Wesley are friends, but he always trolls him hard."

"You've been warned, sports fans! Go to a Longdogs game and you might be accidentally entertained. Btw, Wes doesn't like puppies either. Or pudding."

"I don't think you should worry about it, Britt. He's just one voice."

"Except he has a megaphone."

"So do you. Your actions at the ballpark are gonna speak louder than words. Just focus on what you do best and let the results speak for themselves. And don't talk to Wesley unless you really want to. He's not running your company—you are."

Britt thanked her profusely for the call, the advice and the support. More importantly, she promised they'd go out for dinner as soon as she got a free night.

As Ninah rose to go inside, she dropped the bottle of nail polish and watched helplessly as it rolled off the side of the porch. Jumping down to retrieve it was easy, but she didn't trust the rickety railing to hold her if she tried to pull herself back up.

"She's gone, hurry," Emmy said as her front door squeaked open.

Ninah reached the steps just in time to meet Emmy's secret boyfriend, who was as shocked to see her as she was to see him. "Well, look who it is."

"Ninah…"

She couldn't resist singing his name. "Ike Ike bo-bike… banana-fana-fo-fike."

He managed a sheepish smile, looked back at Emmy with a shrug, and scampered down the steps. "See ya later."

"Oh shit! Ninah…" Emmy clutched fistfuls of her hair and contorted her face with dismay. "I thought you'd gone inside."

"So I gather. What's the big deal?"

"Ninah, you *cannot* tell Mom. Or Dad. Oh my God, but please not Mom. Promise me. Or Carly either, because she'll tell Mom."

She had to admit it was amusing to see the normally chill Emmy in such a state. "I'm not gonna tell anyone anything, but why all the secrecy? You can't possibly be worried about what your mom will think."

Emmy collapsed on the porch swing and gave it a kick. "She wouldn't understand."

"Because Ike's black?"

"No! Because he's a *barista*."

From the way she snarled the word, it wasn't clear to Ninah who considered that a problem, Emmy or Justine. She stifled a laugh and motioned for her to scoot over so she could join her on the swing. "Don't look now, but I think your mom actually married a barista."

"It's not the same. Carly graduated from U of L and worked all over the world before she came back to Leland and bought The Bean. Besides, owning a place is a little different from making the lattes."

"Okay, I'll grant that Carly's a special case, but she'd be the first to tell Justine what a great guy Ike is. And even if he weren't the 'World's Greatest Barista,' his songwriting makes him special. How many guys in Leland can say a Grammy-winner sang one of his songs on tour?"

"I think he's special, but…" She was clearly anguished, almost to the point of tears. "Ever since I came back to Leland, Mom's been on a mission to marry me off to every new doctor in town."

"With this ring, I thee obligate half of my astronomical student loan."

"Ye-ah! It almost makes me wish I'd taken that job in Indianapolis. At least I wouldn't have her watching over me all the time."

"Don't bet on it. She'd have sent a drone with a camera." Justine had been ecstatic when Emmy chose the Grace Hospital pharmacy job instead of the one in Indy. She couldn't stand the thought of her future grandchildren being so far away. "Are you planning on keeping Ike a secret forever or just till you get jammed up for a babysitter?"

Emmy threw a sharp elbow into her side. "For your information, we aren't all that sure we even want kids."

The surprising admission seemed to suggest their relationship was quite serious, which presented a segue to something that needed to be said.

"I remember when I came home from college and told my parents I was in love with a girl. All Mama could talk about was Matthew Shepard, that kid in Wyoming who was beaten to death for being gay."

Emmy scowled. "I know what you're doing."

She wrapped an arm around Emmy's shoulder and hugged her hard. "I'm giving you a window into my world is all. There are shitty people out there who think they have the right to police the rest of us. Your mom and Carly know how that feels, so they're gonna worry about you. Just please don't take your safety for granted."

Emmy nodded tersely without looking up.

"That's all I have to say about it, Emmy. Except…I think it's cool that two people I really like found each other. I'm in your corner all the way."

"Thanks, Ninah. Maybe you should break it to Mom and Dad."

Ninah hardly wanted that job, but she wouldn't mind being a fly on the wall when it happened. "I wouldn't worry. I think they're gonna be thrilled to find out their baby girl met someone she loves enough to talk about not having babies with."

CHAPTER SEVENTEEN

After three days of craning her neck to see the field from her office, Britt enlisted Archie to help push her desk up against the window. The continuous action below—currently practice drills by the visiting Cookeville Moccasins—was inspirational to her creative efforts.

She'd spent the last hour rehearsing remarks to the players, who'd finished their midday practice and retreated to the clubhouse. According to Archie, players barely cleared a grand a month, most of which they paid to Coy in clubhouse dues. Word had it they lived two or three to a bedroom in cheap apartments behind the shopping center, sharing everything from toiletries to clothes. Britt had a plan for earning players extra money through promotional appearances.

Archie knocked softly and cleared his throat. "You ready, boss?"

"Perfect timing." She followed, taking only the list she'd compiled through a day's worth of cold calls to local businesses.

The clubhouse was beneath the concessions concourse in the bowels of the stadium, two levels below the administrative offices. They took the elevator, exiting through a back door that opened into a hallway reeking of onions.

"Maybe you ought to wait here, boss. I'll run ahead and let the boys know you're coming. They can be sort of careless in the locker room, if you know what I mean."

"Of course." If there was one thing she didn't want to see, it was a bunch of naked men.

The painted cinderblock wall of the hallway was covered with framed photos of past teams going all the way back to 1985, the Longdogs' inaugural year. They'd had a good run in the early aughts, winning two league championships and three other division titles. Nothing of note since 2006.

"All set," Archie said.

They walked through double doors into a large open area lined with lockers. About two dozen youthful ballplayers were seated on benches and eating off paper plates. Several were shirtless, some wearing only towels around their waists. Obviously, she'd caught them after their shower.

"Sorry they're not all dressed," Archie said quietly. "Everybody comes running when Coy puts the spread out. Otherwise there's nothing left but peanut butter and jelly."

Two long tables in the middle of the room held a sparse buffet of white bread and condiments—which included the pungent onions—but the cold cuts and cheese tray had been picked clean, as had the chips bowl. There were also apples and oranges, and a bucket-sized jar of generic peanut butter with swirls of grape jelly already mixed in. To say the spread was unappetizing would have been too kind.

The sports websites she'd explored were rife with first-person accounts of life in the minors. A shabby buffet such as this one was considered a rite of passage, motivation to work hard in order to move up the ladder of success.

"Gentlemen, I'd like you to meet Miss Brittany Iverson. Her father Vernon, who is currently recovering from brain surgery, is our new owner."

Someone let out a wolf whistle, prompting several others to laugh. There was no way to pinpoint who it came from, only the general direction.

"Show some respect," Archie snapped. He whispered to her, "These guys just got here a couple of weeks ago. They're a little rough around the edges."

She had her own answer for that, the list in her hand. "Good afternoon, gentlemen. I won't keep you long. Archie tells me you're—"

Someone farted loudly, triggering another burst of laughter.

Archie pointed toward the source and said sternly, "That's enough, guys."

"It's all right, Archie," she said. "Farting is perfectly normal teenage boy behavior. It usually stops once they get interested in girls."

A chorus of appreciative hisses was followed by, "Oooh, better get some cream for that burn."

The reddest face belonged to Troy Cline, the right fielder who'd stumbled on his way to the plate in last night's game. He didn't seem quite so amused with himself now.

She began a slow, deliberate stroll down the buffet table, pausing to note the *ON SALE TODAY* sticker on the white bread. Probably days old. The fruit left in the bowl was bruised. It was hard to feel anything but sympathy for guys who paid half their salary to eat such disgusting crap.

"I came by to introduce myself, since you'll be seeing me around. I'm new at this, but I'm excited about the potential of the Longdogs. My job is to bring people out to the ballpark to cheer you on."

Cory Hanover, the star pitcher everyone was raving about, stood to toss his plate in the bin. He'd been wearing only a towel, which he deliberately allowed to drop. Turning toward her, he badly faked a sheepish grin. "Oops."

Unfazed, she looked him directly in the eye and continued her thought. "If we both do our jobs well, I'd love to share the rewards. I can get you coupons for freebies from some of our advertisers"—she held up her list—"Guido's pizza, The Bean coffee shop, Tacos Chalitos. I'm also lining up public appearances at local businesses where you can earn cash signing autographs and posing for photos. Obviously, I'm only interested in those who can put the best public face on the Longdogs."

Her message was clear: Adolescent ass-clowns need not apply.

She found herself standing over Oscar Lopez. "Oscar, I read today where someone said the wagon race was to blame for causing you to get a bad hop."

A Latino player sitting beside him translated her words.

"No ma'am, my bad," he answered, patting his chest.

"But it did loosen the dirt around third," Cline said churlishly. "It's hard to get traction to run when it's like that."

"I understand, and I—"

"Yo, Cline!" The roar of a deep male voice was followed by the appearance of a middle-aged man Britt recognized as Hank O'Neal, the team's manager. "How many professional baseball games have you played in?"

Cline glanced uneasily at his teammates before meekly replying, "One."

"And how many times have you fucked up?"

"Uh…once?"

"Great, so you're batting a thousand on fuck-ups." He stalked through the room looking down at each player with the scorn of a drill sergeant. "Whose job is it to smooth the dirt under your feet? You better know the answer to that, 'cause that other son of a bitch out there is doing all he can to fuck you over. He's gonna spit, and dig holes out there with his cleats. Hell, he'd drop a turd if nobody was looking. That's your mess to deal with every time you take the field." He came to a stop in front of Cline, who was staring at the floor, his cheeks aflame. "If your peachy ass was good enough to play in the major leagues, you'd be there already. But it ain't. So you better learn from every fucking mistake you make, or your baseball dream is gonna end right here in Leland."

Britt was almost afraid to breathe in the presence of this powerful figure. In the back of her mind, she'd already started plotting her revenge, which would have been to freeze out the clowns who couldn't behave themselves. She liked Hank's ending better.

Taking a step back toward the door, she said, "Just to reiterate, I've got a handful of opportunities for players to show up at places in the community and earn a few bucks just for being a Longdog. Check with Archie for a signup sheet if you're interested."

Hank had returned to his office, but his voice carried just the same. "And don't let me catch any of you saying fuck in front of women."

CHAPTER EIGHTEEN

Almost overnight, the Longdogs were all the rage in Leland. Eleven games into the season, they were in first place in their half of the Valley League at 9-2. And Oscar Lopez already had fourteen home runs.

While there were still plenty of seats available, especially in the bleachers, Britt was thrilled the more expensive club seats behind home plate were starting to fill up, thanks in part to the three-hour flash sale on Monday that slashed season ticket prices by twenty percent. She'd make up that discount in a week's worth of concessions.

"Right this way. We'll take the elevator to the top floor." Along with Carly and Justine, her special guests in the owner's suite tonight were the Hendersons, Joe and Margie. Dr. Joe Henderson was the administrator at Grace Hospital, seventy years old at least, and according to Justine, nearing the decision to retire.

"Hold up," Carly said. She hurried over to the box office to buy a ticket.

"You didn't have to do that," Britt said when she returned. "You're my guest."

"I can't accept freebies. I'm a public official."

"But you aren't here as a—"

"I know, but Tiny Watson has been pissed ever since I beat him in the election. He'd love to call me out for an ethics violation. It's not worth the hassle over a three-dollar ticket."

In the elevator, Joe Henderson asked, "So how's Vernon doing over at the rehab? Justine said he had a seizure."

"Yes, three nights ago. Took everyone by surprise. Dr. Dhawan thinks it was just a one-time thing, but he's put Dad on some medication just to be safe. He's still having a few speech problems and a little weakness on his left side, but they said another week there ought to iron out the wrinkles."

The seizure had scared her half to death until the doctor assured her it was common after brain surgery. Even if he stopped improving now, his other problems were manageable.

She led the small group from the elevator to the private suite. It was hardly luxurious, but cushy armchairs arranged behind three tiers of counters gave everyone a splendid view. She'd arranged a spread of fajitas and spicy slaw from a local food truck, and stocked the mini-fridge with beer, soda, and bottled water.

Her plan, which she'd already played to perfection several times, was simple: Butter up potential advertisers with VIP treatment, promise them the moon, then hit them up to sign a multiyear contract. If the Longdogs kept playing like this, she'd hit her season target in only a matter of weeks.

Convinced years ago by Candice that she was no good at sales, she'd surprised even herself with her early success. The whole week had been a baptism of fire, much of it spent cajoling local businesses who felt Duffy's mismanagement of the team had tarnished their brands. They were excited over her plans to attach their names to fun promotions and giveaways.

"Can I get drinks for anyone? Beer, Coke, water?"

Dr. Henderson answered first, ordering also for his wife. "Beer for me, Diet Coke for Margie."

Britt almost felt guilty about taking advantage of Justine's friendship, but Grace Hospital was the county's largest private employer. If she played her cards right, they could be her biggest advertiser too. She owed it to Justine to go the extra mile and deliver big on her promises.

"I'll have a Sun-Drop," said Carly. As part of The Bean's promotional deal, she'd agreed to sponsor a souvenir coffee mug giveaway at the ballpark. They'd also dreamed up a gimmick, whereby any Longdog struck by a pitch—called a bean ball— got a free coffee at The Bean, as did one lucky ticket holder. It wasn't much in revenue, but it paired the Longdogs with one of the most popular shops in town.

"Something for you, Justine?"

"Bottled water if you have it. It's nice watching from up here. I feel special. Isn't this nice, Joe?"

"I could get used to it."

"Hi, everybody." Ninah waved from the doorway.

Britt completely forgot everyone's drink order, so distracted was she by Ninah's unexpected appearance in the suite. They'd spoken on the phone and traded dozens of texts, but Britt's brutal work schedule made it nearly impossible to make social plans. She was looking forward to tomorrow when the Longdogs left town on an eight-game road trip. First up was a small dinner party at Carly and Justine's.

Ninah politely greeted the Hendersons before addressing Justine. "I picked three gallons of strawberries this morning at Burgess Farm. Want me to bring dessert tomorrow night?"

"Yes!" Carly's eyes went wide. "I love strawberry shortcake."

"But don't bring too much," Justine said. "It's just six of us. I decided to keep the party small so we could all talk and get to know each other."

As Carly and Justine returned to their seats, Ninah took a tentative step toward the door and said to Britt, "Sorry, didn't mean to butt in. I can see you're busy. I just needed to ask about dessert."

"I don't mind at all. You can stay if you like. Carly said you gave your tickets away to one of her employees."

"That's right, Ike Martin and his brother Thaddeus. I thought I'd watch the game from the press box. Carly says you're pitching a big idea to the hospital."

"They don't know it yet, but I'm going to sell them a gigantic, *expensive* digital display of the wait time at their ER, so big they'll be able to see it from the shopping center across the street."

"Break a leg—but not really. Broken legs can be hard to work around." The last bit was accompanied by a subtle wink.

Britt stared after her as Ninah exited the suite and reappeared in the press box. More than once she'd caught herself daydreaming about what they might be doing had she not come down with a severe bout of conscience. She couldn't lead Ninah on, and she'd never bought into the friends-with-benefits game. Sex was for special relationships, those with the potential to last.

"Look, it's the Brownies. Aren't they adorable!" Justine exclaimed.

With the crowd captivated by the endearing performance of the Brownie Scout troop singing the national anthem, Britt pushed thoughts of Ninah aside to focus on her sales pitch.

It proved far easier than expected, since Justine loved her idea and Dr. Henderson simply deferred to her judgment. A mere five minutes into the game, the Longdogs were thousands of dollars richer.

Carly patted the chair at the end. "What's up with you and Ninah? Did I see a little…" She wiggled her eyebrows.

"You might have. So what's her story? How come a woman like that is single?"

"How come you are?" Carly mocked her with a smirk.

"Touché. I'm single because my ex is a pernicious, self-absorbed opportunist and I'm apparently a doormat wearing blinders. By the way, don't ever let Justine come to work with you at The Bean. You can be lovers or business partners, but not both."

"Too late for that. We're already partners in everything." Carly's contented gaze drifted to her wife. "Having said that, she's pitched in a few times at the shop when we were short on help. Let's just say I'm glad it doesn't happen a lot. But I love her to pieces."

"You guys are cute together. Gives me hope." She would have loved a role model couple like Carly and Justine in her life, women who so obviously cherished one another. In her circle of friends in San Diego, couples were always breaking up, switching partners. "Candice and I probably would have split up four or five years ago if we hadn't been in business together. Our relationship really suffered for it, and so did our business. I made too many decisions based on what kind of projects she wanted to work on, not what was good for the company. Now it's all in the toilet."

"And lucky you—the Longdogs dropped right in your lap. Now all you need is to round it out with...Ninah?"

Feeling suddenly uneasy, Britt pretended to watch the game. "I wouldn't go that far. We've only known each other, what? Two weeks?"

"Two weeks, two years. It doesn't matter with Ninah. What you see is what you get." She paused to watch the Longdogs turn a double play for the first two outs. "Ninah Faust is a prize. I'm not kidding. She's one of the nicest people I know. Smart, interesting, sweet. If I were single and twenty years younger..."

"Which begs the question... Come on, she can't be perfect."

"If there's a knock on her, it's that she can sometimes be... let's call it inflexible. She has her opinions, and there's not much gray area."

"You're saying she's hardheaded."

"Or she's principled. You have to respect somebody who sticks to their guns when it's not the easiest choice." Carly leaned forward to scan the crowd, counting in the air with her finger. "See that aisle where the peanut guy is right now? Count up eight rows from the bottom, that woman in the blue T-shirt at the end."

Britt followed her eye and counted. "In the red cap?"

"Yeah, that's Teri Kaufman, Ninah's ex. She's an imaging technician at the hospital. Probably did your dad's CAT scan. Justine runs into her all the time."

The crowd gasped as the batter slapped a line drive down the first base line. Scotty McCall lunged and snatched it out of midair for the final out.

"Teri's one of those life-of-the-party types, always clowning around. Lots of laughs. She comes on a little strong for some people's tastes, but she's not hard to get along with. At least she wasn't."

Britt got a better look when everyone stood and cheered the Longdogs as they ran into the dugout. Teri had a prominent nose with rosy, cherubic cheeks, and a long dark ponytail that looped through the back of her cap. Not as pretty as Ninah, but reasonably attractive. "How long were they together?"

"Six or seven years, I think. Not married though."

"What happened?"

"Look at her again. Notice anything special about that cap?"

Britt strained to bring it into focus. Lots of people were wearing Longdogs caps. Those were dark red with a black dachshund logo and the Longdogs name in black lettering. Teri Kaufman's hat was bright red with white lettering that said... "You can't be serious. She's a—"

"I believe the word you're looking for is Deplorable."

CHAPTER NINETEEN

Ninah lit the last of the citronella candles on Justine and Carly's deck where a round table had been set for six. Justine, a venerable entertainer, was inside tending to a stuffed pork roast and vegetable soufflé. Tonight's dinner party was a notch above the casual cookout they'd enjoyed last week, with white linens and china.

The creases in Britt's pink shirt suggested it was new, something to tide her over until the weekend, her planned return to San Diego to collect her belongings. Ninah couldn't resist fixing a wrinkle in the collar, though she'd vowed not to flirt tonight, no matter how much she wanted to. "How does it feel to have a night off?"

"I'm not sure if I'll get a real night off all summer. Even when I try to relax, my brain won't stop. You wouldn't believe how much there is to do."

"At least it's paying off already. The crowd's gotten bigger since opening night, fans are getting involved. Oh, and that beauty contest was hilarious. How did you convince those guys to walk out there in bikinis and high heels?" Before Britt could answer, Ninah interrupted. "Listen to me...I just congratulated you on getting a night off and immediately asked you about work. Forget I said anything."

Britt examined an unopened bottle of chardonnay resting in an ice chest. "La Crema...this is good stuff. Would you like some?"

"Sure. Carly said she was serving California wines in honor of her guests."

"This Dorie and Margot, are they friends of yours?"

Ninah accepted a glass and settled onto half of Carly's cushioned porch swing, an open invitation for Britt to join her. "They come to all the holiday parties, but I'm trying to think if I've seen them since Christmas. Dorie's interesting. She edits for popular science magazines, like *National Geographic* and *Scientific American*. I guarantee you'll like her. You'll like them both."

She hoped her slight of Margot hadn't left the wrong impression. Margot was nice as well, but passionate about horses to the exclusion of almost everything else. At a typical party, the horse fanatics tended to cluster together in what the others jokingly called "the paddock."

Carly came out carrying a relish tray, followed by Justine with a cheese board.

"I texted Margot and told them to pull all the way around to the back, that we'd be out here on the deck," Justine said. She relaxed in a chaise lounge, leaving room for Carly to sit at her feet.

"Think the Longdogs will keep the streak going tonight against the Oil Cans?" Carly asked.

"We're driving over to Ashland for the game tomorrow night," Ninah said. "But I just promised Britt we wouldn't talk baseball tonight. She hasn't had a moment away from it since the season started."

"Great idea." Justine likely felt the same way about baseball that Ninah did about horses.

Britt's invitation to the road game had come as a pleasant surprise. A two-hour drive each way, plus three hours for the game. It was a real chance to deepen their friendship.

"But I can still follow the game online, right?" Carly held up her phone and looked sheepishly at her wife. "Ninah showed me where the scorekeeper site was. I just wanna see if Oscar can hit like that in somebody else's park."

"I defer to Britt. She's our guest."

"Fine by me. Let me know if he jacks one out."

The sound of crunching gravel signaled the arrival of Margot's pickup, a dual-wheeled monster she used for towing a horse trailer. From the looks of it, Dorie wasn't with her.

"Hey, everybody!" Margot yelled as she started across the lawn. Her face was tan against a buttoned-down white shirt, and her curly dark hair still dripped from her shower. In her hand was a colorful bunch of wildflowers that looked suspiciously like the ones growing along Pinckard Road.

Justine and Carly rose to meet her on the top step. "Where's Dorie?"

"Dorie is…how did she put it? Pursuing other priorities, I believe she said. She left about five weeks ago, went back to Long Beach. I started to tell you on the phone the other night, but I thought what if they don't want me by myself? I didn't want to find out so here I am." Margot held her arms wide as if ready to take a bow.

"Oh, my goodness." Justine stomped down the stairs and pulled her into a hug. "You poor thing. You should have told us. All this time you were sitting out there in that house all by yourself. We'd never have let you do that."

"I know. I just needed a while to get my head together." Margot turned toward the swing. "Hey, Ninah. Good to see you. And you must be Britt Iverson, all the way from San Diego. Welcome to horse country."

Britt met her with a hand extended. "California's no stranger to horses, but I suppose you know that."

They bonded quickly over a shared familiarity with thoroughbred farms on the West Coast, none of which Ninah had heard of before. Temecula, Hemet, Aguanda.

Then as usual, Margot was "off to the races" with endless talk of her work as barn manager at Hickson Farm. Thankfully, she waited until the end of dinner to detail her feed schedule, how she rotated horses in and out of certain pastures because the grasses had a natural laxative effect.

Britt asked, "Did you know that pasture along Pinckard Road belonged to my father till a few months ago?"

"Get out! So that's what Clyde meant when he told Jamie to get it done, whatever it took. Small world, isn't it?"

Too small, Ninah thought miserably. She was trapped in the paddock during old home week.

"Speaking of your dad, how is he? Justine said he had some kind of surgery."

Britt briefly described her father's health scare.

"God, you must have been worried sick. And coming home to find out you own a baseball team. And I thought *my* world had been turned upside down." Margot barely drew a breath, changing the subject before anyone else could jump into the conversation. "Hey, the Longdogs are on a road trip all week, right? Why don't you come out to the farm? I'll give you a tour. Hell, I'll even saddle you up a mount. You ride, don't you?"

Britt laughed and held up her hands. "No thanks. I've ridden a few times but I don't think I could handle something that fancy."

"I can talk you through it. Come on, how many people get to sit astride a thoroughbred racehorse? What are you doing Saturday?"

A mysterious grating sound grew louder before Ninah realized she was grinding her teeth. She darted a glance toward

Carly and plucked a leftover strawberry from the bowl. What she really needed was another glass of wine. Or three.

"I can't," Britt replied. "I've got a sales meeting on Saturday morning. Then I'm off to San Diego for a few days."

"When you get back then. Just let me know."

Justine stood to clear the dishes. "Would anyone like coffee, or more wine? I can open another bottle."

"Sit down, honey. I'll clean up. Ninah won't mind giving me a hand." Carly tipped her head toward the kitchen. "Right?"

"Of course." She jumped at the chance to escape Margot's endless equine endeavors but felt guilty for leaving Britt to endure them.

In the kitchen, Carly quickly said, "Just so you know, I had no idea about Dorie."

"Did you see Margot's face light up when she saw Britt? I'm surprised she didn't go back to the truck for her lasso." Confident, smooth-talking, *endless*-talking Margot. "Margot's practically throwing herself at her. Mark my word, before this night's over she'll—"

"Forget it. Britt gave me the third degree about you last night. She can't imagine why you're single."

"Oh?"

"So I pointed Teri out to her and she got a load of that MAGA hat. Fair to say Britt admires your politics."

"She was asking about me? What did she say?" It was middle school all over again. "Never mind, what did *you* say?"

"I told her you were a prize." Carly's grin suddenly faded. "And maybe a little hardheaded."

"Hardheaded? Thanks a lot."

"Because you're principled. Which is why you broke up with Teri." Carly craned her neck to check the action through the window. "Damn, that woman can flat-out talk."

Ninah grunted. "Am I imagining things or are they hitting it off?"

"Stop it." Carly finished loading the dishwasher. "Margot's got a cool job but it's all she knows. Unless you're into horses—and I don't think Britt is—that's gonna wear on you after two hours, three at the most. There's only so much horse shit a girl can take. Just ask Dorie."

CHAPTER TWENTY

For the third time, Britt summarized the contents of their phone call in an effort to encourage her newest advertising client to stop his blathering and hang up. "I think that covers it, Rich. I'll make sure you have three players in uniform at the Ford dealership a week from Saturday, ten o'clock. Thanks so much."

Seeing Ninah at the door, she waved her into the office and tried to focus on Rich's last bit of tedium. It proved a challenge, since Ninah's outfit instantly commanded her attention—tight white jeans with a red Longdogs jersey specially styled for a woman's figure. Her hair was freshly cut, and her face glowed with a low-key hint of blush and shimmering bronze shadow that made her hazel eyes pop.

"What a great view," Ninah said, gazing out onto the field.

"*I'll say,*" she replied to herself. "I like that jersey. It'll come in handy if Hank needs to pull you out of the stands to pinch hit."

"I don't get to wear it to home games now that I'm official scorekeeper. Can't have people thinking I'm biased."

Britt nodded toward the field, where Pervis was putting up a new billboard. "Keep an eye on Pervis. He goes bonkers when the sprinklers come on."

"That's cruel…in a hilarious sort of way."

Britt came around her desk and gestured at what had become her standard office fare, trim black pants and a fitted shirt. "Will you go with me like this? I can probably find a Longdogs T-shirt in the storage room. I reached the bottom of my suitcase about nine days ago."

"I think you look great. Besides, you're one of those people who can get away with wearing a grocery sack."

"Is that a commentary on my wardrobe?" she teased.

"No, I just put you in that rarified air with women who make their clothes look great instead of the other way around. Like Justine Hall."

"Wow, I'll take that any day." She surreptitiously studied Ninah's figure in the form-fitting jersey, remembering exactly what was underneath. "In case I haven't said it, I really do appreciate all you guys have done to make me feel at home. I realize I haven't exactly been gracious about it, but I'm starting to feel that coming here was the right thing to do."

"Don't be too hard on yourself. Your whole life was upended." With a mischievous laugh, she added, "If I were a better person, I'd feel guilty for being glad about it."

It was the second time Ninah had casually tossed out a hint of flirtatious innuendo. A part of her wanted to answer back and let the chips fall. That would complicate their friendship if Ninah developed expectations.

"I guess we ought to hit the road." On the way out, she grinned smugly and dropped a contract form on Misty's desk. "Got us another one, Misty. The Ford dealership."

"If they were fish, they'd be jumping in the boat."

Ninah bounced ahead down two flights of stairs. "You're not fooling me, Britt Iverson. You enjoy this baseball business."

"As JT Sharpe made very clear, what I do has nothing to do with baseball. As long as I don't tear up the field, that is." She nodded ahead. "By the way, the rental car company picked up my Toyota this morning. Thought I should warn you."

"Does that mean you want me to drive?"

"And miss the chance to go in style?" Outside she clicked her key fob, causing the lights on her father's Silverado pickup truck to flash. "This baby's got every luxury feature you could possibly imagine. I feel like Cleopatra being carried around in one of those golden carriages."

"A palanquin."

"Are you kidding me? Who knows trivia like that?"

"A history teacher."

Ninah's sunglasses dropped and skittered across the parking lot, sending her in pursuit. As she stooped to retrieve them, Britt's uncontrollable libido filled in the visual details from behind. That settled it. Next time Ninah flirted, she'd remind her they were in the Friend Zone. Or maybe she was reminding herself.

On Main Street, they rolled to a stop at a crosswalk, where a slender black youth made eye contact with them and waved. Britt thought briefly it might be one of her ballplayers, but they all were in Ashland. "Am I supposed to know that guy?"

"He's one of my students. Pull over a sec." Ninah hopped out and met him at the corner for an animated chat that lasted less than a minute. When she returned, she explained, "That's Thaddeus Martin, younger brother of Ike. Remember him? Carly's barista. Thaddeus was president of the GSA last year, but he's off to Berea College in the fall. He asked if you were my girlfriend, by the way."

"What did you tell him?"

"I told him no, and that he ought to tie his shoes before he tripped over the laces."

"I guess that's nicer than mind your own effing business." Britt almost remarked about the gossipy nature of small towns but didn't want to start another quarrel about Leland.

At Leland's last stoplight, Ninah waved to a pair of teenage girls on the sidewalk.

"More grist for the gossip mill?" Britt asked, trying not to sound annoyed.

"Probably. Juicy stuff spreads faster around here than head lice. It's worse because I'm a teacher. Students always find it fascinating to realize their teachers have lives outside of school."

"It must be weird living in a fishbowl. What do they think about you being gay?"

"The usual, I suppose. Some of them probably snicker about it but not where I can see them. I've never regretted coming out. They need to see how normal it is. Teri and I—that's my ex, we split up three years ago—we used to go to football games together, or band concerts, whatever. All the kids knew we were a couple."

"Carly pointed her out to me the other night."

"Yeah, she said. In all her MAGA hat glory. She's still on Justine's List so you'll run into her eventually, probably at the Pride picnic next month."

"I can't fathom why a queer person would vote for Trump."

"Oh, Teri didn't just vote for him. She drove to four different states to go to his rallies, and she wears that stupid MAGA hat everywhere she goes. I got home from school one day and there was this big-ass Trump billboard in our front yard. That was it for me." As she spoke, her voice rose with disgust. "It was sickening. I mean physically sickening. Imagine watching the person you're supposed to be in love with morph into a sycophant for that flaming orange asshole."

"And you had no idea she felt that way?"

Ninah shook her head. "Not really...that's on me though. I knew she could be a jerk sometimes, like she called all Latinos Jose and Carlita. Blacks were either homeys or baby mamas.

I'd scold her and she'd laugh it off. I should have taken it more seriously. When you're with somebody like that for six years, people think you must be a closet racist too. Even now, it embarrasses the hell out of me."

"Six years." Not as long as she'd stayed with Candice, but a long time. "Carly said you weren't married."

"No, thank God. I owe her and Justine for that. If they hadn't been so adamant about wanting their marriage license issued here in Leland County, Teri and I might have followed the crowd and gotten married in Lexington. We were tied together with a mortgage though. We built our house on land her father gave us, so we couldn't sell it to anyone else. I had to give up most of my equity just to get away from her. Like a fox gnawing off its own foot to get out of a trap."

Britt had been forced out of her house too, since she couldn't afford to assume the mortgage on her own after Candice gutted their business. "At least you landed on your feet. You've got a good job and lots of friends."

"Can't complain there. I just wish I didn't run into her every time I turn around. The ballpark, the grocery store."

"Do you still speak?"

Ninah shook her head. "It's probably best if we don't. I wouldn't say nice things. What about Candice? Are you still in touch?"

"She pops up at parties in San Diego once in a while. I manage to be civil but I don't go out of my way to talk to her." Her attitude toward Candice was hard to explain without sounding soulless. The urgency of trying to sell the house and save the business had helped her avoid confronting the emotions over their breakup. Once those crises passed, the only thing left of their relationship was ambivalence. "We had eleven years, Candice and me. With absolutely nothing to show for it."

"Oh, I don't know…these scars have to count for something."

CHAPTER TWENTY-ONE

The farther they got from Lexington, the more sparse the countryside, with fields giving way to forests. Past the Licking River, they climbed the Cumberland Plateau to the worn mountain ridges that held Kentucky's rich coal deposits. Ninah knew it all like the back of her hand.

"I just had a flashback," Britt said. "The last time I came down this road was on a school bus when my senior class took a field trip to Washington, DC. I forgot how rugged it was in this part of the state."

"Welcome to coal country," Ninah said, gesturing toward the exit ahead. "You up for a little side trip? It won't take long."

They glided off the ramp, where a road sign indicated a left turn for food and gas. "Coal Springs, four miles. Just promise you won't get us lost out here in the middle of nowhere."

"We're not lost. I could drive this road blindfolded."

The winding road that connected the interstate to the town of twelve hundred ran parallel to a wide ravine known as Stone

Holler. Spring rains had brought the usual rock slides that gouged holes in the pavement.

The speed limit dropped to thirty-five as they entered a short commercial stretch marked by the ubiquitous signs of economic struggle. Junk cars, abandoned storefronts. A thrift shop, a payday lender that cashed checks and wrote money orders.

"Welcome to Coal Springs, my hometown," Ninah said, now second-guessing her impulse for the detour. Britt couldn't possibly react with anything but despair. "Both my parents grew up here. Go back two or three generations, and I'm probably related to half the town. Lucky for me, I was a pretty decent softball pitcher, good enough to get noticed by the college scouts. If not for that I might still be here."

"Do you still play? They have recreation leagues, right?"

"Yeah, but I dropped out about four years ago. Some of the women I played with like to smoke weed, do a few pills. I can't be a schoolteacher and be around that sort of thing. Anyway, now you see why I like Leland so much."

Britt groaned. "I'm really sorry, Ninah. I never should have said those things about Leland."

"No, that's not what I meant. I don't blame you for feeling that way. Yours was a different reality." Their friendship had made her more protective of Britt's comfort zone. "I only brought you here because I feel the same way about Coal Springs as you do about Leland. Not the traumatic memories, but it distresses me sometimes to be here. Even when I visit Mama I can't bring myself to stay the night. I'd never come back here to live."

"Is this a coal town?"

"Used to be. The last mine closed about fifteen years ago. All they have now are a few trout farms. Opioids hit this whole area pretty hard but it seems to be leveling off. Mama says that's because the people most at risk are dead already."

From the main road, there was nothing in the town's landscape that looked anything like hope. No flowers. No parks or playgrounds. Just the fenced-in field by the Baptist church where Ninah had honed the skills that got her into Western Kentucky on an athletic scholarship. She guided Britt to the church's gravel parking lot.

"I was out here till dark most nights with my dad. He taught me how to play ball, drilled me over and over till I could do it in my sleep."

"JT said he played in the major leagues."

"He was a catcher for the Minnesota Twins...sort of." Staring out over the field, she could almost picture him squatted behind a cardboard cutout of home plate as she whirled the ball underhanded. Thousands and thousands of times. "Let me put it this way, he's on the books."

"What does that mean?"

"Daddy got drafted by the Twins out of high school, made it up to Double-A in Charlotte. They had him working with their pitching prospects. Then he got drafted for real—by Uncle Sam. This was Vietnam. Mama kept hoping the Twins would put in for a deferment. When they didn't, Daddy figured they must not have expected him to develop much further. He always said if he'd gotten a deferment, somebody else would have had to go in his place."

"Sounds like a decent guy."

"He was." Talking about her father stirred both sadness and comfort. "About a week before he was supposed to report, right out of the blue, the Twins called him up. An hour later he's on a bus to Minneapolis. The next night they stuck him in a game as a pinch runner and announced to the crowd that he was due to report to Fort Jackson in a few days. He got a standing ovation, and then another one when he scored. I'm sure it was part respect, part PR gimmick, but it still gives me goose bumps to think about it."

"You must have been really proud of him."

"I miss him every day." She patted her chest and blinked back unexpected tears. "He and Mama loved watching the

Longdogs. They used to come visit in the summer so they could go to the games."

It surprised her to realize how much she'd wanted Britt to appreciate her father's story. Perhaps it was a subconscious craving for reciprocity, given that she held Vernon in such high regard.

"Is your mother still here?"

"In the same house." She hitched a thumb over her shoulder. "It's a little ways down that street we just passed. My sister and her boys are living there with her now, but don't get me started on that."

"Would you like to—"

"Absolutely not." Ninah added a sardonic laugh. No way was she taking Britt into that circus. "Last time I was here, all the cash in my wallet went missing. I mentioned it to Mama in case it was one of my nephews. I figured you wouldn't want a kid walking around with a couple hundred bucks in their pocket, right? It worried Mama too so she asked Leah about it, and Leah went ballistic. Called me a terrible aunt for even suggesting one of her little angels would do something so underhanded. Which is fair, I guess, since it was probably Leah who took it."

"Oh no!"

"Hey, I warned you not to get me started. I'd like to believe Leah will get her act together eventually. She's just taking the scenic route."

Britt's face fell as she took in their stark surroundings. "Don't take this as an insult, okay? I'm impressed as hell by what you've done with your life. You were looking at some pretty incredible odds."

"I'm not insulted." On the contrary, she felt nothing but pride at knowing she had Britt's respect. "But credit where it's due, Mama and Daddy always pushed us in school so we'd aim higher than Coal Springs. I owe it all to them."

"Not all of it. You obviously worked hard too." Britt eased the truck back onto the road toward the interstate and craned her neck for a glimpse of the houses on the street where Ninah's mother lived. "Other than my mother being a lunatic, I had a lot of lucky breaks growing up. Dad was always there to hand me everything I asked for. I don't know if I could have done it on my own like you did."

"You went to California all by yourself. That took a lot of guts for a kid right out of high school. I'd have been scared to death to venture that far from home."

"Not if being at home made you as unhappy as it did me." They rode back through Stone Holler in silence, reaching the interstate before Britt elaborated. "What I remember most about my first year at San Diego State was feeling safe for the first time in my life. Truly safe, like I could be myself and not have to worry about being ostracized. Was it like that for you when you went off to college?"

"Most of the time, yeah. I hung out a lot with my teammates, most of whom were gay. Everybody was cool, even the straight players and all the coaches."

"What about when you went to class? Were you out?"

"Not exactly. I didn't lie or anything, but my sexuality wasn't relevant in the history department, so I never brought it up."

"But it was relevant on the softball field?"

"I see what you did there."

Britt flashed a sheepish grin. "Sorry, I was just making a contrast. Because once I got to California, I was able to be out everywhere. I wore Pride pins to class, put a bumper sticker on my car. The point is I felt utterly safe there. Most people didn't care one way or the other, but the ones who did care were supportive. When I compared that to the church culture here in Kentucky, the thought of ever coming back was purgatory."

"Mmm...I could see that maybe fifteen years ago, but it's not like that now."

"Sure it is. Didn't you tell me your kids got heckled at Pride Night? That the churches came out and protested? And you know they're getting it at home too. Maybe not as bad as what my mom did, but still. It's oppressive."

Ninah grudgingly nodded as she recalled the GSA's roundtable discussion of problems they faced for being queer. All of them related to the pain of rejection, even those whose families had gradually come around to support them. "We're making progress though. Fifty-one percent of Kentuckians support same-sex marriage. Do you realize what a big deal that is?"

Britt tilted her head skeptically. "You wouldn't just make up a number like that, would you?"

She smacked Britt's shoulder playfully. "I can't believe you just called me a liar. My civics class had a debate about it. It wasn't all that long ago that a majority of Californians passed Prop 8, so give us some time. All it takes is critical mass, getting enough people to stand up for themselves."

"I have to admit, I'm in awe of people like you and Carly and Justine. You read about gays who get their houses spray-painted and their tires slashed. It takes a lot of courage to put yourselves out there like that."

"Somebody has to, especially at school. Otherwise we're teaching the next generation they should expect to be shamed."

Britt's brow furrowed and she drummed her fingers on the wheel. "How do you think Longdogs fans would react if they knew I was gay?"

"Honestly? With a yawn."

"So it wouldn't make a difference one way or the other."

"I didn't say that. It's always good for queer kids to see that people just like them can grow up and be leaders in the community. They can point you out to their parents and maybe take their anxiety down a notch. And it's good for queer adults to know their family just got a little bigger. So yeah, I think it would be cool to have that be part of your public persona."

"Mmm."

"Something to think about. I'm not gonna judge you one way or the other."

"Easy to say. What you guys think of me matters a lot, but not as much as what I think of myself. I don't want to be a hypocrite. I just have to figure out how to do it without turning it into some big production."

Ninah laughed. "Ha! Don't worry, come tomorrow it'll be all over town."

CHAPTER TWENTY-TWO

Sitting in club seats behind the Longdogs on-deck circle, Britt scouted ideas from the Ashland Oil Cans, anything she could poach for entertaining the home crowd and boosting revenue. Ninah helped by rating the "fun quotient" for each.

"I'm glad you came along. Makes me less annoyed that I'm actually here to work."

"That's why you're glad? Boy, aren't you a silver-tongued charmer."

"I hear that a lot."

"I bet you do," Ninah said, adding an eye roll. "If you want my opinion—since you're *working* and all—this is one of the better ballparks in the Valley League. I like that you can look out over the mountains from the stands. Some ballparks, all you see are strip malls and people's backyards."

"I couldn't agree more," Britt replied. "All that clutter detracts from my billboards."

After the heavy conversation coming out of Coal Springs, they'd both made a concerted effort to lighten things up. Too bad the Longdogs weren't playing along. Their four-game winning streak was in peril, as they trailed 4-1 in the top of the seventh inning.

"Leading off for the Longdogs, first baseman Scotty McCall."

"We need some baserunners," Ninah said. "The great thing about baseball is anything can happen. Doesn't matter how many runs you're down, the game's not over till the last out."

"Three up, three down!" yelled a man two rows back. He was a lively fan who clearly loved his home team, but his booming voice had begun to grate on Britt's nerves. "Time to send these *muttsss* back to Leland with their tails between their legs."

Ninah looked warily over her shoulder. "Sounds like someone may have had one too many beers."

Throughout the game, Britt had jotted notes on her phone for ideas to pursue at Leland Field. The kids seemed to enjoy Squeaky, the team's mascot. Dressed as an oil can, he drove around the field between innings on a golf cart and squirted fans with a Super Soaker.

"Think I could have Banger run around and spray people?" she asked absently.

"Or have him pee on their leg. Maybe just the umpires."

"Don't encourage me. Did I tell you I cut a deal with Tacos Chalitos? They're donating two combo dinners for every Longdogs home run, one to the player who hits it and another to a fan. We'll draw ticket numbers during the game."

"Oscar will be eating there every night."

Scotty chased a pitch low and outside for strike one.

The man behind them shouted, "That's it, Ricky boy. This guy can't hit the broad side of a barn."

Britt took a gander at him, a middle-aged guy whose paunchy gut was visible below his T-shirt. "He's definitely drunk. Let's hope he's not driving home."

Scotty connected sharply with a line drive to the gap between left and center. By the time the outfielders chased down the carom and got the ball back into the infield, he was standing breathlessly on third.

Ninah slapped her program against her knee. "Didn't I tell you? A couple more timely hits and we are back in business."

"Now batting, right fielder Yuki Yakamoto."

"Gooky Yakamoto!" the man yelled.

Britt twisted again in her seat. "You've got to be—"

Wesley Hodges suddenly materialized in the aisle beside their seats. "Taking in the competition, I see. Not a bad idea."

He wore a lanyard that marked him as press, along with khaki chinos and a seersucker shirt that mostly forgave its wrinkles. His expression was odd, as if he were trying to smile through a scowl.

Britt accepted his offered handshake, if only to push it away from Ninah's face. It was bad enough he invaded Ninah's space—he didn't even acknowledge her. "It's…Hutchins, right?"

"Hodges. Wesley Hodges, Leland *Gazette*," he said coolly. "Wondered if you might be ready to schedule that sit-down we talked about. It'd be a great chance for you to make your case directly to the fans for why they ought to come out to the ballpark and support the Longdogs."

"A case that you undermined, if I recall…which makes me a little wary of talking with you again."

He shook his head and muttered, "That explains the attack dogs."

"Excuse me?"

"Right, I'm sure you have no idea what I'm talking about."

Britt grunted as Yuki popped up to the second baseman. "I'm afraid I don't."

Feigning indifference, Wesley pushed his hands into his back pockets and looked away. "You're saying you didn't put Kip Barlow up to writing that letter to the editor? He basically called me a jerk."

"Correct, I did not do that. In fact—in case you'd like to take out your phone and record this—I don't know anything about it. I'm aware that Dr. Barlow often brings his family to the ballpark. Perhaps they enjoy some of the entertainment you belittled as distracting and trivial."

His ears and throat burned red at her scolding.

She cut him off as he opened his mouth to reply. "Since you obviously have an ax to grind over the so-called *fun quotient* at the ballpark—that was very disingenuous, by the way—I'm concerned that whatever I say will get twisted into fodder for another hit piece."

On the field, Hank inserted Austin Farmer as a pinch hitter for Angel Alvarado, who'd limped off last inning after a collision at home plate. Farmer had three homers this season, the only Longdog other than Oscar to show power at the plate.

"Down in front!"

Hodges squatted in the aisle, still not acknowledging Ninah's presence. "My blog is only meant to start a conversation. Thing is, I'm a sportswriter. I go for the game, not the sideshow. Maybe that's a guy thing. But I'll admit you have a point about there being all kinds of people at the ballpark, and I know it's your job to entertain all of them. That's why I really want to hear where you're coming from."

Surely he realized his condescending sexism only made matters worse. Ninah could probably run circles around Hodges and his "guy thing" when it came to baseball.

"Here, take my card," he said. "Call me and let's set up something for next week. Coffee, lunch…I'm up for anything at all."

Britt dropped it in her purse without giving it a glance. As much as she wanted to blow him off completely, she couldn't ignore his potential for influence. Sooner or later, she needed to submit to his questions. "I'll be out of town for the next few days. Perhaps when I get back, I'll have my secretary arrange a meeting in our office."

"Okay, but don't cancel on me this time. You'll give me a complex." He was too awkward to effect genuine humor.

Farmer slapped a ground ball down the first base line, scoring Scotty McCall and giving the Longdogs another baserunner with one down. DeVon Holliday came to the plate representing the tying run.

"I can't believe you were so nice to that jack-wad. After what he did with that blog, I'd have told him to drop dead."

"I wanted to, but it's not too smart to make an enemy of the press. I might need him someday."

The man behind them cupped his hands and yelled, "Let's go, Ricky boy. Give this ape your fastball."

Ninah suddenly dug her fingernails into Britt's forearm. "Oh…my…God. He did not just call DeVon Holliday an ape."

Shocked as well, Britt looked around expecting to find someone, possibly one of the man's friends, calling him out. What she saw instead turned her stomach—literally no one seemed to mind his racist slur. If anything, his friends were amused.

Encouraged by their laughter, he began to grunt and scratch underneath his armpits.

"No fucking way," Ninah said, pushing up from her seat.

Britt caught her shirttail and pulled her back down. "Don't."

"What do you mean, don't? We can't just let people get away with that shit."

"I know, I agree with you. But please…don't." With as little fanfare as possible, she snapped the man's picture with her phone. "Let's get out of here."

She hurriedly led Ninah down the stairs and toward the exit.

"Britt!" Ninah stubbornly stopped on the ramp. "I can't believe you're just gonna walk away. We have to stand up to these assholes, or we're no better than they are."

Judging by the collective grumble of the crowd, the Longdogs had done something good, a stolen base or a hit. Britt no longer cared about the game.

"I promise you I'll deal with it. Section E, row eight, seat two. I even got a photo of him doing that stupid ape impression. I'll send it to the Oil Cans' owner and ask him to handle it, but I don't want either of us in a confrontation with a man who's obviously drunk, and whose friends think he's funny. That's not going to end well."

"These assholes are always counting on people being too polite to call them on their bullshit. That's how we got in this mess, and it's only gonna get worse."

"It's not about being polite, Ninah. It's about living to fight another day. One look at that Longdogs shirt and that crowd wouldn't have cared what he said. *You* would have been the enemy." As they passed through the turnstile to the parking lot, she put a friendly arm around Ninah's shoulder. "I admire your principles and your courage, but what mattered most was getting out of there with all our teeth."

CHAPTER TWENTY-THREE

Ninah's cell phone service faded as they left the confines of Ashland. On her last refresh, the Longdogs were coming to bat in the top of the ninth, trailing by two runs. The final score would have to wait until they got more bars. Sadly, even a win wouldn't be enough to erase their appalling ballpark experience.

Nestled in the cushy passenger seat, she could feel her entire body drooping with shame. "I hate giving in to bastards like that. I can't get over how everybody else just sat there, not saying a word. How can people listen to garbage like that and not even care?"

"You know *I* care, right?" Britt patted her thigh, which Ninah decided to accept as a heartfelt show of support rather than a patronizing brush-off.

"Of course, and you were right to drag me out of there. There's no telling how ugly it would have gotten because I was about to get in his face." She kept thinking about Seth's despicable remark, and how customers at The Bean sprang to

Ike's defense. "There was a time—not that long ago, in fact—when most people followed a basic moral code that said you weren't supposed to drag your prejudices into the public square. Even if you had bigoted thoughts, you kept them to yourself."

"Because you knew it was wrong and that other people would think less of you."

"But now, no one gives a shit. They say whatever they want, no matter how rude or obnoxious, and there aren't any consequences at all because people just don't care anymore. I can't believe it's gotten this bad." She laid most of it at the feet of Trump, who'd drastically changed the tenor of the nation's discourse. "If anything cuts your heart out, it's waking up to the fact that almost two-thirds of your neighbors voted for a racist. Not only that, his racism is one of the things they *like* about him. But don't you dare call them racist. You have to use code words like, 'he says what he thinks' or 'he doesn't try to be politically correct.'"

Recognizing that she was angry enough to cry, Ninah took several deep breaths and closed her eyes. In a twist of irony, she opened them just as they passed the Coal Springs exit. There was little doubt in her mind who her family had voted for, but not discussing it with them let her hold on to hope that they hadn't.

Britt sighed, and in a pensive voice said, "I'll be honest, it creeps me out to know I'm surrounded by people like that here. Most of my California neighbors reject that kind of thinking. Not everyone, obviously, but enough to make people think twice before shouting out something racist in public. If that guy had pulled that kind of crap at a Padres game, the crowd would have turned on him."

"Sounds like nirvana."

"I wouldn't go that far. California has its share of problems. Taxes are brutal…traffic is barbaric. And a halfway decent house is half a million dollars."

"But it must be worth it if forty million people choose to live there."

"Have you ever been?"

"No, the farthest west I've been is El Paso. Our softball team did a swing through Texas." That was fifteen years ago, she realized. "I always wanted to see the West but Teri wasn't much for traveling. Airplanes freaked her out, and she never got off work long enough to take a driving trip that far."

"What if…" Britt's fingers fluttered on the steering wheel, as if she were tapping along to music in her head. "How about coming with me to San Diego?"

"You don't mean tomorrow?"

"Sure, why not? I don't know why I didn't think of this before. If you help me pack, we'll have plenty of time to see the city. I think you'd love it."

An invitation to see the place Britt called home? Ninah already loved it.

"Assuming I say yes—which I intend to do, so you'd better mean it—what time do we leave?"

Britt laughed and clapped her hands against the wheel, her smile glowing in the dashboard light. "The flight's at five o'clock tomorrow. Changes in Dallas and gets into San Diego at eight thirty Pacific Time."

"All right, let's do it." Ninah began to squirm with excitement, her mind already racing with ideas of what to pack. "How long will we be there? What all do you have to do?"

"I've got it all planned out. Pick up some boxes to pack my clothes and personal stuff. That shouldn't take long because I know exactly what goes where—it's literally everything in my closet and bathroom. Then I need to ship it all back here, either FedEx or UPS." She went on to explain that everything else—furniture, kitchenware, linens—would go into a storage unit she'd already rented over the phone. "I have a couple of guys coming Monday morning with a truck. After that, we'd have the rest of the day for sightseeing. Then we come home Monday night on the red-eye."

"Two days, are you kidding? That's a long way to go for such a short time."

"I know, but I need to be back here by Tuesday. Dad's getting out of rehab."

It would have been nice to stay a few extra days, but Ninah wasn't going to pass up this chance for a glimpse of California through Britt's eyes. "Then we'll have to make the most of it."

"We will, I promise. My friend Holly's getting some folks together Sunday night at Gossip Grill. That's our main dyke bar. You'll love it. I can't wait for you to meet everyone."

Of all the things they might have done, meeting Britt's hip lesbian friends at a trendy bar was at the bottom of Ninah's wish list. Nothing in her wardrobe was suitable for such a place. She'd embarrass herself and Britt too.

"Are you sure we'll have time for that? It sounds like there's a lot to do."

"Some things you make time for. Friends especially, since I don't know when I'll get back for another visit. Sundays are great at the bar, kind of low-key. More talking, less getting wasted. Everybody has to be at work the next day."

Obviously it was important that Britt have a chance to see her friends, so Ninah would have to deal with her trepidation. "It's sweet that your friends are coming together for a sendoff."

"More like bittersweet, I'd say." Her tone held a trace of melancholy, and she paused a long moment before elaborating. "Candice always handled the social end of things. She cared about it more than I did, so I usually just went along with whatever she wanted. No matter what it was, she needed to be in the middle of the action. A real FOMO."

Ninah knew from her students that meant "fear of missing out."

"We fought about it sometimes, how she'd appoint herself emcee at parties so she could lead the songs and make the speeches. Such a ham, but nobody else seemed to mind—she had the personality for it. I thought she was being conceited. She'd get up there and tell stories about herself. Who does that on somebody else's birthday?"

Ninah had seen for herself that Britt could be deferential if she thought she was out of her depth. Still, it was hard to imagine her doing that in a romantic relationship with such a narcissist.

"Things got tense between us when we were breaking up. We both dumped about eleven years worth of petty resentment on each other, and Candice had a real gift for sarcasm. She apologized for dragging me out to parties all those times when I clearly didn't want to go, and for making me get to know people I didn't care about. She said if it weren't for her, I wouldn't have any friends at all, and I'd probably be happier."

"I think most breakups are like that. The gloves come off." Britt would be horrified to know how close she'd come to throwing dishes at Teri's head when Teri low-balled her on her half of the house. Ninah had stormed out the back door, shaking so hard she couldn't even drive off.

"I wasn't going to let what she said be true. So after she left for Reno, I made a point to focus on my friends. Not fifty of them like she did, just three or four women that I honestly liked. That's Holly, Izzy, Kim…Lourdes. I really will miss them. I'd like to think they'll miss me too."

"For what it's worth, you can have as many friends in Leland as you want. You won't find any better than Carly and Justine."

"And you. In fact, if I were making that list today—what's good about Leland—you guys are definitely one of the best things about being here."

Ninah liked knowing Britt felt that way, even if she'd been lumped in with Carly and Justine. "I can't speak for the rest of Leland but getting to know you is one of the best things that's happened to me lately. I just wish you could feel better about being there."

"Who knows? It could happen, I guess." Said with absolutely zero enthusiasm. She groped behind her for her purse. "Hey, do you have a signal yet? You need to go online and get your ticket. Here, the flight info's in the calendar on my phone. And use my credit card. Then I can work you like a dog and not have to feel guilty about it."

"Hmm, luring me with sightseeing in exchange for a little work. Isn't that how human trafficking usually starts?"

"Damn, I'll never get you inside the storage unit now."

"What are you gonna do with your car?"

Britt listed her options, each with pros and cons. "I don't have time to drive it back here, so I'll probably end up having it shipped on a transport. Which is one more thing I'll need to take care of on Monday before we leave. The company said it could take a while, since they won't go until they have a full truck."

"I don't have anything pressing next week. What if I drove it back?"

"Pfft. Four days on the road by yourself? That's insane."

On the contrary, Ninah envisioned a glorious road trip, the ultimate American experience. It would be great to finally see those parts of the country, even by herself. "No, it'll be fun. I can take my time and see a few sights. The Grand Canyon, the Petrified Forest, the Gateway Arch. As long as your car has a stereo, I'm good to go."

"It would solve a few problems," Britt admitted. "And I wouldn't have to ship my stuff back. I could just pack it all in the car."

"It's settled then. All I need is a one-way ticket." Nearing the outskirts of Lexington, her phone had three bars. "Well, would you look at that? We picked up three more runs in the ninth and Dunwoody got the save. The Longdogs are on fire."

"Making my job easier every day."

CHAPTER TWENTY-FOUR

"Mocha latte for Khaleesi!"

"What the heck?" Emmy asked as Ninah stepped forward and snatched her drink.

"The World's Greatest Barista was too distracted by his girlfriend to notice me sneaking by with a fake name." She witnessed a surreptitious look between Emmy and Ike. "I don't get why you guys are torturing yourselves with all this secrecy."

"It's on our calendar to come clean, if you must know. Two weeks."

"That's the Pride picnic."

"The day before, actually. Dad at lunch, Mom at dinner. Ike finishes that week at Leland Tech, so at least he'll be able to wave around an associate degree in business. And don't say, 'Then what?' That's for Ike to answer. I'm proud of him no matter what he does next."

"So am I, Emmy." Ninah used a napkin to wipe off a table by the window. "You know, it's possible the answer's staring both of you right in the face. Carly's got more than she can handle over at the courthouse. I bet she'd be glad to have Ike's help to manage the store."

Emmy shook her head vehemently. "I can't go asking Carly to give my boyfriend a promotion. That's taking advantage."

"Not if it's family. Look at your brother. JT set him up at the law firm. I bet he's already started shuffling over his clients for when he retires. And there's Britt, who's now running her dad's baseball team. That's how a lot of the world works."

"Carly's got her own family. That cousin of hers with the furniture store, he's got kids."

"Don't look now, but I'm pretty sure Carly considers you family, whether you do or not." She instantly regretted her blatant shaming. "Not that it makes any difference, since I hear your mom owns half the place. But what do I know? Maybe running the most popular business in town isn't the sort of career Ike has in mind."

"Are you kidding? You should hear him talk about what he'd do if The Bean were his." Emmy pointed to the elevated platform in the corner. "Like get a wine and beer license and bring in bands every weekend."

"There you go. But none of it happens until you—"

"Shh! Carly's coming."

With the Saturday morning rush mostly over, Carly had doffed her apron and turned over the store to Melanie and Ike. "Thanks for waiting. Let's get out of here before there's another stampede. Justine said she'd meet us there."

"You know," Ninah said, "I really don't need a whole committee to help me pack. I've been dressing myself for thirty-five years."

"That's not what you said an hour ago."

Her exact quote was that Britt's friends probably looked like the women on *The L-Word* and they'd all think she was a bumpkin. All she needed was help choosing an outfit that would pass muster when they went to the dyke bar Britt had raved about.

Once outside, Carly mumbled through gritted teeth, "Don't look now, but your favorite person is heading right this way."

Ninah groaned. "Quick, let's cross the street."

"Too late, she's seen us."

So what if it was rude? She didn't need Teri Kaufman blotting her day in that hateful MAGA cap. When they crossed paths, she kept her gaze straight ahead and continued on several feet, stopping to wait as Carly and Emmy modeled better social skills.

"That's it, Ninah. Just act like you don't even know me. Real mature."

"Actually, I'm standing over here because I *do* know you."

Teri shook her head and turned to Carly. "Isn't she ridiculous? Six years with somebody and she can't even try to act like friends. Would you guys please talk some sense into her?"

Carly held up her hands. "This is for you two to work out. Don't put Emmy and me in the middle of it."

Feeling guilty for dumping this mess on her friends, Ninah sauntered back to where they stood. "Go on, guys. I'll catch up in a minute."

"See, was that so hard? You don't have to keep dragging our friends into this and putting them on the spot like that."

It was all Ninah could do not to tell her how many of their friends wanted to gag every time they saw her in that despicable hat. "You're the one dragging them into it, Teri. How about next time you just carry on with your little chitchat and let me stand quietly out of the way? Ignore me like I'm trying to ignore you."

Teri sighed dramatically and folded her arms. "You are so fucking childish, Ninah. Three years of this."

"And three years of hate, lies, and stupidity."

"Aw, get over it already. I have a right to my own opinions."

"And I have a right to think supporting a racist for president makes you deplorable. Are we good?"

"Little Miss Perfect, always think you're right about everything, that we're all racist for wanting our jobs back, or for thinking people ought to stand for the national anthem after soldiers died for it."

"What I'm right about is Trump dished out a plateful of hate and people like you ate it up. Now I've got high school kids chanting his name while they torment their classmates like it's *Lord of the Flies*." Ninah could feel her chest heating up, which meant her face was probably bright red.

"You think that's my fault?"

"I think when they see you prancing around in that *fucking* hat, they feel emboldened to do it because they know you've got their back."

"Well so does two-thirds of Kentucky. You're the odd one out here."

"And I'm damned proud of it." She whirled away and tried not to stomp as she made her retreat. It would be just her luck to trip over a crack in the sidewalk.

Of all days to get sucked into an ugly confrontation with Teri. That two-thirds of Kentuckians agreed with her was an inescapable fact. No wonder Britt preferred California.

She walked briskly to her house three blocks away. "Sorry, guys," she called as she let herself into Emmy's apartment.

Emmy met her at the top of the stairs. "No prob. At least she doesn't come to the hospital in that hat. Come on, let's find you something to wear."

Willing Teri from her thoughts, she eyed the array of clothes spread out on Emmy's bed. "Okay, but we need to hurry. I have to be at Britt's house in two hours and I can't show up looking like a bumpkin."

"Stop calling yourself that. If you're a bumpkin, Carly and I are bumpkins too."

"I've been called worse," Carly said flatly, peering up from the *Gazette* over a pair of cockeyed reading glasses.

Rummaging through her closet, Emmy said, "Is a bumpkin an actual thing, or just a stupid-sounding name?"

"It's a yokel, a hillbilly," Carly said. "A hick, a hayseed."

"Enough already." Ninah groaned and fell back on the bed. "I hate you both."

Carly bounced on the springs beside her. "Come on, what's the big deal? She wants you to meet her friends. Are you honestly worried she's gonna hold you up for ridicule?"

"I'm worried I'll do that all by myself. Once she gets me there side by side with those other women, it's gonna hit her what a…what an apple-knocker I am."

"For God's sake, Ninah." Emmy's voice was sharper than usual. "You make it sound like you're dating out of your species."

That was rich coming from a woman who was sneaking around to hide her boyfriend. "We're not dating. But if we were, some differences would matter. Class, culture…perceived status. Or don't they?"

Emmy sneered at her with one eye shut and almost smiled.

"Emmy's right, Ninah. My company sent me to live in Bolivia when I was twenty-four years old. Talk about feeling self-conscious…but I got through it. Then it was India, Shanghai, Johannesburg. Turns out you can feel at home anywhere as long as you're comfortable in your own skin."

"I'm excited and all…I just don't wanna embarrass her in front of her friends."

Emmy began plucking things from her closet. "Which is why we're here. Now start trying this stuff on."

Only two years out of pharmacy school, Emmy had a more youthful sense of style. Too bad she was six inches taller. "Don't bother with the pants. I'd have to pull them up to my armpits."

After trying on a dozen combinations, they settled on an off-the-shoulder top in a leopard print, which she'd wear over black leggings.

"I don't think I've ever worn anything so dainty in all my life."

"It's not dainty, it's hip," Emmy proclaimed. "I'd take you anywhere."

Ninah had to admit it was a thousand times classier than anything she could have managed on her own. "I'm taking you with me next time I go shopping."

"Hello!" Justine called from downstairs.

"Come on up, sweetie. We're playing Dress the Bumpkin."

"They've turned me into a home-ec project," Ninah groused. "Or a reality show…Straight Eye for the Queer Gal."

"This is darling," Justine said as she fingered the silky top. "Bet you get lucky."

"God, I officially hate all three of you. If we have to talk about sex lives, let it be somebody else."

Emmy waved her finger wildly. "Oh, no you don't. Because somebody else would mean either me or those two. I can't even."

"Never mind," Justine said as she fell across Carly's lap. "I wanna hear you swear you aren't moving to California."

"Why would I do that?" Clearly they thought she and Britt were going down a different road.

"I talked to Britt a little while ago during my cool-down. Said you took her to Coal Springs."

Ninah loved that Britt had forged a special bond with Justine. But then Justine had a magical way of making everyone think she was their best friend.

"I was trying to make a point with Coal Springs. I wanted her to see what a *real* small town looked like. At least now she totally gets why I think Leland is the cat's meow."

"She'll fall to our charms one of these days."

"The flip side of that is Teri Kaufman." As Ninah changed back into her own clothes, she provided a quick rundown of their annoying encounter. "Right there's the downside of living in a small town. There's no getting away from people you can't stand. Teri's gonna be in my face for the rest of my life."

As Emmy put some things on hangers, Justine carefully folded the rest. "I know you don't wanna hear this, sweetie—

Lord knows I don't wanna be the one to say it—but you and Teri need to have a come-to-Jesus meeting. The way you light each other up, that's not good for either of you."

"We just had one. I told her from now on she could pretend I wasn't even there and I'd do the same."

"While the rest of us stand around choking on the ice in the air? You're both gonna have to do better than that."

The words hit Ninah like a bad stew. Did Justine honestly expect her to put her principles aside for the sake of harmony over potluck dinners? "I can't show her respect and dignity while she's denying it to other people."

"All I'm asking is for you to see if there might be a way to make peace with her. We're surrounded by Trump people, Ninah, all of us. How do you think I feel sitting across the table from Trey's in-laws? Or Joe and Margie Henderson, whom I love with all my heart? We can't let politics tear us up like this. We've gotta find a way to get along without being at each other's throats."

"So I'm supposed to just roll over while she shoves that stupid MAGA hat in my face? It's deliberately provocative. I stood outside the courthouse in the snow protesting against Tiny Watson for not giving y'all a marriage license. Now you want me to sell out my integrity so people don't have to feel awkward."

Carly spoke up, "Ninah, that's not what Justine's—"

"Forget it, Carly. It's no big deal." She collected the borrowed items and readied to leave, but stopped in the doorway to add, "Lord knows we shouldn't make people feel uncomfortable over something as harmless as racism. Next time you wanna invite Teri somewhere, just give me a heads up and I'll skip it."

CHAPTER TWENTY-FIVE

Britt hoisted her suitcase from the carousel and rolled it alongside Ninah's to an area outside the ladies' room. Ninah had gone inside to repair what she called a "balloon face," the result of a day's worth of tears. Nothing Britt said would calm her distress over a morning quarrel with Justine.

Justine, of all people, she'd wailed.

Inconsolable, Ninah had called her from the Dallas airport during their layover, gushing a tearful apology. Then with characteristic kindness, Justine forgave her unconditionally, which spawned fresh tears of gratitude. The moment they'd touched down in San Diego, Ninah promised to put the incident behind her so they could enjoy what little time they had here.

Britt couldn't wait to show off her city. Her exhilaration at being back in San Diego convinced her this was her true home, and no amount of success in Leland would change that.

"Thanks for waiting. I look human again."

She spun to find Ninah refreshed and smiling, and it triggered an impulse to hug her. "You look great. How are you feeling?"

"Justine texted me a virtual box of chocolates. I love that woman so much. I wouldn't have slept tonight if she hadn't forgiven me. I have to learn to think before I speak." She grasped the handle of her suitcase and snapped her heels at attention. "But it's all settled now, so as of this minute, I'm completely yours. And I can't wait to see your beloved San Diego. Lead the way."

"Unfortunately, we can't see much at night. The Coronado Bridge is lit up, but you don't get the same impression as when you see the whole harbor on a sunny day. It's breathtaking. But don't worry, we'll have time on Monday." She ordered their Uber as they crossed the skyway to the ground transportation area. Along the way, she shared her disappointment that Holly hadn't yet answered her text to confirm the gathering tomorrow at Gossip Grill. "Sundays are laid-back but they can be iffy too, especially if it's been a busy weekend. I hope it works out. You'd like it there."

"I came to see your city. Everything else is icing on the cake."

After only a short wait, they climbed into the back of a Nissan Rogue driven by Julio. Ninah asked, "How does it feel to be back?"

"I've got about six different emotions going on all at the same time. It's hard to pick just one."

"Tell me all the good ones."

"I feel at home, obviously. That's probably the main one. And I'm excited you're here with me because I get to see it through fresh eyes." They exited the airport onto North Harbor Drive toward the Eight, a ten-lane freeway that divided the county into north and south. "But it also makes me feel conflicted about committing to a couple of years in Kentucky. I thought I'd made peace with it, but being here again is stirring up doubts."

"It would be weird if you *didn't* feel all those things, especially since your dad getting sick forced the issue. You didn't get to think it over and weigh all the pros and cons. But you did the right thing, don't you think?"

"Sure…but probably not for the right reason." She confessed to losing out on the Regent job the very same day she learned about the Longdogs. "It was the perfect job for me, and I would have nailed it. If they'd hired me, I'm pretty sure I'd have told Dad and JT to find someone else."

"You're perfect for the Longdogs job too. Every day you go to work, you make that team more valuable. It's gonna be worth millions, Britt. Would you really have left all that money on the table?"

"Money only matters if it lets you do the things you want. I think I'd have chosen the job that let me stay here. That's how much it meant to me. I only said yes to the Longdogs because my finances were circling the drain."

"If that's the case, then what you did was a no-brainer. Stop torturing yourself with doubts. You made the only real choice you had."

"What I really torture myself over is how I got myself in this position. I should have been more insistent with Candice about expanding our client list so we wouldn't be so vulnerable. She didn't want the responsibility of taking on staff. I always said if Teem Toys got bought out by somebody, it would wipe us out. In the end, we were both right. She got what she wanted and I got wiped out."

After pointing out San Diego State, her alma mater, she fell silent. Dredging up her failures triggered a wave of frustration, perfectly timed to spoil her happy homecoming. On the surface, she could convince herself the opportunity in Leland was too good to pass up. Underneath, she knew the bitter truth, and now so did Ninah.

They exited the freeway onto a divided boulevard lined with big box stores and chain restaurants. But for the palms and junipers, it could have been suburban Lexington, an observation she decided to keep to herself. Their ride ended in the parking lot of her modest two-story apartment complex, where all the units faced inward to the courtyard.

"Welcome to my humble abode," she said glumly as Julio drove away. "And I do mean humble."

"Nothing wrong with humble. I've read about California's exorbitant rents. You lucked out to get a place this nice."

Britt wouldn't dare say what she paid for a mere six hundred square feet, the best she could find on short notice. At least the building was quiet and well-kept.

Bags in tow, she led Ninah down a winding walkway lined with palms and flowering shrubs. A pristine pool occupied the center of the courtyard, surrounded by lounge chairs and an iron fence with its posted list of what wasn't allowed. No alcohol. No diving. No swimming after 9 p.m. One could reasonably think they didn't want tenants to use the pool at all.

"I should warn you, my apartment is super tiny."

"You've seen mine. It's not exactly palatial."

"But yours looks like someone lives there. When Candice's mom died, she inherited all her furniture, dishes, artwork, everything. We had to sell off our stuff to make room for it. So of course when she left, there wasn't anything to divvy up because it was all hers."

Her living area was outfitted with a cheap burgundy love seat, perfect for hiding spills. The ottoman doubled as storage for magazines and a pile of remotes for the wall-mounted TV. In place of a dining set was her Scandinavian desk and file cabinet.

"Did I mention this is also where I work?"

"I can tell." Ninah looked around and smiled. "I may have had more furniture than this in my dorm room. That's an observation, not a criticism. And I appreciate that you seem to be obsessively neat, like yours truly. It won't take long at all to pack this up."

"Most of what you see here is cheap. Except the sheets. I'm a sheet snob. Which reminds me…"

Ninah peeked through the doorway into her bedroom, also sparsely furnished. A queen-sized bed, sans headboard, sat between two sets of drawers made from collapsible cubes. "I've got no problem sharing the bed, if that's your question."

"It was." They shared a laugh that lifted her mood. Before she could offer a glass of wine, her cell phone rang. "I bet that's Holly. I asked her to call."

Ninah silently mouthed "little girls' room" as she slipped into the bathroom and closed the door.

"Hey, thanks for getting back to me."

"You there with your squeeze?"

"She's *not* my squeeze, and she's in the other room. I just wanted to touch base about tomorrow. What time are people coming?"

"I've got a better idea. Let's skip Gossip Grill. How about we meet for dinner at BB's? Izzy and Kim said they'd come too. It'll be easier to talk. We want to hear all about Britt Iverson, sports mogul."

BB's was Baja Betty's, just down the street from the bar. A brunch favorite, it also happened to have the best margaritas in town.

"Why don't we do both? We can meet at BB's for an early dinner and walk down to Gossip when we're done. Ninah's never been to California. I want to take her to a first-class dyke bar so she can see what she's missing."

"We can't do Gossip Grill, not tomorrow." Holly's voice fell. "Fucking hell, I was going to lie and tell you everybody had the flu."

Britt's stomach tightened and she braced herself to hear that her so-called friends were too busy, which was the same as saying they had better things to do. After being gone less than a month, she hardly expected anyone to have missed her that much, but Holly should have been able to coax a few of them out for a sendoff once they heard she'd be gone for a couple of years.

"So no one's coming."

"That's just it, they are. Penelope's doing up a big-ass welcome home party for Candice. The bitch is moving back to San Diego."

"You can't be serious. She's only been gone eight months." For a split second, it crossed her mind to reach out to Teem Toys about picking up their work again. That was her homesickness talking. "What does she think she's going to do back here? I've been working this event market for eight months. It's booked out three years already."

"She, uh…fuck me, Britt. I hate being the one to have to tell you this. I'm so fucking sorry. Candice got that Regent job you wanted."

CHAPTER TWENTY-SIX

"This is magnificent," Ninah said, taking in the panoramic view of the Pacific Coast from Torrey Pines State Park. "If I lived in San Diego, I'd be out here every weekend drinking this in."

Britt smiled weakly and nodded. "I had a feeling you'd appreciate this more than the harbor or Balboa Park. Dad loves it too. I bring him out here every time he comes to visit."

Kentucky had its own natural beauty but nothing to rival the raw grandeur of the gnarled pines and sandstone sculptures lining the coast, bent and worn from the brisk wind blowing in from the ocean. At the Yucca Point overlook, it was as if they were standing on the edge of the world.

Britt reluctantly agreed to a selfie, though after three tries Ninah gave up on eliciting anything resembling a genuine smile. There was no cracking her sullen mood, which had settled like a pall after Holly's call. Absorbed in misery, she'd barely spoken as they packed, dividing their tasks so they worked in separate rooms. Every snippet of conversation was muted by the knowledge that Britt's thoughts were elsewhere.

Ninah had no idea how to comfort her, or if she should even try. In a moment of candor, Britt had described an overwhelming sense of humiliation. Candice had bested her at every turn—claiming their friends, winning the job—even stealing the one lousy afternoon in which she might have had the spotlight to herself.

The movers had arrived at seven thirty that morning, making quick work of the sealed boxes and furniture. By ten, the apartment was empty, the car packed to the gills. Eager to put the incident behind her, Britt had changed her overnight flight to one that left at three p.m. She'd be back in Leland tonight.

For the stroll back to the car, Ninah looped her arm through Britt's and was pleased that she didn't pull away. Even as a gesture of friendship, it was exciting to do such a thing without fretting over a stranger's judgment or insult. This was the joy she felt at a Pride celebration, made even more remarkable for its apparent normalcy. "I like it here."

"There's so much to see in California. I hope you'll drive up the coast before cutting over to the Grand Canyon."

"About that...I think I'm gonna skip the sightseeing this trip and come straight home. Maybe you'll come back with me one of these days and we can see it together."

"I'd love to show it to you, all of California."

"It's beautiful, but there's also an aura about it that's special. I felt it almost as soon as I got here. I can see why it means so much to you."

Had Britt just offered to show her California or was that wishful thinking? After sleeping together for two nights—close enough to hold one another—she wanted to think they were moving toward something more serious. But Britt was emotional right now, much as she'd been the last time they'd—

"I was never able to make Dad understand what this place meant to me. To him, home was where you were from…and where you're supposed to go back to, obviously."

"You need to stop worrying about Leland, Britt. I know, easier said than done, but you've got the opportunity of a lifetime. If the Longdogs had landed in Candice's lap, I bet she'd have squandered it. You won't. So picture her haughty nose when she finds out you're a multimillionaire. Bye, Felicia."

Britt rolled her eyes and sighed. "If I quit sulking, will you quit patronizing me?"

"Maybe," she replied drolly, adding a lighthearted smile. "I wasn't trying to be patronizing. I was just pointing out the obvious, that you've managed to charm everyone in Leland not named Wesley Hodges. However long you stay there, I hope you'll end up being glad you did."

At a fork in the trail, Britt steered them toward another overlook called Razor Point. By her silence, she was either considering her fortunes or hoping Ninah would drop the subject.

"Britt, we don't have to keep talking about this if you're sick of it, but if it's stuck in your head, you might as well get it out." Getting no reply, she added, "I get the feeling I'm dancing on your last nerve."

"It's not your fault. It's just that…God, I can't possibly say this without sounding like a shallow, pompous twat."

"Go for it. If you really are a shallow, pompous twat, it's gonna come out sooner or later. And now's as good a time as any, since I'm willing to overlook a multitude of sins in a gorgeous place like this."

That put a tiny crack in Britt's stern facade, but it didn't last.

"You're right about the Longdogs, it's the opportunity of a lifetime. I should feel good about it but everyone knows it was handed to me on a silver platter. And I had to go crawling back to Leland to get it. In my book, that's called failure."

Everyone knows. What she really meant was *Candice knows*. It was killing her to think Candice was taking a victory lap at her expense. That wasn't failure. It was wounded pride. Ninah thought better of saying so.

"I'd have taken that Regent job in a heartbeat. Call me crazy, but I'd rather have lived here and made thousands than in Leland making millions. If I was going to prove myself, it had to be here on my own."

"We aren't here to prove ourselves, Britt. We're here to live life and be good people. Besides, what Candice did, that's a relationship failure, not a business failure."

"She knows how I feel about Kentucky and why. I'm sure she's heard the news by now. I bet she had an absolute field day, probably told everyone I've gone back to the cult."

Plainly, Britt was hurting on so many fronts. Ninah couldn't help but think her presence made it worse. Britt had been bursting with excitement to show off the great life she had in San Diego, and Candice had turned it into a shit show.

"I hate what she's done to you, and what she's still doing. Especially how she came between you and your friends, but that's on them too. It's hard to believe they don't know what an asshole she is, but sooner or later they will."

When they reached the second overlook, Britt led her all the way to the edge, where she folded her arms and tapped her foot defiantly. "I need to get over it. Maybe I ought to start over somewhere else…make some *real* friends."

"You have real friends here, Britt. The others don't count."

Britt answered with a scornful grunt.

"It's beautiful here. Who knows? If all the dominoes fell just right, I could learn to love this place too."

Had those words actually left her lips? She'd practically offered to move to California if it meant a future with Britt. *Bold*. Or maybe foolish. Either way she felt no urge to walk it back. It hardly made a difference that she'd said it, since Britt gave no indication she cared one way or the other.

CHAPTER TWENTY-SEVEN

"Dad wanted to welcome himself home with another dinner party but I put the kibosh on that."

Ninah laughed and plugged her phone into the dashboard jack that allowed Britt's call to come through the Prius's stereo system. "It's good to know he's back to his old self."

"And he's dying to go to the ballpark, but I'm making him wait a couple of days. The doctor said he had to take it slow, but he didn't think there'd be any more seizures."

Their conversation was delayed while a double haul oil truck passed Ninah on the left. Their jockeying had become a game of sorts, her passing on the incline and him rolling past on the downslope.

"Die, you fucker!" Britt suddenly yelled. "Sorry…mosquito. I'm sitting out here in the gazebo drinking the last of your Blue Moon ale. That got me wondering what you thought about while you were driving all alone through Bumbletucky, New Mexico."

She was delighted to find Britt in such a cheery mood. "As you can probably tell, I'm not alone. I'm locked in mortal combat with half a dozen trucks that keep passing me and slowing down. You'd think I was driving around topless."

"Now there's a visual. My head just exploded. Now all the little water moccasins are swimming to the surface to eat my brain bits." She animated the image with nibbling sounds. "How far are you going today?"

"Tucumcari."

"Gesundheit."

Britt related the results of her sales meeting that afternoon with Kroger, during which she'd learned the value of holding out premium space for those with deep pockets. She could have sold a full-season sponsorship package for top dollar had she not already sold off pieces to smaller advertisers. "But they bought out the rest of the season on the back page of the program, and I agreed to make them my first call next year."

"Wow, it's like your secretary said. The fish are jumping in the boat." She gunned it to get past the double truck at the crest of the hill. "I checked the box score this morning. Oscar hit another one last night against Spring Hill. That's what, twenty-two homers in fifteen games? He needs to chill, or he's gonna get himself called up."

"That would be a disaster. I hope you didn't just jinx us. We sold twenty-eight more club seats for the season. People are jumping on the bandwagon because of Oscar."

Ninah had always found it frustrating that the team's breakout stars were usually whisked away to Bradenton or Altoona as soon as they showed promise, but that was the nature of the league. The Pirates didn't care if the Longdogs were in first place or last. Players in the Valley League weren't there to win, but to develop. Guys like Oscar were more valuable up the chain.

"You're sounding awfully chipper for somebody who got home so late. You must have been dragging."

"I'm sure it'll hit me later tonight. But I have to admit, I felt better about getting back here than I expected to. After our talk, I mean. It was good for me to hear all that, so thanks for ignoring my cranky mood. I'm more settled about being here…for the next year or two anyway. I have to focus, because if the Pirates don't renew their contract next year, all this is for nothing—*and* Dad loses his investment."

Ninah was pleased to hear her resolve. "But keep an eye on the job listings in San Diego. You'll see how long it takes Regent to fire Candice and advertise that job again."

"Wouldn't that be a scream?" Britt's voice abruptly turned serious. "Ninah, I've been thinking about what you said at Torrey Pines, about the dominoes falling a certain way. Would you really consider moving to San Diego someday, or was that just…"

So she *had* heard. Ninah didn't want to have this conversation on the phone at eighty miles an hour, but she'd never forgive herself if they put it off and it never came up again. If Leland was the only thing keeping them apart, she needed to lay her cards on the table.

"Let me put it this way, Britt. We all have to do what makes us happy. I like living in Leland, but it's not the most important thing in my life. I realized that when Teri and I split up. I came *so* close to leaving. All that stopped me was not having another job lined up." Again she waited while three trucks barreled down the hill beside her. "You still there?"

"Yeah. Does that mean—" The next part was muffled, as if Britt had her hand over the phone. "Sorry, Dad was yelling at me from the back deck. I need to go in and see what he needs or he'll try to get it himself."

"Go. We can finish this tomorrow." Except she probably wouldn't sleep all night unless she put it out there. "Wait a second. What it means is, where a person lives might not matter as much as who they live with."

"Hmm…that would make a nice tattoo."

Ninah swore she could hear Britt smiling.

CHAPTER TWENTY-EIGHT

Despite having more official duties than her father, Britt had saved him the largest of the executive offices. He too had a grand view of the field, where Pervis was busy mowing his checkerboard outfield.

The doctor had okayed his coming to the ballpark starting at two hours a day, increasing a half hour each day as his energy allowed. He had to save some for physical therapy.

"You doing okay over there?" she asked, looking up from the ad galleys. She'd sold four more pages for the next home game program.

"I'm fine." He nodded out toward left field. "And if I'm not, you can run me over to the ER, where the wait time is less than three minutes. I can't get over you squeezing that much money out of Joe Henderson. That man's so tightfisted, he sneaks his own popcorn into the ballpark."

Britt was glad she hadn't known that ahead of her sales pitch. It would have made her anxious. "I think my success there had more to do with Justine Hall. She was the first person I talked to when I got to Leland, and she bent over backward trying to make me feel welcome."

"That Justine's always been a sweetheart. Carly too. I had a feeling you'd like them."

"They hardly gave me a choice. Had me over for dinner twice, introduced me to their friends, including Ninah Faust. Oh, and somebody named Margot who manages the barn at Hickson Farm. Margot called this morning, by the way. Apparently Clyde and the boys are off to an auction tomorrow in Saratoga Springs. She's invited me out to the farm to ride. It's just for a couple of hours."

"Don't go getting yourself hooked on thoroughbreds. That's one hobby that costs more than a baseball team."

"I'll keep that in mind." She caught him up on her progress with ad sales, including Carly's travel mug giveaway. "Then she hooked me up with all the other downtown merchants. I expect to sell out that second row of billboards by the Fourth of July."

"You're not gonna leave me anything to do, Britt. I might as well retire, read a book."

"Don't worry, I've saved you plenty. For starters, one of us needs to set up an interview with Wesley Hodges. I've put him off a couple of times already. I thought it was best to have you do it in case he starts asking about bloopers and dingers and frozen ropes. He actually used all of those in one story. I had to get Ninah to translate."

She'd mentioned Ninah several times since coming back from California, drawing no reaction at all. Given his friendship with her, she'd have thought he'd be pleased they were friends too.

"So Dad, I was wondering what you thought about—"

"Did you see that story this morning on Boomer McBride? I can't imagine the brass in Pittsburgh is happy about that."

She kept up with baseball news on ESPN's *Sports Center*, which had become part of her morning routine. "I hate to laugh at something so crude, but that video was hilarious."

An All-Star slugger for the Pirates, McBride had a "bad boy" reputation that included drinking, brawling and now, disorderly conduct. He'd managed all three last night in Miami. Ejected from the Marlins game in the first inning for cleating the second baseman on a high slide, he'd watched the rest from a bar on South Beach. His third act—urinating off his hotel balcony while singing "Raindrops Keep Falling On My Head"—had been captured on a video that went viral overnight.

"Surely he'll get suspended a few games," she said. "The Pirates can't let him get away with that. Can you believe he's making twenty-one million?"

"He didn't actually rain on anyone's head, so that's in his favor. But he's already been suspended twice this year, so they'll have to put some real teeth in this one. I 'spect they'll hit him extra hard in the pocketbook."

"What he needs is a good spanking."

Her dad began laughing to himself. "Archie came by the hospital that first week, said you showed the boys a little tough love in the locker room."

She'd almost forgotten that incident. After Hank's swear-a-thon over the players not minding their dirt, she'd gone back to her office fuming that she hadn't stood up for herself. As the executive in charge, she couldn't allow sexual harassment in the workplace to go unpunished. With a call to Pervis, she'd cut the hot water to the locker room, resulting in cold showers after that night's game. "Hey, tough love works. Hanover and Cline came into my office the next day and apologized."

Her father's face was frozen in a broad grin. "I'm so doggone proud of you, honey. I don't know what I'd have done if you hadn't jumped in and taken over. You saw what a mess this was. How you got it going so quick, I can't even begin to imagine."

Despite what she'd said to Ninah about needing to prove herself in San Diego, not Leland, her father's praise filled her with pride. "It's what I do, Dad. I'm glad for the chance to show you. In fact, I want to go over a few ideas to see what you think."

Group ticket sales would flourish on her dad's longstanding relationships, she explained. A Rotary member himself, he'd be a welcome guest at civic clubs where he could market the team as a community asset.

"What about church groups?" he asked. "I bet that's the biggest untapped market in town. We could host a different congregation every night, put them in the right field bleachers. They'll eat a barrel of hot dogs and popcorn."

She'd already been invited to speak at the monthly Faith Luncheon, a gathering of Leland's spiritual leaders, but the idea of going before a group of church elders to pitch them on a ticket package set her teeth on edge. Even if she got her father to do it, she didn't like the idea of being ingratiated to a bunch of holy rollers. "Let me think on that one, Dad."

"I'll handle it if you like."

"We have to consider the potential for conflict. I know churches are popular around here, but not everyone's on board. What if they complain about beer sales? Or Pride Night for the LGBT community? What if they want to have a prayer beforehand and some fans are disrespectful? We need to be careful about putting ourselves in the middle of that."

He nodded along, though he obviously was not convinced. Nor was she, to be honest, since churches were probably good for a hundred tickets per night under the right circumstances. Over the course of a season, that was a hefty chunk of change.

"What else do you want to tackle, Dad? Systems and accounts? Capital improvements?"

"Both of those. And I suppose since I wrote an actual book on how to be a food entrepreneur, I should take on concessions. Lord knows that could use an overhaul."

"You can say that again. Archie can help you with the vendors, but you ought to see if you can get some of the food trucks to bring their kitchen inside. Especially the fajitas." She checked the doorway to make sure their GM wasn't lurking. "Archie's good with the travel logistics, but that's not a full-time job. We might need to have an uncomfortable talk with him about his future. Could be he's ready to cut back anyway."

"Best we see how the summer goes. I don't want to get caught shorthanded if you decide to go back…"

"You won't get caught shorthanded, Dad. I gave you my word I'd see this through, as long as we're still on the same page." She was a little concerned his emotions would get the better of him in the wake of success on the field, that he'd want to keep the team instead of selling it. "Our goal here is still to build the team up and make it attractive to a buyer who will keep it in Leland, right?"

"And get the Pirates extension," he added. "We sure picked a good year to buy. It's been fifteen years since the Dogs were in first place. I can't wait to see this Oscar Lopez. JT says he can hit the ball a country mile."

"And then some. Fans like the Hanover kid too. You'll see him Friday night. He's pitching the opener against Spring Hill, but you have to rest up if you want to come out for that one."

"I'll be here. You bet on it." His excitement was palpable. "I guess before long you'll be wanting to get paid."

"It crossed my mind. This jet-setting Leland lifestyle comes with a price tag, as you well know. How do you feel about me taking over your basement? I can get my own apartment if you want. I don't want to cramp your style."

"Well, well. And here I thought I was cramping yours. I heard you might have a girlfriend."

She felt herself blush at his playful query. "I might be dating someone but I wouldn't go so far as to call her my girlfriend." She'd definitely need her own apartment if she wanted to have secrets.

Archie appeared in the doorway, red-faced and out of breath. "Bad news...Boomer McBride...twenty game suspension. They're calling up Oscar...sending a plane for him right now... he's going straight to Miami."

CHAPTER TWENTY-NINE

By the time Ninah crossed the Sherman Minton Bridge into Kentucky, she was as good as home. Hugging the Ohio River along Interstate 64, she skirted Louisville and calculated a six o'clock arrival in Leland. Twenty-one hundred lonely miles in three days and five hours. It was worth every mile to help Britt feel anchored in Kentucky instead of California.

She closed her navigation app as a call beeped in from Carly, who'd texted earlier to commiserate about Oscar Lopez. "Hey, Bean Lady. Tough day for the Longdogs, huh?"

"I'll say. I'm sad to see him go but proud of him too. Did you hear what he did last night?"

"Britt said they pinch hit him and he homered in his first major league at bat. We knew it on day one, didn't we? She's really bummed her dad won't get to see him in a Longdogs uniform."

"Yeah, Justine told me Vernon got home from rehab the other day. How's Britt doing? I haven't talked to her since she got back. Everything go okay out there?"

Ninah didn't feel it was her place to share how Candice's unexpected return had soured their weekend. "It's gorgeous, Carly. The water, the sailboats, the weather. Everything looks so crisp, like God just took the cellophane off. I even told her I might be willing to move."

"Seriously? Did something happen out there? You can tell me. I won't tell anyone but Justine."

"And she'll tell JT, who'll tell everybody." She didn't actually care who knew they were dating. Assuming they were. "But to answer your question, no. Nothing happened. But it might."

"Margot's gonna be so disappointed."

"Speak of the devil, Britt was taking off a couple of hours this afternoon to go riding at Hickson Farm. Can't wait to hear how that went."

"I bet Margot's taking her through the sperm collection process right now, and she's got Britt holding the collection bottle."

"I'm telling her you said that."

"Ask her if they watched mare porn first to get him excited."

"I worry about you, Carly. Does your wife have any idea how deviant you are?"

"You know, that's what I love about Justine. Everybody thinks she's so innocent. That woman has more kinks than a water hose."

Ninah was laughing so hard, she could hardly catch her breath. "You must be home alone, because if Justine were there, she'd box your ears."

"Nah, she's having supper with JT so they can talk about Emmy. It's pretty obvious she's got a new boyfriend but she isn't telling anyone who it is. Justine's freaking out thinking it might be a married man."

"That's ridiculous. Emmy would never do such a thing." Though admittedly Ninah had wondered the same thing before she found out it was Ike. She grinned at the sight of the Leland exit. "I'm on the last fifteen minutes of a thirty-two-hour drive."

"You wouldn't happen to know who Emmy's seeing?"

"Don't drag me into this. You think I'd squeal on somebody who could make my life a living hell with a pair of tap shoes?"

"God, Justine's gonna be so relieved. Because you obviously know who it is, and you explicitly said Emmy wouldn't date a married man. So I can tell Justine that much and she'll be able to sleep again."

"I can't help what you *inferred*, but I want the record to show that I did not reveal anything."

"On that note, I'm hanging up so I can text her with the good news."

It was all Ninah could do to hold her speed down as she neared the turnoff for Sandstone Drive. At the end of the street, the garage door stood open with Vernon's truck inside. Her Subaru was parked right where she'd left it, now sitting alongside…Margot's truck.

"Are you kidding me?" She'd told Britt she'd arrive around six. Why on earth would she invite Margot to be here?

The front door opened to a blur, Britt leaping from the porch to meet her as she wearily pulled herself from the car. "I'm so glad to see you."

"Me too." Ninah whimpered with pleasure as Britt hugged her and rubbed her tired, stiff back. "The closer I got, the faster I drove. I'm lucky I didn't get a ticket."

"I'd have paid it. Are you hungry?"

She stepped back to appreciate Britt in her denim shorts and tank top. Her hair hung like silk around her bare shoulders. "I could eat…but it appears you have company."

"We have pizza." The house smelled of garlic and herbs, thanks no doubt to the large pizza box on the dining table. "This is so weird," Britt said, keeping her voice low and her eyes affixed to the back door. "I went riding today—it was fun, I'll tell you about it later—and I told Margot about Dad doing physical therapy to improve his balance. Next thing I know, she's standing at the front door with a pair of magnetic horse boots that he's supposed to wrap around his ankles to improve circulation. She spent forty-five minutes telling him how they supposedly work, which—I looked it up while she was talking—is basically junk science. He finally ducked out to use the bathroom and didn't come back."

That sounded just like Margot, fascinated by the sound of her own voice. "How long do you think she's gonna be here?"

"Who the hell knows? I thought she'd leave when he did. I took his pizza upstairs and when I got back she'd wandered out to the gazebo. That's when I heard you pull up."

"You want me to start a brush fire by her truck? That'll get her out of here."

"What I want is this." Britt lifted Ninah's chin and planted a light kiss on her lips. "Can you tell I've been thinking about you?"

"That makes two of us. Wait, that didn't sound right. I was thinking about *you*." She could hardly think straight. It would serve Margot right for them to head down to the basement and lock the door.

The object of her scorn walked in from the back deck and placed an empty beer bottle and plate on the counter. "Hey, look who finally got here. The road warrior."

"That's me, fresh from a four-day battle with five thousand trucks. I bet it takes the next three days for me to stop hunching forward and clenching my teeth."

"Sounds just like riding a horse. Once your butt gets attuned to being in the saddle, nothing else feels quite right."

Britt shot Ninah a wink as she went to work straightening the kitchen. "You want a slice of this before I put it away?"

"No thanks. I ate half a pound of M&Ms in the car. So tell me about your ride today. What was it like?"

"I'll let Margot tell you. I need to go up and get Dad's plate."

Ninah could have kicked herself. She'd stupidly opened the door for Margot to talk about horses.

"For a beginner, she's got a pretty good seat," Margot said. "A little intimidated, but who wouldn't be riding such a magnificent beast? I've been riding almost forty years and I'm still in awe of them. You need to respect an animal like that."

Why hadn't she asked about Vernon or the Longdogs or the fish in the lake or the guy who delivered the pizza? "I can't imagine Britt was intimidated for long. From what I've seen, she takes command of whatever she gets her hands on."

Margot cocked her head and grinned. "Can't argue with you there. Anybody who kisses like that knows all about being in charge."

Ninah's chest filled with a volcanic rage as Margot nonchalantly helped herself to another beer. The very idea that Britt would kiss her was more than she could stomach. Apparently *going for a ride* meant something different in the Golden State.

CHAPTER THIRTY

Britt turned off Main Street onto Monroe, mildly steamed that Ninah had left so abruptly. She was exhausted, of course. Who wouldn't be after such a grueling trip? And no doubt annoyed that Margot was there. But to leave without even saying goodbye? And then not to answer her phone.

She recalled the day Ninah had marched off from the gazebo, when she'd gone to her house to apologize. No question that one had been her fault, but not this time. Margot had complicated matters by downing her second beer and then insisting she couldn't drive home for a couple of hours. Britt waited helplessly, enduring a mind-numbing ramble on how to tell whether a horse had colic or gastric ulcers.

Ninah's car was in the driveway and the lights were on in her apartment. That didn't mean she was in the mood for visitors. If she wasn't answering her phone, she might not answer her door either.

When she reached the porch, a man's irate voice caused her to freeze. "We can't keep doing this, Emmy. Either you tell them tomorrow like you promised or we might as well forget it."

"Ike, wait."

He stepped outside—the barista from The Bean—and his eyes went wide with surprise. "Hello."

A young woman appeared at his side, obviously Justine's daughter. Same good looks, for sure, and sporting a look of pure panic. "Hi, you must be Britt Iverson. I'm Emmy Sharpe. I think you know my mom, Justine. Right?"

Britt summed up the situation in seconds.

"And this is Ike. He works for Carly at The Bean."

"That's right, I work for Carly," he snarled, flashing Emmy an angry look. "I'll be going along now so I can work for Carly tomorrow."

As he stomped down the porch steps, Emmy closed her eyes and sighed. "In case you didn't catch that, I'm the biggest asshole in all of Leland. I know it. Ike knows it. And now you know it. Ninah too."

Britt held up her hands. "I really don't know anything."

"I'll let her fill you in on the gory details. But the bottom line—like I said, I'm an asshole." She retreated and closed the door, leaving Britt to reckon that her current drama with Ninah paled compared to this powder keg.

She announced herself and stepped inside Ninah's apartment to the sound of water running in a distant room. "Ninah, it's me. Is everything okay? Ninah?" On her way to the bedroom, she kept talking so as not to startle.

Ninah stood at the foot of her bed sorting the contents of her suitcase into laundry piles. In the adjoining bathroom, the tub was filling.

"Ninah, what's this about?"

She glanced up only briefly and kept sorting.

"I get it. You're upset about something. Whatever it is, let's please just talk about it. If I've done something wrong—"

"If you've done something wrong?"

"I'll try to make it right," she continued evenly. "I don't want to fight with you, but we can't resolve anything if you go running off. Don't I at least get a clue what this is about?"

"You should ask Margot."

"Ugh, Margot. I told you already, I didn't invite her to the house. She just showed up out of the blue with those stupid magnets. Dad and I were having a beer and waiting on the pizza when she got there. Then it came and it felt rude not to offer to have her join us. Granted, I should have known she'd take it as an invitation to hang around and regale us with her infinite knowledge of horse physiology. But I figured once you got there she'd—"

"She told me you kissed her."

Britt stopped short, taking in the fury on Ninah's face. Precious seconds ticked by as she weighed whether to challenge her assumptions or calmly explain.

"Obviously I misunderstood what we were saying the other day. I'm thirty-five years old, Britt. I'm not interested in dating someone who's still playing the field."

"Is that what you think?" This was utterly ridiculous, and Britt briefly considered throwing up her hands and walking out. But she couldn't stand to have Ninah think she was so shallow. "Have I said or done anything to make you think I'm remotely interested in Margot? Or that I'd go and kiss somebody else after making it clear how I felt about you?"

"So she's lying then." Ninah retreated into the bathroom and turned off the water.

"There was a kiss," she admitted grudgingly, taking a seat on the edge of the bed. "It happened in the barn when we were getting ready to mount up. I didn't see it coming, but as soon as I realized what she was doing, I pushed her back. Not hard, but enough that she got the message."

"Obviously not or she wouldn't have followed you to your house."

"I know this about Margot—she's into games. I told her that instant that I was seeing you, and that you were plenty to handle at one time."

"So you joked about it." She emerged from the bathroom with her hands on her hips. "Would you have been making jokes if a guy had forced himself on you like that?"

Clearly Ninah wasn't going to be happy no matter what answer she gave. "She got in my face all of a sudden and did it. Yes, it was inappropriate and yes, I was annoyed. But I wasn't threatened by it. I handled it. Are you saying I should have stormed off like you just did?"

"At least you can tell when I take something seriously."

"Too seriously in this case. I thought I made it clear that I'm interested in you, not her." From the redness pooling around Ninah's nose and mouth, it looked as if she might burst into tears at any moment. Britt let go of her frustration and wrapped both arms around her shoulders. "I'm sorry she got under your skin. If it helps at all, I'm pissed off she said that to you. Obviously she was trying to provoke a fight between us and it worked."

"I hate her."

"No need for that. Hating people uses up too much energy. But I promise I'll handle this if and when I see her again."

Ninah groaned and her shoulders slumped. "You don't have to. I'm just mad for walking into her trap. I always knew she was a yammering bore but I had no idea she had such a mean streak. She's probably home right now licking her chops."

"You're probably right." Britt cradled her head against her shoulder. "I'm sorry you came home to that. Believe me, it's not the homecoming I had planned. I've been counting the hours till you got here. I was so excited about us dating again."

"And then I threw a tantrum."

"I won't lie, it bothers me you ran off that way. If you'd stayed, we could have driven her sorry ass home. And I could have done this."

She took Ninah's face in her hands and kissed her. Light brushes to the corners of her mouth, a gentle nibble of her lower lip. Then the velvety texture of their tongues together. One hand slid around to the small of Ninah's back and urged her closer as the other dropped to graze her breast through her T-shirt.

"I've wanted this every day since the night you were here, Britt."

"What happens next is up to you."

Ninah made her wishes known by raising Britt's shirt over her head and relieving her of her bra. In mere seconds, she'd made a pile of their clothes on the floor. Then she took Britt's hand and led her into the bathroom, where the tub was almost overflowing with bubbles. She lit a half-dozen candles and turned out the overhead light.

"A candlelight bath. Very romantic."

"Mmm." She stepped into the center of the tub and held Britt's hand as she got in behind her. "I think this'll do us both good."

"I'm not the one who drove all day."

Ninah's lips curled with the hint of a grin. "And I'm not the one who smells like horse."

CHAPTER THIRTY-ONE

The powder-blue shirtwaist dress, with its hem well above the knee, was arguably the only one in Britt's newly filled closet that was suitable for meeting a roomful of ministers. Especially since Ninah had dissuaded her from her first choice, a T-shirt that proclaimed her a "vagi-tarian."

Presbyterian minister Jerry Creach had invited Britt to address the Faith Luncheon, which was held in a private room at Guido's Italian Café and Pizzeria. Present today were eighteen men sitting packed together at two long tables. All were Protestant except the Catholic priest, Father Joseph. The only other woman in the room was Pearl, a middle-aged waitress who kept the red plastic glasses filled with sweet tea.

Despite her misgivings, Britt was ultimately convinced that a targeted appeal to area churches would not only bring more fans to the ballpark, it would elevate the team's standing in the community. Once she grudgingly accepted that, she set aside her general animosity toward organized religion and prepared a pitch that emphasized her quest for family-friendly entertainment. So far, the presentation was going better than expected, though she found herself fighting the heebie-jeebies at being confined in such a tight space among men who, like Brother James so many years ago, would be itching to cast out her lesbian demons had they known she was so possessed. She'd pared her comments to ten minutes, hoping to be long gone when they started praying over their pasta.

"I'm proposing a special 'Focus on Faith' section in the stadium that will seat up to two hundred fans. That's the bleacher section in right field behind the Longdogs dugout. Come next season we'll add seat backs to make those benches more comfortable. We can rope off the entire section if you have a really large group, and even limit beer sales there if you like."

She'd handed out brochures with all the particulars, including discounted tickets and recognition of their church on the website and by the public address announcer. Those were extras she offered to any pre-registered group of twenty-five or more. The featured church got the added bonus of delivering a brief invocation before the national anthem. It was a painful concession, one she had to rationalize with the knowledge that she'd pocket thousands of dollars if she managed to book a group every night.

"And finally, we'll give lucky members of your congregation the chance to participate in some of the contests and games we do between innings while the teams are warming up. That's another chance for you to publicize your church. Think about it. Fans will see you out there having fun and think, 'Hey, I'd like to go to a church with people like that.'"

Around the room, heads bobbed in agreement, and she congratulated herself for sufficiently sucking up to their interests in a way she wouldn't have thought possible a month ago. Maybe one of these days she'd even put the past behind her and learn to respect those with—

"Point of clarification, if I may," one of the pastors blurted as he scraped his chair back and rose. "Brother Ned Coppins, Assembly of the Holy Word."

Her stomach tightened as she realized she wasn't going to make it out without having to face the very thing that made it nearly unbearable to even be in this room. Ninah had warned her to watch out for Ned Coppins, who'd organized the protest at last year's Pride Night. *Brother Ned.* Why did these creeps always presume to be her brother?

"I have heard a rather unsavory rumor that the Longdogs are planning on holding another of those L...T...BQ alphabet soup *pride* carnivals at the ballpark." In an obvious effort to show his disgust, he choked out the words and paused for a gulp of tea. "Now I hear you're from out there in California where anything goes, so you might not be aware of the conflict those of us here in the Christian part of the country have with these misguided kooks trying to cram their homosexual lifestyles down our throats. I for one don't believe Assembly of the Holy Word ought to align itself with the Longdogs if they're gonna turn around and give the same recognition to people who are out there flaunting their unnatural sexual perversion in our face."

Britt had prepared for the possibility this issue would be raised and had practiced her response no less than twenty times in front of the mirror. Feelings of anger and insult were unavoidable, but she'd convinced herself she could control her verbal response if she just took a deep breath and reminded herself that she wanted their money, not their blessing.

"Thank you for your concern, Mr. Coppins. In promoting the Longdogs as an asset to the entire community, we're mindful that baseball fans come in all stripes. Thus we feel it best to focus on the things we share in common, such as wanting the team to play well, to avoid injuries, and to exhibit sportsmanship that our children will grow to emulate. I think if we can get behind that purpose—"

"Why yes, I think we can agree that all those things would be to the glory of Christ Jesus. However"—his voice took on a fiery tone that signaled God's wrath—"we are not called to abandon our righteousness for the sake of uniting in sport. On the contrary, the Apostle Paul directed the Corinthians not to associate with those guilty of sexual immorality. To the Thessalonians, he commanded they not walk with any brother not in accord with the teachings of Christ. And to the Galatians—"

Reverend Creach abruptly rose and proclaimed, "Before you get the wrong idea about our group, Miss Iverson, we often engage in robust discussions of our theological differences. Several of us represent congregations that are welcoming to the LGBT community."

Coppins twisted his portly torso toward the other table and sneered. "The Word of God is sacrosanct, as Brother Jerry well knows. Betraying that under the guise of theological differences denies the authority of the Holy Scriptures. Be assured that we at the Assembly of the Holy Word shall lift those congregations in prayer that God might light for them a pure path through Christ Jesus."

A wave of restlessness from both tables seemed to suggest impatience with Coppins's holier-than-thou manner, though Britt knew better than to think it was a rebuke to his views. She had one last arrow in her quiver, which she hoped would put the matter to bed.

"If I can clarify, we're guided in this instance by Major League Baseball's inclusion policy, which prohibits us from discriminating against specific groups—by race or ethnicity, by gender, age and sexual orientation." She glanced at the other table and weakly added, "It even protects the Presbyterians."

While her quip didn't get a raucous laugh, it seemed to dispel some of the tension, and it prompted some good-natured ribbing at the expense of Creach and the other Presbyterian minister in attendance.

"The Longdogs organization would love to welcome your congregation, and we hope you'll take advantage of this opportunity for a night of family fun at the ballpark. All the information is there in the brochure. Just call our office and we'll put you on the schedule."

"And for those of us who follow the Good Book," Coppins continued, "can you guarantee that our worshippers will not find themselves being forced to associate with those who do not walk with Christ Jesus?"

"If you're asking not to be scheduled on the same night as LGBT Pride, I'm sure we can make that accommodation," she replied coolly, taking a step toward the door in hopes of getting out of there before she lost her—*oh, screw that.* "But if you're asking to be shielded from having to share company with those who live proudly and openly as members of the LGBT community, I'm afraid that won't be possible. Because I plan on being there every night, Brother Coppins. With my girlfriend."

The silence that ensued was shockingly satisfying. Even Pearl stopped filling tea glasses and stared at her, mouth agape.

Britt slung her purse strap over her shoulder and collected the unused brochures from the end of the table, wishing she'd followed her gut in the first place and steered clear of this group. No amount of money was worth their pompous sanctimony.

"I appreciate your time, gentlemen. Enjoy your lunch." And *your petty theological squabbles,* she thought miserably.

"I have one more question, Miss Iverson, if you'd be so kind." All eyes turned toward a white-haired gentleman who wore an old-fashioned seersucker suit with a bowtie. His face red from the heat of tight quarters, he fanned himself with a brochure. "Lawrence Dalton, Friendship Christian Church. I was friends with Charlie Iverson, your granddaddy."

She steeled herself for another diatribe, this one probably even more vicious now that she'd sullied her grandfather's good name by having the audacity to be gay.

"I just wanted to ask, if Brother Ned here doesn't wish to take advantage of his invitation, would you consider allowing Friendship to sign up for his night too?" He shook his finger at the others around the room. "And I'll make that offer for anyone else here who wants to sit this out. I've been to some Longdogs games this season. Folks are having more fun than pigs in the mud." He pounded the table with his fist. "And by golly, the Dogs are winning."

The tenor of the room relaxed dramatically as others began to chatter and grab for the brochures.

"Call my office when you're ready to schedule and I'll give you as many nights as I can. That goes for everyone here. If we fill up, we'll open another section. How's that?"

Walking to her car, she couldn't help but notice pep in her step. She felt as if she'd gone into the lion's den, tossed them catnip, and scratched their little chins. Her dad would be pleased. Ninah would be astounded.

The drive from Guido's to the ballpark was all of five minutes. Her father was waiting by Archie's office when she entered from the stairwell. "Get in here, Britt. You're gonna wanna hear this."

Archie was wrapping up a call. "Yes, sir. Yes, sir. We'll be ready."

"What's going on?"

He rubbed his hands together excitedly. "Tell her, Archie."

"You're never gonna guess who I ran into this afternoon at The Bean—Boomer McBride."

"The guy who peed off the balcony in South Beach?"

"The very one. I started to speak to him and this other fellow got between us, like he didn't want me to bother him. Turned out it was his agent, and when I told him who I was, he said—you're not gonna believe this." He looked to her father and grinned. "You tell her this part, Vernon."

"The Pirates sent him down here to Second Dawn. That's the substance abuse treatment center off Barnard Road. He's been there a week, and they're moving him to outpatient as of today. Which means—"

"He'll be in uniform for the Longdogs tonight," Archie blurted.

"Are you kidding me?"

"The Pirates want him out of the spotlight while he works through the program, but they need him to stay in shape. So we've got him for the next three weeks."

"I can't believe this," her dad said. "A Major League All-Star playing for the Longdogs. You know what this means, Britt?"

"Yeah…standing room only."

CHAPTER THIRTY-TWO

Ninah carried a pair of lattes to a tall table by the window where Britt was watching Hanover, Cline, and Holliday sign autographs and pose for photos with fans. "Here you go. I bet Carly's ecstatic. She's always busy on Saturday but I've never seen The Bean this packed."

"I just hope they're all spending money. I'd hate to put her through this circus for nothing."

"It's fun seeing people so excited over the team. That said, I love my Longdogs, but I'll be glad tomorrow when they hit the road. I've hardly seen you since we got back from California."

"That isn't true," Britt demurred. "You saw every inch of me night before last when I sneaked you into my basement at midnight. Took me back to my teenage years."

Ninah laughed. "Not this teenager. I didn't have sex till I was twenty."

"Guy or girl?"

"Do I have to answer?" She looked askance, feeling herself blush. "Fine, I'm a Lone Star Lesbian. One guy. It was terrible."

"And you waited till you were twenty? That should have told you something right there. If you'd really wanted to be with a guy, you'd have done it way sooner than that."

There probably was a lot of truth to that, since Ninah had spent most of her adolescence trying to convince herself she wasn't sexually attracted to women. It wasn't easy given how often she saw them naked in the locker room. "I suppose you have a pristine record."

"Gold Star all the way. First sex at fifteen."

"Aren't you the early bloomer!"

DeVon Holliday, the Longdogs center fielder, appeared at their table and asked Britt to take a photo for a family who wanted to pose with all three players.

"All right, but Annie Leibovitz I ain't."

Ninah chuckled over the likelihood that DeVon, a nineteen-year-old from Muscle Shoals, Alabama, even had a clue who Leibovitz was. It was fun to see Britt hanging out with her team, especially after the rude welcome they'd given her in the locker room. She'd been so intimidated back then, not by the testosterone, but by baseball itself. It was a game she didn't play, a language she didn't speak, a song she didn't know. Now it was in her blood.

Even Wesley Hodges was convinced. His glowing profile of the Iversons had rightly credited her as the driving influence behind the Longdogs' turnaround to profitability. Quoting Vernon, he'd written that Britt's focus on improving the ballpark experience was key to keeping the team in Leland, and that Longdogs fans were lucky to have lured her back from California.

"Hey, you get ditched by your girlfriend?" Carly said as she dragged a stool over from a counter along the wall. She'd taken off her apron, and somehow the polo shirt underneath was splotched with spills and splashes.

"I was just looking at her and thinking how much fun she's having. Remember that night at your house when we all met for the first time? She was so miserable. I didn't think there was a snowball's chance in hell she'd still be here six weeks later, let alone enjoying herself."

"We told her she'd like it here once she got to know people. And obviously it didn't hurt that you two…" She made a raunchy two-handed gesture to simulate sex.

"Stop it." Ninah looked around sheepishly, always expecting to find a group of her students nearby.

Britt returned, slapping Carly on the back. "Stop what? This lady bothering you?"

"She's being crude, rude and uncalled for. I don't know how Justine puts up with her. Where is Justine anyway?"

Carly grimaced. "She's out on a run. A long one up at the logging trail."

"She's amazing," Britt said. "I have a couple of friends in San Diego who are into running, but I don't think either of them trains as hard as she does."

"She's not training today. This is how she copes with stress, by running and running and running until her muscles won't fire anymore. It's even worse when she thinks she's done something wrong, like she's required to go out there and punish herself."

"What's she upset about?" Ninah asked.

Carly looked back over her shoulder, where Ike was wiping down the espresso machine. "Emmy came over last night and finally told us who she's been seeing for the last five months. I couldn't believe it—Ike Martin."

"I know," Ninah said. "About a month ago, I accidentally caught him trying to sneak out of her apartment."

"I wish you'd given me a heads-up."

"Sorry, it was Emmy's news to tell."

"Yeah, I guess. I've never seen so much tension between Justine and one of her kids, and believe me, there were some really hairy moments with Trey when we first got together. She was trying so hard to say the right things but her face gave her away. Emmy got upset, accused her of being a phony liberal, wanting acceptance for herself while denying it to others. Justine was so afraid of saying the wrong thing that she just disappeared into the bedroom and shut the door."

"Wow. Talk about awkward." Ninah couldn't help but be disappointed in Justine, especially since she'd encouraged Emmy to tell her. Addressing Britt, she said, "You said you heard them arguing the other night. What were they saying?"

"Yeah, I was on Ninah's porch," she explained. "Ike sounded frustrated about her hiding it from her family. He even said maybe it was Emmy who had the problem."

Carly grimaced. "I wondered the same thing, if you wanna know the truth. Why else would she wait five months to tell us?"

"Maybe she was worried her mom would freak out...which it sounds like she did."

"I wouldn't call it freaking out. She was surprised is all. I know Justine better than anyone, and she doesn't have a bigoted bone in her body."

"Emmy thought she'd more upset over Ike being a barista."

"*I'm* a barista!"

"My words exactly."

"What happens now?" Britt asked. "Is there anything we can do?"

"No, she has to process this by herself. She told me later it was her fear talking, that she pictured Emmy and Ike being harassed by some of the rednecks here in Leland. We don't have many mixed-race couples around here, but there was one at her church a few years ago. They woke up in the middle of the night and somebody had torched their car in the driveway. The police never arrested anyone."

Ninah wondered if Seth and his friend had been in Leland back then. It was easy to imagine them intimidating Emmy and Ike if given the chance.

A surge of new customers streamed through the door and Carly rose. "Guess I'd better get back to work. Thanks for bringing me all this business, Britt. Keep this up and I might get to retire early."

When she'd gone, Britt said, "You're annoyed, I can tell. Do you really think Justine would have a problem with a black son-in-law?"

"Of course not, but it's obvious we have a long way to go before we're truly colorblind." She nodded toward the players, who were sitting on the stone hearth chatting with young fans. "Look over there at DeVon Holliday. Those kids he's talking to don't care that he's black."

"No, but take away his uniform and his white teammates. How do you think these same people would react if he was walking down their sidewalk?"

The answer was obvious. And depressing.

Cory Hanover pressed Britt into service again, this time for a photo with a group of kids who'd arrived at The Bean on skateboard. It was good for people to see the players out and about as part of the community, especially the ones who didn't look like everyone else in Leland. Now if they could just get back to being the team they were at the start of the season. They'd struggled for wins after Oscar's departure, even with the addition of Boomer McBride.

"What's up with the Longdogs anyway?" Ninah asked when Britt returned. "They ought to be going gangbusters with Boomer. He's hitting even better than Oscar but the rest of the team is letting him down."

"Archie says there's bad chemistry in the locker room, that the guys don't like him."

"I can understand a little professional jealousy, seeing as how they're all making about seven thousand bucks this year and he's making twenty million."

"Dad thinks it's more than that. Hank's been pounding it into them every day what a precious opportunity this is for them. They feel like Boomer's taking up a space for a kid who deserves a shot."

"Yeah, I get that. We were all excited a couple of years ago about getting to hire a new social studies teacher. They wasted it on Tommy Britton. He's a decent basketball coach, but he doesn't know jack shit about world civilization. Really makes you stop and think how we glorify these sports guys…and it's always guys, isn't it?"

"Oh shit," Britt mumbled, craning her neck at a commotion on the sidewalk. "Speak of the devil and there he is."

Boomer McBride had picked this moment to stop in for coffee, effectively spoiling the planned appearance of his teammates as fans abandoned them mid-sentence to rush outside. Angry and humiliated, the three younger players prepared to leave.

"Quick, come with me," Ninah said as she hurried to catch DeVon by the elbow. "Wait, guys. I'm a huge fan. I've been dying to get some pictures but you were swarmed by all those kids."

Troy Cline grumbled, "Wouldn't you rather be out there with Mr. Big Shot? Everybody else is."

"Nope, he's a Pirate. I'm a Longdogs fan." She posed them for several photos, including some she promised to give Carly to frame for her wall. "You'll have to come back and sign these. Someday it's gonna be you drawing crowds like that. I'm glad I got my chance to meet you."

"You made their day, Ninah Faust," Britt said. "I love how you do that."

"I don't know what you're talking about. I saw an opening to have them all to myself and I took it."

"Right…then in that case, I love your quick thinking. Especially when it just happens to make other people feel good," she added, sticking out her tongue. "I'm glad their morning ended on an up note. Between us, I like having a full house at the ballpark, but I'll be glad when Boomer goes home."

Ninah felt the same on principle, but there was one thing she was happy about—Boomer's last scheduled game in Leland was on Pride Night. That all but guaranteed the biggest crowd of the season would be there to see her GSA members celebrate Pride and present their check to the library.

CHAPTER THIRTY-THREE

In the owner's suite, Britt corked the bottle of Black Stallion Cabernet Sauvignon and set it aside to enjoy at home later, ideally in the gazebo with Ninah. She should have known better than to offer fine wine to these particular guests, a group of wannabe jocks representing a sports media group interested in acquiring the broadcast rights for all Longdogs home games. They preferred Corona with lime, especially with the taco bar she'd arranged from Tacos Chalitos.

Like everyone else in the ballpark, they were keenly focused on Boomer McBride, who entered the batter's box with runners on the corners. The Longdogs were clinging to a one-run lead over the Terre Haute Wabashers in the bottom of the eighth. After three straight losses, fans were anxious for a win.

"What do you think, Dad?" she asked, keeping her voice low as the two of them huddled at the back of the suite out of earshot of their guests. It was a whole different experience to be on the receiving end of a sales talk.

"We can't sell hot dogs to people listening to the game at home."

"No, but it might build fan loyalty, which would help with merchandising. Plus we get paid even if the team sucks…which right now, they do." She went on to describe a chart of Ninah's that showed a marked increase in fielding errors since Boomer joined the team. "Ninah thinks he's a distraction, that the others are focused on competing against him instead of working together as a team."

"Archie talked with Coy, the clubby. He says the real problem is they miss Oscar. He used to gather the team in a circle after every game and lead a prayer. It was broken English, but the guys didn't mind. They helped him out. Archie said they liked how it brought everyone together. Boomer's not like that."

She fought the urge to roll her eyes. He knew how she felt about empty religious rituals.

"You can understand it from their point of view," he went on. "They're a long way from home, so they need to feel that connection with each other."

"They shower together. How much more connected can you get?"

He chuckled. "Oscar was authentic, Coy said. And humble. And when he got called up, some of them felt like it was his reward for doing what God wanted."

"Some reward. They've used him what, four times as a pinch hitter? He was better off here in Leland where he got to play."

"I'm just saying the boys looked up to him. He was a spiritual role model."

She found the whole topic irritating, especially after capitulating to the ministers who wanted to give the invocation on their church night. "I just wish they'd do it on their own time instead of in our locker room. I'm fine to let them have their space if that's their thing, but we have to consider the others too." She gestured toward the on-deck circle, where Troy Cline was swinging a bat with a weighted donut. "Take Cline for example. What if he's an atheist but he feels pressured to join the circle and pretend he's praying too? Or suppose one of the guys is Jewish and the others go on about Jesus this and Jesus that? Is that fair to them?"

"Technically?" He crossed his legs and folded his arms, a stall tactic she recognized from her childhood when she asked permission for something and he didn't want to give it. "It's probably not fair. But we all have to navigate the world with our peculiarities. Sometimes that means going along."

Her throat suddenly burned with anger and she gritted her teeth so their guests wouldn't hear. "Seriously, Dad? You think I should I have gone along with Mom and that insidious cult leader of hers?"

"Britt, that's not what I meant. I would never—"

"Suppose their little 'Jesus circle' decides they need to pray over Cline and cast out his demons so he can hit a curve ball?"

"You've made your point." He abruptly rose and joined the men at the front of the suite, playing the charming host again with an offer to fetch them another beer. As he reached for the cooler, he cast a hurt look at Britt.

"Way to go, asshole," she grumbled to herself. The one person who'd been there for her all her life, and she'd taken him down with a thoughtless absurdity.

A crack of the bat brought a gasp from the crowd, who rose as one to watch Boomer's shot clear Grace Hospital's towering digital display in left field by twenty feet at least. It was by far the longest homer Longdogs fans had seen all summer, and it boosted their lead to four.

"Now batting for the Longdogs, right fielder Troy Cline."

As her dad negotiated the broadcast rights, she quietly scolded herself for her tirade. So what if they wanted to pray together? No one had complained. She'd created a problem where there was none.

She cleared her throat to catch her father's eye. When he turned her way, she patted her chest and mouthed, "I'm sorry."

"Me too," he silently replied, with the gentle smile he always seemed to give when she needed it most.

Behind him on the field, Cline suddenly went sprawling to dodge a fastball that tailed up and inside toward his head. Within seconds, Boomer charged out of the dugout on a beeline toward the Wabashers pitcher. The infielders collapsed around the mound to protect their ace as more Longdogs rushed the field. Shoving became punching became stomping as the infield erupted into a full-blown brawl.

After almost ten minutes of mayhem, Boomer, Cline, Holliday and three of Terre Haute's players were ejected to loud boos. With order finally restored, the final four outs of the game were recorded and fans headed for the exits.

"I'm going down to find Ninah," Britt said to her dad. "I'll meet you at the car."

"Don't worry about me, honey. I'll get Archie to drop me at home."

She cut through the press box to reach Ninah and Carly at the club seats.

"Hey, Britt. Too bad about the ugly finish," Carly said. "Otherwise we got a good win."

"And probably a suspension or two," Ninah added.

Britt found the whole thing childish. "Which means this win streak is over at one. What did they expect, sending a brawler down to Leland? How am I supposed to make a marketing pitch for the Longdogs being good, clean family fun if they're going to act like a street gang?"

Ninah nodded toward the field, where Wesley Hodges was holding out his phone to record an interview with Boomer. Cline stood beside him, sporting a swollen nose and bloody shirt. "Let's go down and hear what they're saying."

"Boomer, this isn't the first time you've mixed it up on the field. What was going through your head when you charged the mound?"

"He threw at my guy here." Boomer hooked his arm around Cline's neck. "I'm not going to let anybody get away with that. Teammates stick together."

"And what about you, Troy? Did you know that pitch was coming up and in?"

"I figured it might. Boomer smoked his ass with that homer. Probably sucks to give up one that deep."

Britt made a mental note to ask Hank to talk to the younger players about the language they used with the press.

"Lots of ejections tonight, including you and Boomer. Do you think that was fair?"

"Hey, whatever happens, happens. If they come at us, we're not just going to sit back and take it. I saw him take a swing at Boomer, I wasn't thinking about getting thrown out. Your guy's getting swung at, you jump in there and crack heads."

"There's a good chance the league is going to hand down suspensions. That means the Longdogs will probably be shorthanded tomorrow night in Cookeville, with three starters on the bench. Was it worth it?"

"Heck, yeah!" Boomer said with a laugh. "Besides, it won't matter. There's plenty of guys on this team that can play. Once they get out there and show how good they are, the three of us are going to have to bust our tails to earn our jobs back. That's why we're here, to toughen up for the majors."

Cline jostled him. "It's not why *you're* here, Boomer."

"Oh, yeah. Forgot about that."

Britt leaned into Ninah's shoulder. "Never mind what I said about good, clean family fun. Looks like we've got our team chemistry back."

"And just in time to make a run for the playoffs."

CHAPTER THIRTY-FOUR

Carrying a canvas lawn chair over her shoulder and a tub of Mexican corn salad, Ninah walked the five blocks from her apartment to the park for the annual Pride picnic. Justine coordinated the effort jointly each year with Rob Freeman, who owned a B&B on Lake Leland and managed an email list of the town's gay men. Last year's picnic had drawn over a hundred men, women and children from Leland's LGBT community, and this year's event promised even more. Ninah couldn't wait to see Britt's reaction to the crowd.

Underneath the pavilion, the buffet was being set up on a long picnic table covered with a patchwork of tablecloths—red-checkered, blue-checkered, white and rainbow. After wedging her dish into a spot between the salads and the other vegetables, she peered out into the sun in search of familiar faces.

Carly yelled from atop a ladder, where she was stringing a volleyball net across a sandy court. "Hey, Ninah! Grab me a Sun Drop."

As she rummaged through one of the coolers, Teri arrived balancing a large bag of ice on each shoulder. "Yo Ninah. Give me a hand with this, will you?"

Remembering Justine's encouragement to restore some civility to her dealings with Teri, Ninah grabbed one of the bags and propped it by a cooler. Irked by the ever-present MAGA hat—at the Pride picnic, of all days—she just couldn't bring herself to actually speak.

"You're looking good, Nines."

"Thanks," she managed to mumble. The compliment surprised her, given their acrimonious last encounter. It was true she'd been paying more attention to her appearance since getting involved with Britt, fussing over her face and hair, and choosing clothes that showed off her work at the wellness center. Still, she'd hardly expected Teri to notice.

"Appreciate the help, those were heavy. You know me—too lazy to make two trips."

No. She would not be drawn into a conversation that might normalize their relationship, not if it meant looking at that symbol of hate.

"Still the silent treatment, huh? Suit yourself."

"I have no desire to make small talk with anyone who'd wear that hateful hat."

"That's a real fetish with you, isn't it? You really ought to get some help for that."

"If one of us has a hat fetish, it's you. You had a choice this morning, Teri. You could have worn a Pride cap, a cowboy hat, even a fucking helicopter beanie. No, you chose to go with a *fuck you*, because you know the very sight of it makes most people here wanna puke."

"I don't dress myself for most people."

"Oh, I think you do. Maybe *you* should think about seeing a therapist. They could help you understand why you have a sociopathic need to rub people's noses in it."

"I can tell you why. It's because I'm not gonna give assholes like you the satisfaction of taking it off. The more you bitch about it, the more it makes me wanna wear it. In case you haven't noticed, people have been treating me like shit for three years. Mostly thanks to you, the way you've trashed me to everybody. Why should I care about their feelings?"

"Because you hurt them. You sided with a man who takes sadistic joy from being cruel to people he thinks are beneath him, including our whole community. I didn't trash you—you trashed yourself. Decent people respect others' humanity."

"What about respecting my humanity, Ninah?"

Ninah was sick of having this conversation over and over, as if it ever would end differently. "We all respected you before you sold us out. If you ever want our respect again, you'll have to earn it."

By the time she got across the field, Carly had finished with the net and was sitting in a lawn chair beneath a maple tree with Justine. "Come join us. You and Teri fighting again?"

"I'm so tired of her shit."

"Apparently, shit is contagious," Justine grumbled, intercepting Carly's Sun Drop for the precious first swig.

Carly had warned her that Justine was still in a funk over Emmy and Ike…or more precisely, over her reaction to the news they were dating. She was angry with herself, even questioning her own convictions.

"How are things with Emmy? You guys getting it worked out?"

"I don't think she's mad at me anymore but I can tell she's disappointed…which, for the record, is a thousand times worse. Not that I blame her."

"I'm sure it'll all work out." A tepid response was the best Ninah could manage, since she too had been disappointed in Justine's reaction. "But whatever you said or didn't say, you can't possibly compare yourself to Teri Kaufman. You're not even in the same ballpark."

"I wish I could believe that. For about three seconds, there wasn't an inch of daylight between Teri and me. I didn't think Ike Martin was good enough to date my daughter, and Emmy saw it all over my face."

"You are *nothing* like Teri. She embraces all that hate. You're repulsed by it."

"She's right, sweetheart." Carly pulled her into a hug. "If you were anyone else, you wouldn't have raised Emmy to be the person she is. Three seconds won't erase that."

"I won't be surprised if she freezes me out of her love life. It's exactly what I deserve."

"I don't think that's gonna happen," Ninah said. "Considering they're planning on stopping by the park this afternoon together to show their support. Don't forget, Ike's brother Thaddeus is gay too."

Justine's face lit up with a bright smile. "They're both coming here? Are you sure?"

"Uh-oh, I think I just spoiled their surprise."

"Oh my God, that's fantastic! Did you hear that, Carly?"

"I'll go fetch the extra chairs from the car."

"Ninah, you have no idea what a relief that is. This means she's giving me a second chance." She pressed her hands together and looked skyward. "Lord, please don't let me screw this up."

"Just do me a favor and act surprised. Hey, I have an idea. Wednesday's Pride Night at the ballpark. Vernon's gonna be up in the VIP suite, and I already asked Carly to help me keep an eye on my GSA kids in the stands. How about you take our tickets and go with Ike and Emmy instead of sitting with the Pride group? Enjoy it together, the three of you. Your own little mini-Pride section. It'll be a big crowd that night, Boomer McBride's last game in Leland."

"You are so sweet, Ninah." Justine stretched over to squeeze her hand, then nodded toward the parking lot. "Speaking of the Longdogs, isn't that Britt coming back with Carly?"

"*Day-um!*"

"I'll say."

Britt wore short denim cutoffs that showed off her long, shapely legs, and a dainty white sleeveless top. Her hair cascaded from beneath a floppy straw hat, and half her face was hidden by oversized sunglasses. It was impossible not to notice the heads turning as she and Carly crossed the open field.

Also hard to miss was the sight of Margot bolting from her group of horse lovers as if it were suppertime in the barn.

"Oh shit." Calculating the distance to intercept, Ninah bitterly accepted there was no point in racing to meet them as she couldn't get there fast enough. "There goes an hour Britt will never get back."

Margot headed them off and stopped directly in their path. To Ninah's delight, Britt and Carly barely broke stride, offering only smiles and a perfunctory greeting as they sidestepped her and continued across the field. Margot got the message apparently and trotted back to her herd.

"Hi, beautiful," Ninah said, eyeing Britt lasciviously. "I think I'll stick close to you today. I have a feeling you're gonna make a lot of new friends. I want them to know you already have a girlfriend."

"I certainly do." Britt kissed her on the lips before bending down to plant another on Justine's cheek. "I can't get over how many people are here. Who knew there were this many queers in Leland?"

Justine visibly shuddered, prompting Carly to say, "She hates that word."

"Sorry, I meant lesbian, gay, bisexual, transgender, intersex, nonbinary, pansexual, asexual, questioning people. I probably left out half a dozen. That's why most of my friends in California just say queer. We've taken the word back from the haters. If we reclaim our own language, they can't hurt us by calling us names."

"I know, I know," Justine muttered. "With any luck, I'll be hard of hearing by the time everyone starts using it."

"I take it those are the coupons." Ninah gestured at the small stack of cards in Britt's hand. "Britt printed up a bunch of two-dollar coupons for Pride Night at the ballpark."

"A hundred and fifty of them. I hope that's enough."

Justine said, "By the way, I talked to Lawrence Dalton, our minister at Friendship Christian Church. He said he'd be honored to do the invocation on Wednesday. If you still want him to, that is."

"Absolutely."

Ninah was surprised to hear that Britt had extended the invitation. "I thought you were only doing the prayer on church nights."

"I am, but I have a feeling Ned Coppins is going to have his holy rollers out protesting again. I thought it would help to hear from the other side." Britt gestured with a tip of her head. "Shall we get started on handing these out?"

Ninah located Margot's group and plotted a course that would make them the last stop. Then taking advantage of their surroundings, she looped her arm through Britt's. "That was a sweet gesture with Justine's minister. I'm very impressed."

"I liked him. He stood up to Coppins that day at the Faith Luncheon. And it was an olive branch to Dad. I think he was starting to worry that I might be the Antichrist."

"I take it you smoothed things over."

"We understand each other better, I think. Dad's always been nice to everyone, no matter their differences, so it makes him uncomfortable when I rock the boat. Even if I don't share their beliefs, I should respect them. Or so he says, live and let live, all that."

"Begging your dad's pardon, that's a lot easier when you're in a position of privilege. He has status and probably holds beliefs that don't violate the norm."

"Exactly. If you're a straight, white, Christian man, you aren't used to being on the outside of an issue, so going along with the crowd isn't hard at all."

Ninah slowed their pace as they neared the parking area, where a group of gay men had set up their own tailgate party. She recognized Rob, the B&B owner, and his husband David. "Surely he doesn't expect you to listen respectfully while folks like Ned Coppins spew their trash."

"I asked him that specifically. Who gets to define which beliefs are worthy of respect? My mom? She's a brainwashed lunatic and Coppins is a hate monger. If religious beliefs are arbitrary, respect should be arbitrary too."

Rob rose to greet them, wearing a tank top that showed off his muscular shoulders. Even in his late fifties, his buff physique held up well to those of the younger shirtless men. "Ninah, good to see you."

She greeted the faces that seemed familiar and reminded them she was the faculty sponsor for the GSA, who'd organized the second annual Pride Night at the ballpark. Then she introduced Britt so she could make her pitch.

"There were some protests by a local church group at last year's event," she explained. "Unfortunately, there isn't much we can do to restrict them since the city owns the park. What we *can* do is come out in numbers to show our support. We all remember what it was like—"

The sound of a car alarm pierced the air, bringing picnickers to their feet. Seconds later, the dark gray Dodge that had stalked Ninah and Thaddeus in front of the high school slung gravel as it fishtailed out of the lot.

One of Rob's young friends sprinted to the parking lot to investigate, and yelled back, "Bad news, guys. We've got a bunch of flat tires out here."

CHAPTER THIRTY-FIVE

Ninah had hoped to avoid the limelight, but incoming president Abby McFarland insisted she accompany them onto the field for the presentation of their check to the library. For the occasion, she'd worn a T-shirt with rainbow lettering that spelled out PRIDE.

"Also representing the Gay-Straight Alliance, faculty sponsor— and longtime fan of our Longdogs—Ninah Faust."

Hoots and hollers erupted from her various pockets of support. Loudest was the cluster of friends sitting in the club seats behind home plate. Tonight, that bunch included Justine, Ike and Emmy.

"...would like to present this check for three hundred dollars to the Leland County Public Library so they can add to their collection of books of special interest to the LGBTQ community. The GSA wishes to thank all those in attendance for coming out tonight to help celebrate Pride Night with the Longdogs."

The ensuing applause was at least polite, if not particularly enthusiastic. More troubling was the scattered murmur of boos. Not as many as last year, Ninah noted as they returned to their seats in the right field bleachers, which had been roped off for their group. Tonight's turnout was at least double what she'd expected. Saturday's vandalism had galvanized support within the LGBT community.

More frustrating than slashed tires was the tepid response of Leland's police department. Two officers came and took statements, but only Ninah had gotten a good look at the car. Despite her near certainty of who the villain was, she admittedly hadn't seen the vehicle's occupants. Officers already had the pair on their radar, they said. Seth Causwell and his brother Kevin, who'd recently moved from Little Rock, Arkansas. They were staying with relatives at a house on Barnard Road, and both claimed to have been at home all afternoon on Sunday. Case closed.

"How about this crowd, huh?" she asked Carly.

"A full house and then some." She waved over toward the club seats, catching Justine's eye. "That was a great idea having Justine use our tickets. She thought about asking Emmy and Ike to sit over here with us, but this being their first night out together, she wanted to make it about them instead."

"You know what I like about sitting in these bleachers? Last night these very seats belonged to Ned Coppins and the Church of the Holy Word. Now our queer butts are scrubbing them clean."

Britt hadn't scheduled an official church congregation tonight but a handful of Ned's flock were outside the stadium holding signs that condemned not only the queer community but their supporters too. While they certainly were obnoxious, their group was pitifully small and largely ignored.

On the field, the teams were lining up shoulder to shoulder along the baselines for the pregame ritual.

"Would you get a load of that!" Carly said, tugging Ninah's arm excitedly.

"What? I don't see anything." She'd been busy firing up the scorekeeping app on her tablet.

"Look what the players are wearing. Boomer, Cory, Troy, DeVon. All of them, even Hank."

White pants…black jerseys. "Oh my God! Abby, look. All the Longdogs are wearing our Pride bracelets." That must have been Britt's doing.

Ninah looked up to the owner's suite for Britt, who was standing with her father alongside a group of VIPs, probably advertisers. After a few wild waves, Britt finally spotted her and grinned as they pointed to their wrists.

"That is so freaking cool," she told Carly. "Can you imagine how much it means to these kids to get that kind of support from a bunch of jocks?" Lowering her voice, she added, "My girlfriend is gonna get so laid tonight."

"Ladies and gentlemen, we ask that you stand and remove your caps. Tonight's invocation is given by Reverend Lawrence Dalton of Friendship Christian Church."

Carly elbowed her. "Better get your mind out of the gutter. God's listening."

The brief prayer focused on sportsmanship and safety, and closed with a message of acceptance of all. Perfect pitch for a Pride event.

"…and we ask these in the name of Christ our lord. Amen."

Before anyone could sit, a quartet from the Friendship choir harmonized on a nice rendition of "The Star-Spangled Banner." The crowd cheered loudly at the close, but not enough to obscure a cry of "Faggots!" from the section adjacent to the Pride group.

Carly whipped around. "Where did that come from?"

Several fans cast scolding looks in the general direction of two young men who sat across the aisle from Thaddeus and his mother. Ninah at once recognized Seth Causwell and assumed the other guy had to be his brother Kevin.

"Carly, it's those guys who slashed our tires." She craned her neck in a futile effort to locate one of the uniformed police officers hired to provide security. "You think we should report them?"

"Poof!" Kevin appeared to be trying to get Thaddeus's attention. He dangled his wrist as he said it again, sending his brother into fits of laughter.

"I'm not sure what the police can do about it. But I'm not gonna let him keep bothering Thaddeus."

"Leading off for the Paducah Dukes, shortstop Emilio Reyes."

Ninah stepped into the aisle to get a better look at the situation four rows up. Thaddeus wasn't their only easy prey. Several others from the GSA were clustered nearby. She was most concerned about Jordan and Trina, since they'd both gotten into trouble at school for fighting with bullies. It was only a matter of time before one of them blew their cool.

She put her tablet in Carly's hands. "Here, keep score while I deal with this. And go sit up there on the end by Thaddeus before something happens."

"Okay, but hurry back. I don't have a clue how this works."

At the opposite end of Thaddeus's row were some of the picnickers who'd come tonight to give moral support, both lesbians and gay men. Ninah climbed over several sets of knees to reach their aisle. "Hey guys, we've got a couple of rednecks over there bothering my GSA kids. I hate to put you in the line of fire, but I can't let anything happen to them. Could I get a few of you to move down to that end?"

"I'll go." The first volunteer was none other than Teri…who for once *wasn't* wearing her MAGA hat. Gesturing at her friends Robbi and Liv, she added, "All three of us will go."

"Great, I'll meet you over there. Just tell the kids on the aisle to slide in toward the middle." She rubbed her hands together.

"Okay, who else? We need two or three cool-headed adults to be a buffer at the end of each row."

A dozen more responded to her plea, juggling seat cushions and concessions to follow her. Carly had already swapped their front-row seats with Thaddeus and his mom.

"Any more trouble?"

"Nothing so far." She pushed the tablet into Ninah's hands. "Take this contraption back before I screw it up."

A ground ball to Castillo at second base ended the top half of the inning, all of which Ninah had missed while she scrambled to deal with the possible threat.

She whispered to Carly, "I didn't tell anyone these were the same guys that trashed their cars. I was afraid it would start a fight."

"Britt would kill us. Although…it might be fun to sneak out and find their car. You wouldn't happen to have a pocketknife on you?"

"You're evil, Carly. I love that about you." She glanced behind her to see Teri and her friends two rows up. "You're aren't gonna believe this. Guess who actually left her butt-ugly MAGA hat at home? I think I finally got through to her."

"Leading off for your Leland Longdogs, right fielder Troy Cline."

She shoved her tablet at Carly again. "Here, take this."

"Wha—"

Ninah climbed to Teri's row and crouched low on the steps. After making such a big deal about Teri's hat, she had to give credit where it was due. "I just wanted to say thanks for jumping in. These guys over here, I've run into them before. They're both assholes and they're looking for trouble. Don't give it to them."

Robbi flashed her wallet to reveal her state trooper shield. "I never leave home without it. If they start something, I'll be on top of it."

"Great, but let's hope it doesn't come to that. I'm gonna text Britt and ask her to keep a uniform nearby. What I'm worried about most is afterward. If you guys don't mind hanging around when the game's over, I wanna make sure all these kids walk out with somebody."

"Sure, we got that," Teri said. Shaking her head, she added, "This kind of shit's getting out of control."

"Yeah…what we need is more people who wanna be part of the solution, so thanks again." Sliding back into her seat, she said to Carly, "I just had an out-of-body experience. Teri Kaufman has suddenly decided she wants to be one of the good guys."

CHAPTER THIRTY-SIX

Peering through binoculars, Britt located the trouble spot in right field. She'd had her eye on it all night, in between schmoozes with real estate agency in the VIP suite. Ninah and Carly had the situation under control for now, they said, and there also was a uniformed police officer stationed at the top of the bleachers in case something got out of hand.

The sold-out crowd was abuzz over McBride's last game as a Longdog, not to mention their winning streak since last week's brawl. Whatever issues simmered in the Pride section, they hadn't spread to other areas of the park.

Her father looked over her shoulder. "Can't we just have those hooligans escorted off the premises? Hard to believe no one's gotten up and punched them in the nose."

"JT says we have to be careful how we handle it. I texted him. He's on his way up."

"While we're at it, tell him to send that church crowd packing too, with all their hateful signs. They've got no right to do that here. We're a private business."

"But we're in a public park," Britt replied. "That's what JT said, that we can't shut down a peaceful protest just because we don't like what they're saying." She raised her binoculars again. "It's still mostly quiet down there. Ninah says it's just a few adolescent insults. We need to get through these last two innings."

The suite door opened to JT and his son Trey. They greeted their real estate friends before joining Britt and her dad in the corner. "So what have we got here, Vernon?"

"I'll let Britt tell you. She's got a better handle on it than I do."

They were interrupted by a deep blast to right field by the Longdogs catcher, a solo home run that tied the game with the visiting Dukes.

"Angel Alvarado and one lucky fan just earned themselves a combo meal from Tacos Chalitos. Join Angel for lunch at Tacos Chalitos, your taco stop in Leland. Now check your ticket stub for this number…"

When the excitement died down, she discovered another text from Ninah and directed their focus to the Pride section. "It's the two guys sitting straight across the aisle from Ninah and Carly, early twenties. They're brothers from Arkansas. Ninah says they've been around all summer, staying with their aunt and uncle out on Barnard Road and working at the boot factory. They're also the SOBs who slashed all the tires last weekend. Except when the police questioned them, they denied it and that was the end of it."

"I got an earful about that from Justine," JT said. "Something about how the cops didn't even search their car for a knife. What are they up to right now?"

"Ninah said they were yelling out slurs earlier, things like faggot, poof, lezbo. They're just making fun of people, being obnoxious and trying to provoke somebody."

JT grimaced and shook his head. "This is a tough one."

"Wait a minute," her dad said. "Are you telling me I can't have somebody ejected if they're sitting down there harassing my customers? They ought to be arrested for disorderly conduct."

"It's a gray area, Vernon," JT said.

Trey, a younger version of his handsome father, cleared his throat. "What Dad means is we have to take into consideration what's harassment versus free speech."

"So they get to sit there and spew their vile garbage and we can't do a thing about it?"

"The problem is they might sue. Their lawyers would argue they were only protesting against the LGBT community. That's political speech, protected by the First Amendment. The court won't care whether it's offensive or not. Now if they were doing something else, something threatening…"

Britt couldn't stand to think of losing a court case to those two bastards. "I was going to have security walk them out, but it sounds like I can't do that. Ninah's worried about when the game ends and they all crowd together on the way out."

"The law's a tricky thing," JT added. "Makes it dang near impossible to pinch the fuse on a powder keg. Gotta wait till it blows up."

"So basically you're saying we need to suck it up and get through this."

He patted her shoulder. "Don't you worry, Britt. One of these days they'll mess with the wrong person and karma will kick their pathetic butts."

"I'm going to head down there for the rest of the game. Maybe I can get security to run interference, keep them busy while everyone else walks out." She thanked their real estate guests for coming and promised to follow up in a couple of days to talk about a sponsorship.

By the time she'd spoken with the police officer on duty and reached the bleachers, the eighth inning was in the books with the score tied.

"At the plate for the Dukes, left fielder…"

"Scoot," she said to Ninah, nudging her down the row. "Everything okay down here?"

Before Ninah could answer, the man across the aisle called out, "Don't tell me you're one of them, beautiful. 'Cause that would be a crime."

She sneered across the aisle to see an overgrown child jostling his junk. "Christ, is that the kind of crap you've been putting up with?"

"Pretty much. I moved Abby McFarland all the way to the other end because he kept going on about how he had just what she needed."

"You should have told me it was this bad." She didn't need JT's legal advice to know that obscene gestures didn't count as free speech. "I'd have had security take them out sooner."

Ninah caught her shirt to stop her from standing. "Please hold off if you can. It's been such a great night. No one on this side of the aisle is paying them any mind. Do you have any idea how dope it is for these kids to look out there and see an icon like Boomer McBride wearing a Pride bracelet?"

"Of course I do, and I don't want a couple of knuckle-dragging mouth-breathers to ruin that for them."

"They won't. What they want most is to get a rise out of us and ruin our night. We've denied them that for three hours. It's just infantile drivel. Kids need to learn how to deal with that kind of nuisance. That's why we all shuffled seats, so those of us who've faced it before could show the younger ones that it's possible to handle it without being confrontational."

Britt wasn't sure which was more infuriating, the harassment or Ninah's surrender to it. "But you aren't handling it. You're letting a couple of douchebags walk all over you. What's the use of having a Pride Night if you don't get to act proud?"

Carly leaned around to speak, "Trust me, Ninah's just as pissed off as you are. I've been holding on to her shirt the same way she's holding on to yours."

"It's like that drunk guy in Ashland, Britt. These kids are having a great time. I'd like nothing more than to send someone over there to crack heads, but I don't want that to be anyone's takeaway from Pride Night. Like you said, we all need to leave here with our teeth."

Britt grunted her disapproval. "At the very least, we should sneak out to the parking lot and slash their tires."

Ninah laughed and jerked her thumb toward Carly. "Great minds think alike. Carly said the same thing."

Shawn Dunwoody, the Longdogs closer, recorded his fifth strikeout of the night to shut down the Dukes, giving Leland a chance to win if only they could score a run in the bottom of the ninth. Britt usually rooted for extra innings since it meant more concession sales. Tonight, she just wanted to be done with it and see everyone safely out.

"Leading off for the Longdogs, third baseman Boomer McBride!"

The crowd responded with its usual Boomer-mania, obviously aware this likely would be their last look at him in a Longdogs uniform. He'd been good for ticket sales, but his biggest contribution was in getting the youthful Longdogs to play as a team.

"I'd take a walk-off home run right now," Britt said.

Ninah elbowed her. "Look, they're leaving."

She turned to see the Causwell brothers walking past security to the exit. As instructed, her uniformed officer followed to ensure there was no mischief in the parking lot.

"Peace at last," Ninah said, stretching to trade high fives with several others sitting along the aisle. "Great job, y'all."

"Am I imagining things or did you just slap hands with your ex?"

"I'll tell you about it later. Apparently she's—"

A curve ball came in slow and hung over the plate. Boomer crushed it, dead center, the walk-off homer Britt had wished for only moments ago. The stadium exploded in cheers as he trotted the bases and proceeded to slap the outstretched hands of fans sitting near the dugout. When he reached the Pride section, the adults stepped back and let the GSA youth storm the front row.

Ninah hugged Britt's waist in a pleasantly surprising display of affection in front of her students and their families. "Talk about a storybook ending. Boomer's now got fans for life in Leland."

"Including me," she admitted.

Carly squeezed past them into the aisle. "I'm off to find Justine and see how it went with Ike and Emmy. Want to come?"

"Sure, I watched them earlier with binoculars from the suite. Looked like they were having a great time."

"What a relief. She was a nervous wreck."

Outside, the parking lot was a mass of taillights as cars slowly crept toward the exit onto Main Street. Justine had texted she was waiting by her car.

Carly walked into a hug and delivered a peck on the lips. "How'd it go, sweetie?"

"I've been a total idiot. Ike's such a gentleman and he's obviously crazy about my daughter. If you ever catch me doubting my daughter again, you have my permission to smack me in the head with an egg."

"Where'd they go?" Carly asked.

"Oh, they're walking back to Emmy's. Ike has to be at work at six o'clock in the morning. I hear his boss is a real harpy."

"You better believe it."

"How did it go with Pride? Did the kids have a good time?"

Before Britt could answer, Ninah said, "Couldn't have been better. The crowd was a lot more enthusiastic this year, don't you think? And the kids were super-excited that all the players took the field wearing Pride bracelets."

"We were all so proud of you out there on the field. That was such a sweet gesture, giving that check to the library. They're good kids, aren't they?"

Outside the entrance, a rumbling vehicle suddenly revved and lurched from the sluggish line. *A gray Dodge!* With tires squealing, it skidded almost half a block in the oncoming lane before swerving onto the sidewalk, where its underside scraped the concrete curb. Then came a sickening *thump*, the unmistakable sound of the car striking something.

Screams, shouts.

"Oh my God," Ninah gasped as they scrambled across the gravel parking lot toward the scene.

The car reversed and then veered back onto the roadway, accelerating past several stopped vehicles before spinning through an opening in traffic to disappear down a side street.

Yards ahead, people were leaving their cars to rush to the sidewalk…some already wailing in horror.

Justine suddenly broke into a dead run. "Emmy! Emmy!"

CHAPTER THIRTY-SEVEN

With the parking lot at Friendship Christian Church overflowing, a handful of teenage boys had begun guiding newcomers into tight diagonal spaces along the grassy edge of Van Buren Street. Britt pulled into a slot, taking note of the people walking past. Young and old, black and white. A community coming together for two of its own.

"You okay?" her father asked.

She'd put the car in Reverse—not Park—her subconscious telling her she didn't belong here. "Maybe I should just drop you off and you can text me when you're ready to be picked up. Would that be okay?"

"Kip Barlow said he'd take me home after the service. He can't do the march on account of his broken toe." He opened the car door but made no move to exit. "What's bothering you, honey?"

"I don't know how you stand it, Dad. I'm not sure I can live in a place that hates this much."

She'd been mired in fury for the last three days, raging at every word in the *Gazette*, every news clip of the shock and horror visited on their "idyllic small town." In truth, towns like Leland nurtured such violence. It was baked into their gun culture, along with their embrace of a racist Confederate heritage and the misguided belief that God was on their side.

"I know this town, Britt. Leland's got its share of problems, but there's no welcome mat out for those boys. Go inside that church tonight and what you'll see is the opposite of hate."

"You know how I feel about churches."

He nodded grimly and patted her hand. "Do whatever feels right, honey. I'm sure JT and Justine would appreciate you being there, but with all that's going on, I doubt they'll even notice if you aren't."

"That's what I'm thinking." They wouldn't miss her at all given the size of the crowd streaming into the sanctuary.

"Sit here a minute and think it over. I'll save you a seat just in case." He got out but leaned back in to add, "Ninah's heading this way. You want me to run interference?"

"Nah, you might as well send her over. I already told her I'd see her here."

"Then I'll save seats for you both."

Like many others filing in, Ninah was dressed casually in jeans and comfortable walking shoes. The prayer service promised to be brief, as the main event was the candlelight march through the neighborhood to the site of the accident on Main Street.

Accident. There was nothing accidental about the savagery the Causwell brothers had inflicted on the town of Leland. That Ike and Emmy's families would answer such violence with a peaceful show of faith left her both bewildered and in awe.

Ninah slid into the passenger seat and greeted her with a quick kiss. "I wasn't sure you'd come. Are you going in?"

"I haven't decided. I want to show support for what they're going through but I don't want anyone to think I'm being flippant about it."

"Meaning?"

"Everybody knows how I feel about this church business. I'd hate it if Justine thought I was there under false pretenses." She'd muddled quietly through her grandparents' church funerals, but this was different. "I'm not trying to make this about me. I only want to be sensitive to how Justine feels. She probably won't even notice if I'm there or not. I'm afraid if she does, she'll think it's disrespectful for me to come to her church at a time like this and act like I belong there."

Ninah's smile was sympathetic, but the shake of her head made it clear she didn't agree. "Look around, Britt. Practically half the town's here, including a lot of people who hardly ever set foot inside a church. If ever there was a right time for a nonbeliever to go, this would be it. It's more about respecting Justine's faith than expressing our own."

"I just don't want her to think I'm being insincere…even if I sort of am."

"Let me put it this way. If this were a Muslim or Jewish service, I'd still go. I don't think you'll be out of place at all.

It was a fair point, and ultimately persuasive. "All right, I'm in. Dad's saving our seats."

Inside, soft organ music set the tone for what was sure to be a somber affair. The sanctuary was filled to capacity, with a large contingent of Justine's lesbian friends from the picnic clustered in the back. Britt would gladly have joined them but for her father, who waved them all the way up to the second row.

Ninah peeled off near the front to greet some of her students from the GSA, including Thaddeus. She hugged them all and shared words that left several of them wiping away tears.

"That's Ike's little brother, Thaddeus," Britt said to her dad. "He was the one who presented the check to the library the other night."

"Look at that. Those kids sure do love Ninah, don't they?"

"And she loves them. They have no idea how lucky they are to have support like that at school."

"I wish you'd had that, honey. Maybe school wouldn't have been so hard on you. And you might not have felt like you had to go so far away when you left home."

Given her mother's betrayal, there probably wasn't anything that could have kept her in Kentucky. Before she could say so, an anteroom door opened to a pair of robed men, Lawrence Dalton from Friendship Christian Church and an African-American minister Britt recognized from the Faith Luncheon, probably the Martin family's minister. Behind them, Justine walked hand in hand with a woman Britt assumed was Ike's mother. Their families followed, JT and his wife, Carly, Trey and his family. Thaddeus joined his parents in the front row.

The congregation rose for a hymn that was vaguely familiar from her childhood, "Love Lifted Me." Ninah finished her hugs and returned in time for the second verse, whispering, "I'm proud of you."

Sitting between her father and Ninah, Britt noted a level of comfort she hadn't expected. The scripture readings, hymns and prayers faded into white noise as she observed the interactions— the smiles, touches, and subtle exchanges—of the two families forever joined by this senseless tragedy.

Following a second prayer, Justine took the pulpit. "We started to take a vote on which one of us should speak this evening, but JT told everybody they might as well pick me because, let's face it, no one's ever figured out how to shut me up." Justine had a charming way of putting everyone at ease, even in the worst of situations. "On behalf of John and Hazel Martin, JT and myself, and these beautiful families God has blessed us with, we thank you all for being here with us tonight. We're humbled to see so many faces. Some of you have asked for an update, so this is what we know. Emmy is facing a series of surgeries, but I'm thrilled to tell you she was moved this morning from the University of Kentucky Medical Center back home to Grace Hospital."

She paused for a wave of applause that was interspersed with a few cries of "Hallelujah" and "Praise the Lord."

"Emmy sends her thanks for all the warm thoughts and prayers, and asks that you please, *please* keep those up for Ike. He's still at UK with internal injuries. Our good news today was that his condition was upgraded from critical to serious, and doctors are extremely encouraged by his progress over the last seventy-two hours. My dear friends…Ike and Emmy both are looking at long roads to recovery. And by extension, all of us as well. In coming here tonight, you've reminded us that we don't face this alone. And for that, we thank you more than we can possibly say."

As Britt observed the bobbing heads, she acknowledged that Ninah was right about tonight's service. It was less about faith and spirituality than a chance for the community to express its support.

"I thank you especially for your prayers because frankly I wasn't up to it. I hate to admit in front of Reverend Dalton that I've had a real hard time talking to God. I don't know how to thank him for saving the lives of my daughter and the young man she loves, since it was that same God who let this terrible thing happen in the first place. To be honest, I still haven't reconciled that but I'm working on it, and I firmly believe God will make it clear in his own time."

Britt was oddly pleased to hear Justine voicing the same doubts she'd harbored about God and his infinite plans. She'd long since given up on getting logical answers to spiritual questions.

"Please know that none of us here take comfort from the horrible crash that claimed the life of Kevin Causwell. At nineteen years old, young Kevin had his whole life before him, a life in which I choose to believe he would have found salvation.

Our march tonight is also for him, and for his brother Seth, who is fighting for his own life at the trauma center in Louisville."

Obviously touched by this generosity of spirit, several in the congregation were choking back tears. Even Britt found herself struggling with her composure as her dad leaned forward to comfort JT with a pat to his shoulder.

"For all my personal struggles with this adversity, I will not let it shake my faith," Justine continued. "I see the hand of God in those who rushed in to comfort our children while they waited for the ambulance to arrive. I see it in the skilled work of the EMTs, of the doctors and nurses, and in all of you who drove to Lexington at midnight that night so you could give blood. And I focus on"—she gestured to the others on the front row—"*we* focus on your prayers and your kind words of support. In times like these, we need one another so very much. You are a well of strength for us all, and I have a feeling we'll be calling on you for quite some time."

"Amen," Hazel Martin replied, dabbing tears from her cheeks with her husband's handkerchief.

"Now this next part...folks, I tried not to go there but this needs saying. We *cannot* sit silently by while our political leaders fan the flames of resentment and racism, stirring up hate that too often leads to tragedies like this one. Feeding that hate is like feeding anything else—it makes it grow bigger and stronger. Many of you have reached out in the last few days to ask if there's anything you can do to help us through this time. There is, my friends. You can feed *love*. Feed it, nurture it, share it with everyone who crosses your path. I promise you that love will grow, and together we'll overcome these hateful times in Leland. That's all we ask of you, to be your best selves and *feed love*. Thank you."

Amid a chorus of cheers, Justine returned to her pew to hugs from the Martins, and an especially moving embrace with JT, in which they both cried. After taking her seat next to Carly, she stretched a long arm behind her to touch fingers with Ninah and Britt, a gesture of affection that again made Britt glad she'd come.

The Martins' minister took to the pulpit as several teens, including Ninah's GSA members, quietly began distributing candles for the march. "As we conclude our service, it's my sad duty to share some news I just received. The Causwell family sends word that Seth was removed from life support at six thirty this evening and passed soon after with his parents at his side. Please pray for the Causwell family, and remember Seth and Kevin with forgiving hearts."

A collective gasp was followed by murmurs of sadness, a remarkable show of compassion for the young men who'd caused so much pain. Their determination to love and forgive was deeply touching. How different her life might have been had her mother followed that credo instead of Brother James.

When the service finished, the church emptied from the front so that Ike and Emmy's families led the march, with Britt's row directly behind. Marchers paused at the door to light their candles before stepping out into the twilight. In a soulful alto voice, Hazel Martin began to sing "Amazing Grace."

CHAPTER THIRTY-EIGHT

As the march dispersed, Justine drew Britt into a hug and said, "I'm so blessed to have such wonderful friends. And a bundle of thanks to the Longdogs for sending all those beautiful flowers. Trey carried them back here in his SUV. Emmy's room at Grace looks like a botanical garden."

"We were happy to do it," Britt replied, though she felt guilty now for not making her own personal gesture. "If there's *anything* we can do to help, all you have to do is ask. And that goes for Ike too. Please let his family know."

"Thank you. Lucky for us, the insurance has most of it covered. But once their rehab starts, all bets are off. I'll be signing all of you up for shifts."

"Put me at the top of the list, Justine," Ninah said.

"You're back in school tomorrow...but you can come over and keep all of us company whenever you want. Both of you."

As the crowd dispersed, Britt took Ninah's hand for the short walk back to her car. "Thanks for convincing me to come.

You were right, this was about supporting the families. I would have hated to miss it."

Ninah nodded solemnly, apparently overcome with emotion. "Are you okay?"

"No...no, I'm not." She looped her arm through Britt's and rested her head against her shoulder. "I'm probably gonna have nightmares tonight."

"How could we not?"

"It seems like no matter how much society evolves, we're always gonna get blowback from hateful people who think they're better than everybody else just because their skin happens to be white...or whatever. They don't have the emotional or mental capacity to adapt. Or in some cases, the desire."

Britt would have said the same thing an hour ago, but the service and vigil had softened her view. Here in Leland, the good outweighed the bad. It wasn't even close.

"We'll never be totally rid of people like that, Ninah. Even in San Diego, we've got gangs of white supremacists shooting up synagogues and setting fire to mosques. That's why tonight's service matters so much here in Leland, because the only way to defeat hate is for decent people to stand up and make their voices heard."

"I've been teaching my GSA kids to come out and be brave. But it makes them targets of violent, unhinged predators like the Causwell brothers." Her voice shook with anger and frustration. "These kids need a protector, somebody who cares about them and understands what they're going through."

Britt processed her words with a ripple of alarm. Ninah seemed to be saying she couldn't bring herself to leave Leland after all.

"It's not just Leland, Ninah. Kids everywhere need a champion like that. Big cities, small towns, even in liberal places like California."

"But don't you see? It matters so much more here because there isn't anyone else to do it. I realized that tonight. When

I went over to talk to my kids before the service, Abby told me they left the game together, all eight of them. They were gonna walk to her house on the very same sidewalk as Ike and Emmy. Imagine if Seth and his brother had spotted the *queer* kids out there, lined up like bowling pins." Her quivering voice grew stronger, as if filling with conviction. "But then Thaddeus reminded them what *I* said, that they should go straight to their cars. If I hadn't been watching out for them, they might have been run down too."

"But they weren't, sweetheart. They're all safe."

"They are this time. Who's gonna keep them safe if I leave?"

There probably was no good answer to such a nightmare scenario, but Britt hated to see fear unravel their future. "It's scary, Ninah. I get that. But if we let ourselves dwell on all the horrors that didn't come to pass, we'd never leave our homes. None of your kids got hurt. Let's dwell on that instead."

At Ninah's house, she parked in Emmy's empty space hoping for an invitation to stay the night. They paused on the porch, as if paying homage to the dark upstairs apartment. Doctors were doubtful Emmy would ever walk on her own again, let alone climb stairs.

"Come sleep with me," Ninah said.

"Are you sure? I don't want to keep you up late. You've got school."

Ninah pulled her down for a kiss. "I don't wanna be alone tonight."

Neither did Britt. "I know it's scary right now, but please don't rush into a decision about staying in Leland. I'm not saying I definitely want to leave, but I'd really like it if we could decide that together. It has to work for both of us."

Ninah sighed and hid her face against Britt's shoulder. There was no way to know if she was conflicted about what to do, or just reluctant to say it.

"Don't cut me out, Ninah. I love you, and I promise to put you at the center of every decision I make. But I need for you to do the same."

"You love me?"

"Of course I do. How could you not know that?" Maybe because she'd been too chickenshit to say it.

"I love you too. I can't believe I finally get to say it." Ninah withdrew from their embrace to face her.

"Why would you…"

"I started to tell you when we were at Torrey Pines, but you weren't ready to start a relationship. That's what you said."

"That was a long time ago. I couldn't let myself fall for you when I knew I'd be waving goodbye in the end. But that day at Torrey Pines, when you raised the possibility of moving to San Diego…Ninah, it changed everything. That's when I started to believe we had a real future together."

"As long as I go back to California with you."

"No, not because you'll go—because you're *willing* to go. Once that sunk in, it hit me that it has to work both ways. I need to be open to staying here. I'm not saying I will, but it's on the table. We'll do whatever's best for both of us." She cupped Ninah's face in her palms and looked for a reflection of the joy she felt at sharing her love. "All this time we've been holding each other at arm's length. I'm not going to do that anymore. I love you. Simple as that."

Ninah hugged her fiercely, squeezing even tighter when Britt began to loosen her hold. Gradually they began to rock and sway, a slow dance set to a shared heartbeat.

CHAPTER THIRTY-NINE

"Ladies and gentlemen, please direct your attention to the mound for a special message from Longdogs owners, Britt and Vernon Iverson."

From the front row of the VIP suite, Ninah rose to cheer. She was delighted by the crowd's warm reception, helped along by Wesley's glowing coverage of how Britt and Vernon were upgrading Leland's ballpark experience.

And certainly, no small part of fans' enthusiasm was due to the team's on-field success, thanks to the Pirates' decision to send Oscar back to Leland once Boomer's suspension was up. After a drought of fourteen years, the Longdogs were playing next week for the championship of the Valley League. Tonight's regular season finale against the Oak Ridge Atoms mattered naught in the standings, since the Dogs had already clinched home field advantage throughout the playoffs.

There was a nip in the air, the first sign of autumn. On the field, Britt was looking borderline glamorous, having dressed for her on-field appearance in skinny jeans with a white shirt and navy blazer. Her hair was piled in a messy updo, the perfect casual touch. She and her father jokingly passed the microphone back and forth as if urging the other to speak. Finally it landed in Britt's hand and she addressed the crowd.

"What a summer, huh? How 'bout those Longdogs?"

In all the years she'd followed the team, Ninah couldn't remember seeing fans so excited. Tonight's crowd was easily the largest of the season, standing room only in the far corners of the outfield, which Britt had opened to fans with lawn chairs and blankets.

"Ladies and gentlemen, on behalf of the Longdogs organization, my father and I are extremely proud to stand here tonight and celebrate this great season of outstanding baseball. How lucky were we for the chance to watch future stars like Troy Cline"—she called out several names, giving fans time to cheer each one—*"Cory Hanover...and for gosh sakes, Oscar Lopez!"*

Conspicuously absent from her shout-outs was Boomer McBride, whose return to Pittsburgh had the Pirates in contention for the National League pennant. The *real* Longdogs were these scrappy, wet-behind-the-ears rookies.

"Dad and I want to take this opportunity to say thanks for all you've done to make our first year at the helm such an amazing ride. It might be our name on the paperwork, but these Longdogs belong to all of you!"

Carly leaned into Ninah's shoulder and said, "Hard to believe that's the same Britt Iverson who just four months ago looked like she was gonna spontaneously combust if she didn't get out of Kentucky."

"Mmm...she's still kind of skittish about it, but she's been pretty chill since the candlelight vigil. I nearly had a meltdown that night over who was gonna take care of my GSA kids if I left. I think it freaked her out."

"You think she's gonna stay?"

"I honestly don't have a clue, Carly. It's like we're both afraid to bring it up, but I'm pretty sure I'd go with her if she needed to leave."

Carly clapped her shoulder. "I don't think there's a doubt in the world about that."

What worried her was the fear of resentment, whether it was hers for feeling forced to leave or Britt's for feeling forced to stay. One thing was certain though—they both agreed their love was too precious to lose.

"Six weeks ago tonight, Leland suffered a tragedy just outside the park. Two young people from our community, Ike Martin and Emmy Sharpe, were struck by a car while walking home from a Longdogs game." The crowd grew solemn as Britt recalled the horror. "Make no mistake, that violent act of hate was meant to tear us apart. That's not what happened though, was it?" She paused for reflection, which gave rise to a rousing round of applause. "Instead, it brought this whole town closer together. People giving blood, sending flowers and cards, holding a march to show our solidarity. And tonight, I'm overjoyed to welcome Ike and Emmy back to the ballpark. Turn around and give them a wave."

Hundreds of faces turned toward the suite as Britt pointed upward from the field. The couple basked in the warm reception, which grew louder as Ike shakily rose, leaning on Emmy's wheelchair for support.

Ninah rubbed her arms to settle the goose bumps. In honor of Ike and Emmy's first outing together, Britt had insisted on using the suite for a private party with family and friends. JT and his wife joined Carly and Justine, along with Trey and his family. Even the Martins were there, having bonded especially with Justine over their likelihood of becoming in-laws. And there was Thaddeus, who'd decided to take a gap year before college. Not only was he helping out at home, he was holding down Ike's job at The Bean until he was able to return.

"And finally, if you've been following the Longdogs over the past couple of seasons, you probably know our relationship with the

Pittsburgh Pirates has been a little…shall we say, tense. We're thrilled to announce that this morning we signed a seven-year extension. That's seven more years of your Leland Longdogs!"

She'd buried the lede—the biggest news of the year, even bigger than the change in ownership. Why had Britt kept such a critical secret from her? Ninah had an ominous feeling about the reason—because it was likely to bring rich offers for the team, offers Britt might find too tempting to pass up.

They left the field to rousing cheers, quieted soon by an invocation from the pastor of the First Presbyterian Church and Leland Middle School's choir singing the national anthem.

"Leading off for the Atoms, shortstop Hector Ortega."

Seven years. Britt's goal all along had been to position the team for an extension. Now she had it. She'd laid a solid foundation—overhauling the vendors, signing sponsors to long-term contracts, filling the event calendar. Even if they didn't sell right away, any halfway competent GM could build on that. She could have one foot out the door right this minute if she wanted.

Carly rose with what was left of her nachos and beer. "I should go help Justine play hostess so she can sit down for a few minutes. You need anything?"

"I'm good."

Shaking off thoughts of Britt leaving, Ninah dutifully focused on the action on the field so she could record the score. Longdogs starting pitcher Ricky Robles had his curve ball going tonight, and he shut the Atoms down in order. Troy Cline led off the bottom half of the inning with a double down the left field line, ratcheting up an already excited home crowd.

Britt set two cups of beer on the counter in front of her and squeezed into the seat Carly had vacated. "Can anyone sit here or are you saving it for somebody special?"

"You look pretty special. Do you have a girlfriend?"

"As a matter of fact, I do."

Ninah boldly gave her a peck on the lips, paying no heed to who might be watching. "You were terrific out there. If I didn't know better, I'd think you liked being the center of attention. Maybe next year you can be Banger."

It sent a shudder to her stomach that Britt didn't respond, not even a smile. Was it the mention of next year?

"So…a seven-year extension?" She gently poked Britt's shoulder, hoping to break the tension. "You'd think something so important would have slipped out during pillow talk."

"I didn't know for sure till this morning. JT's been handling the negotiations since June, but none of us expected it to go through this year."

"I can't imagine why anyone would be surprised. Look how much you've done, Britt. From day one you kept saying it could take two years, maybe three. Look at you, barely four months later. As my kids would say—goals."

A sharp *thud!* drew their attention to the field, where Rolando Castillo was clutching his elbow after being hit by a pitch.

"It's a bean ball! For taking one for the team, Rolando Castillo just earned himself a custom cuppa joe and pastry at The Bean. Get on down to The Bean on Main Street for your own pick-me-up, fixed just the way you like it. That's The Bean, the Official Coffee of the Longdogs."

As the crowd cheered its approval, Carly whooped and slapped hands with everyone within reach. It was just one of many hooks Britt had dropped into the ballpark experience for fans and sponsors, quirky tie-ins that brought a chuckle and boosted the local community. With her zany theme nights and fan contests, she'd mastered the atmosphere of the minor leagues, delivering exactly what she'd promised—a fun night out for the whole family.

Batting third for the Longdogs, shortstop Malik Terry laid down a beauty of a bunt that was bobbled by Oak Ridge's hard-charging first baseman, an error that loaded the bases with no outs.

"*Now at the plate for the Longdogs, third baseman…Ossscar Lopez!*"

"Ninah, what's wrong?"

The question jarred her from her thoughts. Clearly she was the only one in the stadium not caught up in the anticipation of Oscar knocking one out of the park.

"Nothing's wrong. It's all great, in fact. I keep thinking that you've done practically everything you set out to do, which means theoretically…" She stopped herself, not wanting to have what was sure to be an emotional conversation in front of a dozen people.

"It means we could put the team up for sale tomorrow, or I could hire a new GM to take over operations." Britt shifted sharply in her chair and leaned closer, giving them a modicum of privacy. "If I wanted to, that is."

Ninah was afraid to read too much into that, but Britt's twinkling eyes gave her reason to hope. Before she could elaborate, a thunderous *crack!* brought the entire stadium to its feet.

They looked up to see a towering shot clear the fence in right center, a grand slam, and Oscar's thirty-fifth homer as a Longdog. The crowd cheered him long after he crossed home plate, urging him out of the dugout to take a bow.

"I was about to explain," Britt said, "but Oscar said it better than I could."

"You've become a baseball fan. I knew it! This game gets in your blood."

"It's been a great year. Look at these fans—they're having a blast. But you know what keeps me up nights? Worrying about next year when Oscar and Cory and the other guys are gone. We were lucky to have talent like this for a season, and Boomer too, but what happens when the Dogs are mediocre again, or worse?"

Attendance would probably fall off, but Ninah had faith that Britt knew how to bring people out to the ballpark anyway. Or have her GM do it.

After a pitching change for the Atoms, the next three batters were retired in order. That did little to dampen the buzz over Oscar's homer and the Longdogs' four-run lead.

"I understand now what you guys have been saying all along, Ninah. It's not just about baseball." Britt gestured with a hand over her chest. "I could feel it when I was standing out there talking about Ike and Emmy. There's so much more to this job than selling hot dogs and billboards. The Longdogs are a cornerstone of the community. We can't waste that. We have a responsibility to bring people together, whether they're gay or straight, black or white, Mexican or Japanese."

"Christian or atheist?"

Britt laughed. "Especially that. But we aren't there yet. That's what I've come to realize, that the Longdogs will always be one bad season away from ruin unless they're thoroughly knitted into the fabric of Leland. I need to stay here and make that happen."

It all sounded too good to be true. "Is there a catch?"

"What do you mean?"

"Don't get me wrong, Britt. I'm thrilled if this means you're staying, but only if it's what you really want. Nothing's more important to me than you being happy. If you can be happy here, I'm over the moon. But if you aren't…say the word and I'll pack my bags. I mean that, because I'm *not* gonna lose you."

"No, you're not." Britt raised her cup for a toast. "Because a wise woman once told me, happiness isn't about where you are. It's about who you're with. All I really need to be happy is you."

Bella Books, Inc.

Women. Books. Even Better Together.

P.O. Box 10543
Tallahassee, FL 32302

Phone: 800-729-4992
www.bellabooks.com

CPSIA information can be obtained
at www.ICGtesting.com
Printed in the USA
LVHW030055210919
631767LV00001B/2/P